I0680818

Coven of Desire

CLAW

ELLEN MINT

Claw
ISBN # 978-1-83943-958-2
©Copyright Ellen Mint 2021
Cover Art by Erin Dameron-Hill ©Copyright March 2021
Interior text design by Claire Siemaszkiewicz
Totally Bound Publishing

Totally Bound Publishing books by Ellen Mint

Happily Ever Austen
Pride and Pancakes
Rash and Rationality

Coven of Desire
Claw

Collections
Some Like it Haunted: Ink
My Bloody Valentine: Love's Curse

CLAW

Dedication

My dog is demanding pets so I'll make this brief.
Thank you, readers, thank you, editors, thank you
everyone who... Fine, I'll scratch you!

Chapter One

An edge exists between the living and the dead, the celestial plane and the mortal realm, reality and its reflection. Upon that sliver of existence is where the witch —

"Damn it!" I gasped, nearly sending the book flying from the rash of tickles prickling across my stomach. "Ink..."

Breath hotter than brimstone twisted against the back of my ear as two hands caressed down my sides. I bit my lip, the ticklish nerves transforming to a different tremble. He pressed the full breadth of his palm to my jittery belly, working his way under the Bellpeppers uniform top.

Two weeks ago, I would have returned from work, tossed away my pants and fallen to the floor to dig into my nursing homework without a second's pause. Having a personal incubus forever lurking at my elbow was going to take some getting used to, however. Ink's attentions grew in fervor, the man slipping his fingers under my panties. He brushed back my hair with his other hand so he could place a kiss to my neck.

"I thought I was supposed to be studying," I said even while losing to his demonic sway.

He grazed his teeth along my throat. "That's not what you truly desire."

Coming off a ten-hour night shift hauling cargo for the Friendliest Big Box store in the Midwest, I'd thought I'd only desired a quick meal and sleep. But my attempt at microwaving ramen had been foiled by the spell book left sitting on the kitchen table. It had demanded my attention like an obstinate cat about to break a vase if it didn't get what it wanted.

A yawn rounded around my mouth, aching for its release, when Ink dove his coy fingers right to my clit. Holy shit! My body was wide awake now.

"Why don't you sleep on me?" he said, tipping back onto the living room floor and splaying me on top of him.

All the while, he continued tantalizing my clit with a speed usually reserved for a 'neck massager.' I ramped up to orgasm in record time, Ink arching his hips against my lower back to press his monolith erection on me.

Breath sputtered from my lips, my exhausted body springing to life as I ground against him. "Aren't you supposed to be teaching me witchcraft?"

"Interesting," Ink mused in his melodic baritone. "You desire me in a tweed jacket and...carrying a yardstick?"

The flittering thought of Ink as the strict professor having to punish his one student crashed into a pool of guilt. I kept forgetting he could read my every desire, no matter how minute, the second it popped into my head. And he was more than happy to lean into the depravity.

"Tell me, Ms. Leeland." He startled me from my inner turmoil. "What is the counter-ward for the acidic saliva of a manticore?"

"A...a pentagram with—"

"Wrong!" Ink shouted and slapped my inner thigh. It wasn't hard, but loud enough that I jumped in shock. Ink didn't remove his palm, but strained my leg to the breaking point while he caressed and threatened another slap up and down my inner thigh.

"What is the plant that ensures the dead stay six feet under?"

My brain sputtered smoke. I had read something about plants. But then there were all the pharmaceutical questions I'd studied for my real job. Witch hazel? Belladonna? Quinine? Foxglove? Pacific Yew?

"We need an answer, Ms. Leeland," Ink ordered, his voice crackling with a growl as he traced his nails up and down my skin.

"Periwinkle?"

He cupped my chin in his hand, twisting it until I caught his eyes. Flames danced in his irises, and his lips nearly pressed to my cheek. "Nice try, but very wrong."

"Holy fuck!"

With demonic speed, he parted my legs using just his knees and thrust his cock inside me. With one hand, he pinned my hip back against his body so I could feel every thrust from his pelvis cradling my ass. Roughing out of my hair, Ink reached up to grab my hand and pinned me by my wrist.

"Shall we play a new game?" he asked. My body strained at the breaking point, balanced upon the demon dick inside me. Thunderous energy pounded in waves from my heart up to my throat, leaving me clenching my bare toes into the rug while Ink pressed on both of my thighs.

9

"What…what game?" I gulped, the blood pooling in my head and nether regions with alarming speed. If this lasted any longer, I was liable to pass out…or worse.

Ink brushed the length of his sharp nose from the hollow of my jaw up to my ear. "For every answer you get right, you receive a thrust of eternal bliss."

Fuck. I squirmed in anticipation, flexing my fingers inside his grip. But the fact that I'd barely had two seconds to do more than crack open my spell book in days cooled my blood. "And if I get it wrong?"

He released a rumble loud enough to be heard at the end of days. "You shall see," was Ink's response and he drew a single nail across my thigh. "What is —?"

The first five bars of *White Wolves of Winter* blared from behind me. Without a second's thought, I snaked my hand from Ink's fading grip and grabbed my phone. It took a moment for me to read it, fuzz blanketing my brain.

Dana was calling.

"Oh shit!" I shouted. In one deft move, I rolled off Ink to my knees. "I completely forgot." I kept narrating while cramming back on my shitty dark gray jeans. What else did I need? Book bag? Did I load it last night before work?

Of course I didn't. I never plan ahead.

While shoving my mass of books worth the cost of a used car into a flimsy messenger bag, I glanced at the man left lying on my rug. Black hair thicker than a bear's lay in curly waves surrounding his head. A treasure trove of the same caressed down the dangerous muscles of his body, but parted at the monstrous erection prodding free.

Ink wore nothing but a smile when he wandered around my place, no doubt much to the delight of the random saleslady who'd dropped her catalogs for seventy-dollar micro-cloths and run for the hills when he answered the door.

Tearing my eyes off the man ready to pound me to heaven wasn't easy. "I have a study date... With Dana and Fariah."

Curling a hand under his high cheekbone, Ink twisted onto his side to watch me. I kept dashing about the apartment, trying to not glance at his ass. *Do not give in to the bubble, Layla. This is important.*

"We have a test coming up," I kept explaining as if Ink was my keeper, but he wafted a hand through the air like a Roman emperor dismissing a servant.

"Yes, yes, go on to your university issue."

I clung white-knuckled to my backpack. Despite him being an incubus, a literal sex demon that gained energy by fucking, the second I needed to get away he let me go. No questions. No complaints.

If I had any lingering doubts that he could be a human, the sight of him with a giant erection — nearly at the point of no return — and not a single challenge to my exit proved that was impossible. Fisting my keys between my fingers out of habit, I turned to the door.

"What will you do?" I began, my gut boiling as I spun back to the man with a sequoia in his lack-of-pants. "While I'm gone, I mean?"

That delectable and devious smile returned. Ink hopped to his feet, his hands grazing the carpet before he rose to stand before me. The flames had doused in his eyes, leaving only the amber shine behind. "I will wait for you."

A blush burned on my cheeks and I felt like a teenager who just had the hottest guy in school look at her from across the cafeteria. Why did I even think that he'd...? *Never mind.* Shaking my head, I undid the lock on my apartment and moved to slip out without anyone peeking in.

"My bond," Ink called to me. He stared me straight in the eye and curled a hand around his cock. "When you return, the game will resume."

Fuck! Blushing so hard that my black hair turned red, I ran from my apartment and the incubus contained within.

Chapter Two

Witch.

Before Halloween, witches had been green-skinned crones. *And demons didn't screw on living-room rugs.* The night of my twenty-fifth birthday, Ink had appeared literally out of nowhere. He'd told me impossible things. That I was a witch, capable of untold power. That he was a demon, a personification of lust who killed with sex.

I wish I could say that had been the watershed moment, to have gone from an average, uninteresting girl to a witch with a chained-up demon in her bedroom, but I hadn't exactly been ordinary to begin with. None of the picket fences, dog in the yard, suburban past for me.

But I never signed up for this mess either.

Yawning, I leaned a little too hard into my car door and slammed it shut behind me. I jostled the massive bag strapped over one shoulder and aimed for Grizzly's café and caffeine emporium only to be interrupted by the biggest smile I'd ever seen outside dentists' billboards.

"Excuse me, do you have a moment?" the woman asked, somehow thrusting her chest out while handing over a shiny flyer.

"Sorry," I said, taking the paper so she'd leave me be. "I have to get somewhere."

My gruff response didn't faze her, the perky voice not fading. "Greetings of the moon upon you!"

"Yup, sure, whatever," I mumbled. My weary eyes glanced down the paper, noticing a white-haired man swarmed by women before I tossed it to the trash.

It didn't even take a once-over for me to spot my friends and fellow nursing students Fariah and Dana. They sat at our usual table, the one closest to the wall outlet. We'd spent hours chugging caffeine, eating scones and dissecting diagrams of diseased organs there.

"Took you long enough," Dana shouted once she spotted me. She too wore the signs of her getting-by job, a blue polo with the name tag clipped on.

Fariah gave me a kind nod. She wasn't trapped in the same cycle of night job plus morning classes, leaving her looking like a showered and refreshed human being.

I tried to ignore the accusing eyes of my friends and plummeted fifty pounds of knowledge onto the table. But Dana couldn't be shaken so easily. "We've already gone through the practice test. What were you doing?"

I was about to be split in half by a sex demon.

My jaw clenched at the guilty thought roiling through my brain. But the body's strange mechanism to relax itself took over, and my yawn provided an excuse. After shaking it off, I said, "We got a truck in and I must have missed my alarm. Wait, where's Cal?"

"He's running late as well," Fariah said from her perfectly aligned study material. Even the pencil lay parallel to her notebook.

Snorting, I shook my head. "Then why are you busting my balls over here?"

Fariah barely shivered at the curse, but Dana cracked a smile. "Because you're more fun." Before I could call her to task for that, Dana took a long swig of her jumbo coffee and my salivary glands kicked in.

Caffeine! my depleted brain cried out. *Sugar. Fat. Feed me, Layla. Feed me!*

I pulled in a breath, taking in the scents of a coffee shop in early November. "Please don't tell me that's some pumpkin spice bullshit," I said, already weary of autumn's grip on the culinary world.

Dana snorted in her cup, sloshing bubbles over the side. Fariah took control. "I'm trying their maple cream latte."

"Okay, *that* sounds good," I groaned, trying to read the menu. The hand-chalked letters bobbed like those old black-and-white cartoons. *Whoa.* I felt myself tipping to the side, a chair threatening to impale me through my ribs.

A hand wrapped around my shoulder. I whipped my head over in shock, sending the world once again reeling. Eyes blue as an afternoon sky in Iceland greeted me. "Calvin?" I whispered, words clogging in my neurons. My instincts expected to find fiery eyes and jet-black hair. Instead, it was white-blond hair and a face as clear as a glacier lake. Ink didn't have a single mole on his demonic body, but he always carried around a day's worth of stubble regardless of the calendar.

Cal's smooth jaw, sharp as a dagger with nary a hair to disguise it, sent my heart wobbling.

"Long night, Layla?" Cal asked, his half-moon smile in full force. Beyond the clean-cut look fresh from a commercial selling insurance, Calvin always seemed to glow when he smiled, as if the full strength of his bright white teeth turned him radioactive.

And he was still holding me.

"Yeah," I said getting my feet under me and slipping away. "You know Bellpeppers." I tried to shrug it away, when Cal's winter-tan cheeks turned pink.

"It's not the same since they moved you to nights." He didn't lean nearer to me, but he withdrew his striking gaze as if the loss of me sharing his shift struck him deeply.

"I don't know how you can work days and get to class. Not without crashing, anyway." I was running on fumes as the semester wound down, and planned to spend the entirety of Christmas break in bed.

With the incubus?

Shit. I forgot about him. Would I even be capable of leaving bed with Ink around?

"Hey, Ross and Rachel," Dana shouted, causing both me and Cal to whip our heads to her. "Babble on your own time. I have to get to work in an hour."

Cal and I both muttered sorry at her and each other. In trying to slip away, I took a step to him and he one to me. Then he quickly dashed back while rustling a hand through his short hair. "I should... I'll get coffee. Anyone want anything?"

"No!" Dana called, giving him a dismissive wave.

A half-smile crawled up my face. "No thanks."

He beamed his full grin at me and inched away. It wasn't until I turned to the girls that I groaned. "Fuck, I did want that maple latte. It's too goddamn early." With that, I slumped into the chair and pulled out my pharmacy textbook. We fell to studying in silence, only the scratch of pens and clack of keys filling the table.

I juggled my phone over the impenetrable text of the printouts, trying to scan the massive Latin names. The app was supposed to change the font so my brain would stop swapping around letters when I tried to read them. It worked eighty percent of the time. If only I could get them to let me use it during tests.

It felt like hours of a deep dive into the Mariana Trench when a shadow passed beside me. "Which part are we on?" Cal asked. He unwound the scarlet scarf knotted around his neck and unzipped the light coat. A fisherman's cream sweater clung to his body like it never wanted to leave. Not that I could blame it.

"Tobramycin sulfate is primarily used for…?" Fariah prompted.

"Bowel prep before surgery," Cal answered with a smile.

"And to prevent absorption of ammonia in hepatic encephalopathy," I added, my brain kicking out a jolt of knowledge before it fully shut down.

Dana was the one who grunted. "What? Since when?" She furiously flipped back through the pages of the study guide while Cal placed a tall white cup in front of…me?

I stared up at him and he smiled. "The maple latte."

"Wow, that's…thank you." I wrapped my hands around the nectar of Hermes, and a different warmth percolated through me.

"I thought I heard you mention—" Cal began, before he worried his lips to the side and for a second knocked his fingers over mine. "No problem."

Layla, what are you doing? You have a literal sex demon bound to your soul or something. Oh, and you're a witch

17

with ungodly powers on top of schoolwork. This is not the time to go boyfriend shopping.

Reality chucked cold water on me, dampening the flush. I buried my face in my work, trying to ignore the sweet guy a foot away.

After she'd highlighted a mass of text, Dana snapped her piercing gaze from me to Cal and back. "Well?" she said out of nowhere. Confused, I stared at her, waiting for an explanation. "Give me a damn question, already."

"Warfarin is used for—?"

"Blood pressure," Fariah answered before I could finish. "Give us a harder one, Layla."

While I scanned down the list of medications, I spotted Cal staring intently. "I'm complaining of a heart arrhythmia," I prompted. "What would you do?"

"Check your pulse first." Calvin caught my wrist and slid two of his fingers against it. As he leaned closer, I stared deeper into those eyes bluer than a turquoise pool.

"That's..." I gulped, the pseudo-arrhythmia threatening to become real. Cal's warmth washed over my skin. While testing my pulse, his ring and pinkie finger settled in my palm. Slowly, they began to swirl in a circle, casting soothing waves up my arm. "That's not how you do it," I said, even while I didn't want him to stop.

But Cal blushed across his pale forehead and he released his hold. "You're right," he said and leaned forward. His two testing fingers pressed to my neck, right over the carotid artery. His knees bounced into mine, and he gripped the back of my chair with his other hand. All I could do was sit and stare in wonder at his sunny face inching closer to mine.

My tongue darted along my lips, preparing for something I hadn't ever imagined possible. All those long hours with our heads bent together over books, and I'd never once thought Cal would look twice at me. His soft-peach mouth parted as if a sigh was about to release. "Your heart sounds—"

Hands slapped over my eyes. I yanked away from Cal, ready to impale my nails into whoever had attacked me from behind when a thigh-quaking voice whispered in my ear, "Guess who?"

"Ink?" I spun in my chair, smacking my shin into the table, but the pain didn't register as I stared at my live-in incubus standing behind me. "What are you doing here?" My words snarled venom even with the thundering sexual beat kicking through me.

At least he'd put on clothing, his only outfit of a crimson button-up and black silk pants tailored for his ass. Last thing I needed was getting banned from the one good coffee shop in the city.

"Who's this?" Calvin's voice hit a sharp note, whipping me away from the incubus getting looks from all corners of the café.

"He's...um." My brain smashed straight into a brick wall. I hadn't thought of an explanation for my little bondage-demon problem. I didn't think he'd be foolish enough to leave my apartment. He'd seemed allergic to clothing for the past ten days. Why had he figured out trousers now?

The smile that could blind the sun rose and Ink tipped his head to Calvin. "I am Ink, if a name is requested."

Cal snorted and folded his arms. "It wasn't, but that's not an answer."

"Oh, my purpose in this world?" Ink picked up my fingers and brushed them across his cheek while a burn burst over my face. "I pleasure her flesh whenever it's requested."

Pumpkin spice latte sprayed across three pharmacology textbooks. Dana barely wiped her spit-take away before she slammed a hand on the table and rose. Before any accusations could bash through the light chatter of the coffee house, I leapt to my feet and grabbed Ink.

Despite easily having fifty pounds of muscle on me, he gave in to my tugging him to the side. "What are you doing?" I tried to whisper at him.

"You forgot..." he began while raising a book from his satchel. The second I caught the red leather, I slammed my hands over his to ram it back in.

"Why did you bring my—? Just, stand over there a minute. Okay?"

Ink gave a single-shoulder shrug and literally hovered backward to the bookcase. The café was crowded enough that I doubted anyone saw his lack of leg movement, but I still growled at his showing off. That got me a single smirk, setting off another rage incendiary in my chest.

"Layls, what the shit?" Dana demanded, dragging me from one problem into another.

Three sets of eyes stared daggers through me, but it was Cal's I couldn't face. Sadly, that gave Dana all the opening she needed. "Who is he?"

The better question is 'what is he?' but you wouldn't like the answer.

"He's...Ink."

"That isn't a name." Fariah snorted, breaking from her study bubble for my abject humiliation.

"It's just, it's what he wants to be called, okay?" I floundered. There wasn't much of a high horse I had left to sit on. So I had a sex demon living on my couch.

Was that so weird? I didn't expect the Spanish Inquisition for him.

"How long have you two, has he been" — Dana jabbed a finger back and forth between us and her face pickled — "pleasuring the flesh?"

God, my soul cringed at that and I wanted to melt into the floorboards. *Anyone have a bucket of water to throw on me?*

Before I could invent an answer to get me out of this, Ink cheerfully called over, "Halloween. Nigh on midnight. It is the witching hour, after all."

"I'm not a..." I began, only to turn back to my friends.

"Halloween?" Dana looked like she was about to crumble, her lips pursed. "Why didn't you say anything?"

"Because it..." I lowered my voice and tried to huddle them around me. Only Cal remained rooted in place, his arms crossed tight as he watched Ink. "It was supposed to be a friends with benefits. Not even friends. Strangers really."

Dana's dark turn lightened in a second. "Oh, is that all. God, way to make a mountain out of nothing. Though..." She too watched as Ink drew a nail down his exposed forearms, tracing the tattoos without a care. "How can you keep *him* a secret?"

"I have no idea."

"She's going to want every detail, you know," Fariah said and returned to her work. That was as good as a blessing from her.

"Fuck, yes," Dana kept on. "Okay his weird way of speaking is, just so. Ugh. But then again the crazy ones can be fantastic in the sack..."

I let her insinuations continue as I stared at Cal, who seemed to try to avoid the dirty girl talk. "I'm..." A *sorry* lingered on my tongue, but he turned away before I could even mouth it.

"Do you wish me to regale your friends with our sexual conquests, my bond?" Ink asked from clear across the coffeeshop in a voice that'd shatter mountains.

Fuck. Bending my face to the floor, I bull-rushed at him. "No," I said in full scolding mode. Locking on to his biceps with both hands, I tried to drag Ink into the street.

He gave in, but paused to call out to Dana one last time. "When Layla is finished with me, perhaps I could answer your every desire."

"Don't even think about it," I said, a snarl rising as I shoved him out of the door.

Chapter Three

The clanging of chains slapping from the back of a truck reverberated through the alley, leaving me to stare at my impassive and confused incubus. Even in the dark shadows of the crumbling Romanesque buildings of downtown, Ink burned. Shafts of light streaming through rusted grating above our heads found only his cheekbones and full lips. One tried to pierce into his eyes, but his brow wouldn't allow it.

Fire danced among the already unearthly amber irises and I knew what they wanted.

What he always wants.

"Why are you here?" I shouted, my voice spiking as the truck finally vanished around the corner.

"You left without your book." Ink kept on his high horse, as if he was a dutiful boyfriend bringing me my purse. This time I let him exhume the witch's book, my book.

Created from the nether magics for me. Only my eyes could read it, only my fingers could spin it into magic. Or so the incubus said.

23

As I wrapped my palm around the red binding and traced down the spine embedded with vine designs, I felt whole. Weird, I hadn't felt a missing piece before, but now I didn't want to let it go.

"No, this is stupid," I said to myself, but it drew Ink closer. How did I not notice that his hand was already around my hip?

Wiggling out of his grip, I said, "I don't need this." Even with my nerves tingling, I pushed the book back into his arms and let go. "This is my normal time when I don't have to be a witch."

Ink twisted his head until his chin was almost parallel with the ground. It knotted my stomach up, but the inhuman move only lasted a second before he returned to normal. "How can you not be what you are? Witch born, witch bred."

What does that even mean? The exhaustion of an unending day caught up at once. My knees started to bow and I felt myself crunching up into an epic scream. But my friends were still in the shop and I didn't need them rushing to my aid. How in the hell was I going to explain Ink to them?

Said cause of my current stress looked on with his quizzical stare, one hand cupped under his chin and a long finger extending up his cheek. He twitched it back and forth like a broken metronome. "Ah, I understand. You have not yet told them what you are."

I hadn't planned on ever telling them. "Look, I can't just. People nowadays don't believe in magic and demons," I said, waving my hands at him for the last bit.

Ink snorted. "I am as much a demon as you are an aardvark." At my confused look, he continued, "The classification can be apt only if vague generalities are observed."

Here comes the headache again. He was supposed to teach me. Help me figure out my power, understand this new world with nether planes and monsters and demons. But every time he explained something, a rule came with two new rules, which had their own exceptions to those rules. None of it made any sense.

"Contrary to your public assertion, when I last walked the earth, most humans didn't believe witches were real either."

What? That couldn't be right. "Weren't you trapped in hell for four hundred years?"

Ink shrugged as if that was a pittance of time.

"Everyone knows the pilgrims were superstitious," I began. *Why am I arguing this with him?*

Ink laughed as if I too was a moron blathering on about moon fairies. *Assuming moon fairies aren't a thing.* The hairs on the back of my neck stood on end and I glared at him. "What about all those witch burnings? Foolish people murdering innocent wo—"

He flipped on me so fast his body blurred. I only knew I went from standing around the edge of a puddle to my back pressed against the wall. Fires of lava churned in his eyes, the flames reaching into his sclera while he locked my wrist in his grip.

Smoke twirled off his back, rising in thick plumes against the cool November day. I couldn't fight him off, so I stared at him beat for beat, neither of us blinking.

Horns blared from down the alley, and voices rose as what looked like hungover frat guys stumbled onto their dilapidated lawn to shout. I could only watch from my peripheral vision, my body ordering me to not let the rampaging demon out of my sight. Would they see me? Could they even find us amongst the trash and boxes?

Ink's shoulders rose once as if the demon who didn't need oxygen took in a cleansing breath. He broke our death stare, the steam snuffing off his shoulders and the flames quenching in his eyes. But he kept hold of my wrist. "Even a fool can stumble into a win."

That seemed to be enough to deflate the sudden outburst. He stepped back, adjusted the fallen elbow of his rolled-up sleeve and appeared in complete control.

"I understand now. You wish to keep me…and your witch side hidden from potential hunters." His head bowed and he whispered, "Wise."

"Witch hunters died out centuries back." Running a hand through my hair, I tried to ignore the red marks on my wrist. "They're not a thing anymore."

A snort burst from Ink, spurting two puffs of smoke from his nostrils. "I pray you are correct."

"You pray? To what?"

All I got was a slow smile revealing the full row of teeth. Ink slotted his hands behind his back and rose taller. "If your concern does not lie in the hunters putting you to the noose, then why make this harder on yourself with a double life?"

Because I cannot tell my friends that I'm a witch, and I sure as shit can't let them know you're an incubus. "It's not like I can do much to show off and prove it. That's a tall order in this day and age. Oh look, magic, totally real. Here's some sparklers from my fingers to prove it."

"Then show me to them?" Ink grinned wide and moved to walk out of the alley.

This time I grabbed him. Locking both hands around his wrist, I tried to plant my feet to the ground. It didn't prove necessary as he instantly froze at my slightest touch. "You can't, you might…"

His head swiveled around and he spoke in a voice colder than a November rain. "You believe I will harm them."

"It's—" Biting my lip, I shifted on my feet and let him go. In exchange for my learning about witchcraft, to protect myself from the monsters hunting me, I'd have to unbind Ink, willingly let him loose on the world even knowing what he was. And the idea of doing that to my friends, letting him know them, letting them trust him… I couldn't.

Locking my hand around my upper arm, I shrank in on myself. "Isn't that what you do? Kill people with sex?"

"I feed upon their lusts. It is what I am. It is not a choice of my making, as much as you cannot one day decide to transform into a flower and acquire energy from the sun." Beyond the pride in his voice, the demon's ego never far gone, I heard a rattle from him I never expected—*pain*.

Damn it, I was too tired to deal with an angry demon and an upcoming midterm. One had to take precedent and the test couldn't be delayed. "Just…go home. Please. I'll keep the book near me, but I won't have time to study it."

He released the spell book back into my hands and I clutched it to my chest without thought. "No witch should be without it, for her safety as much as anything."

Why didn't he just start with that?

God, I needed a nap. No, I needed a twenty-year-long coma.

Ink didn't move, not that he needed to. He seemed to be able to teleport wherever he wanted, whenever he wished. It was unnerving for my mind to wander a moment to him and have the man walk around the corner. But whenever he did appear, I always wanted him to stay.

"Hey," I said, threading my fingers through his. The demon cupped the back of my head and brushed his pinkie along the baby hairs at my nape, pulling me closer until my wide nose brushed against his ski slope. I flexed my toes in anticipation of the kiss, but he didn't lean in for it.

His eyelids closed, not even a flutter against the light, while Ink felt me breathe. I tipped my head, prepared to get at least one good kiss in before he left. A pinch burst across my ass, causing me to leap in the air. Before I could get away, Ink slapped the offending palm under my buttock and—by that single point— hefted me higher.

"You do not desire a simple kiss," he growled, kicking my heart into overdrive. Surging forward, Ink wrapped his tongue around my lip and guided me to him. I was prepared to give in, when my mind saw a flash of fingers that my eyes didn't.

It caused me to whip my head to the side, implanting Ink's wet kiss into my jaw. He barely blinked at the change, working his way to my ear. But my attention was snagged by a single dumpster among the many.

"You're such a challenge when distracted," Ink purred, his voice cranked to liquid sex. He had obvious intentions to finish what we'd started. But I couldn't look away.

"I keep thinking," I said, furrowing my nose at the idea. Sliding off the man more than happy to do me in an alley, I walked closer to the dumpster. There it was again. A hand, but not really. It felt like someone kept brushing fingers just outside my range of vision. But also right there in front of me.

"I swear, it's like I see…" Shaking my head, certain it was the long night and lack of sleep, I lifted the lid.

"Ah, *fuck!*"

Trash bags barely obscured the mutilated body of a woman with a single hand pressing against the dumpster wall.

Chapter Four

How many ways could I say the same damn thing?

Another bang from the dumpster of interest caused everyone to jump out of their shoes, including the police officer grilling me. He had the kind of features that made me think of a slab of melting clay a kid dug their fingers into for eyes and gave a half-hearted attempt at a nose. There weren't any lips—the skin simply vanished into a wide mouth that wouldn't stop needling me.

"You were in the alley where you discovered the body, because you were arguing with your boyfriend?"

"He's not my…" I began, raising my arm to Ink. He'd had enough presence to blend into the background to the point even I almost forgot he was there. But once Dana had mentioned that 'the new boyfriend' was in the alley with me, the cops had to interview him too.

I had no idea how he was doing, the three of them on the far edge of the sidewalk. I couldn't hear the words, but there was an awful lot of giggling that set my teeth on edge and told me he was fine. As if he could sense my frustration and concern, Ink turned his head and winked at me.

"Miss Leeland," the officer pressed, drawing me back to him.

"Yes, fine, I was in the alley with my boyfriend when I found the corpse."

We weren't in the coffee shop because the owner refused to close, and he sure as hell wasn't going to let the cops take it over for a single dead body. So that left us standing in the parking lot trying to huddle near the forensic team's pop-up canopy to avoid the drizzling rain. Police cars formed a makeshift maze blocking the alley off from any through traffic. Their red and blue lights continually circled off the buildings and puddles. If I stared too long, my stomach began to rotate with them.

"Why did you lift the lid on the dumpster?" The officer tapped a finger against his tablet while focusing his clove eyes at me.

"Because I thought I saw a hand." It'd have been better if I hadn't. No sudden scream that sent people racing to the alley. No harried phone calls to nine-one-one. No hours spent watching as people in plastic suits pulled first the severed chest, then the head and limbs of a woman out of the trash.

"How precisely did you see this hand?" a new voice asked from the side. I moved to face him just as he walked to me. Too close to me. His shoulder brushed mine, but he didn't even blink. Probably. Dark oval sunglasses perched on his nose hid his eyes. No doubt they were as squinty as the other cop's.

Instead of the blue uniform, this guy was in a full-on suit complete with secret agent skinny black tie. He wasn't ugly, but he wasn't my type by any stretch of the imagination. All his features were hard as diamonds, the nose shaved within an inch of its life, his lips knotted into a sneer. Even the cheekbones, that'd make models cry in agony, were too severe. He looked more skull than man.

And he was pressing me for an answer.

"How people see things," I said, hoping my sarcasm and exhaustion would be read as genuine. I pointed at my face and added, "With these."

The man in a suit released the pressure on his lips and they slid not into a smile. It wasn't a sneer either. I couldn't read the expression at all when he tugged off his glasses. Eyes green as a field of clover after a spring rain glared through me and all my confidence sloughed away.

"It's a most curious thing, Miss…"

I folded my arms, unprepared to give him my name, but he didn't even miss a beat as he glanced over at the officer's tablet.

"Leeland." That gave him pause and he quirked his head to the side. But whatever it was he shook off. "According to the forensics team, the victim's hands were both found inside the dumpster, making them obstructed from every angle. Yet, you spotted them while in the throes of an argument with your not-boyfriend."

Every hair on the back of my neck stood on end. I flexed my fingers, digging the long nails into my flesh while I glared at the man playing some Sherlock Holmes bullshit. "Are you trying to say something… whoever you are?"

That unreadable not-smile returned and he slipped his glasses back on. "Merely exercising the facts before the lies get a chance to stretch."

"Detective Stone?" another one of the suits called, furiously waving at a scrap of garbage trapped under the wheels of the dumpster.

That caused the man, Mr. Stone, to turn first in that direction then back to me. "You may go, but I wouldn't plan on any long trips for the foreseeable future if I were you." With that, he turned on his polished heel and walked toward a murder scene.

I tried to shake off the feeling that someone in dress shoes had just tap-danced on my grave, but it wouldn't leave. Thank god I'd left the book with Ink. He could hide anything anywhere. And I should really check on him before I found three drained police officers piled up in my apartment.

"Wait," the officer shouted the moment I took a step. "You can't go. I have more questions."

"Of course," Stone called, his body nearly bent in half for a bow. "Animal Control always shows deference to the local authorities."

The officer growled in his throat as if he didn't buy that deference. I stared at the people with the audacity to use an obviously false backstory. "Animal Control?" I whispered to myself.

"They think something big ripped that girl apart. Mountain lion or wolf maybe. Always calling in those…" He didn't elaborate on what curse word he thought of them. He didn't need to. I supplied my own.

It was obvious, even as Detective Stone crouched over a clue in the case, that he was keeping one ear trained on me. Why couldn't my heart stop beating out of control? My skin burned not only on my cheeks but in my belly and... *It's the cold. Nothing at all to do with me thinking he's a –*

"What are you?"

My mind blanked and, like I'd downed a bottle of vodka, I blearily swung my head to the officer. He eyeballed me up and down and worried his chin in thought.

Don't say witch. Don't think witch. Don't even let the word sandwich escape your lips.

"Excuse me?" I muttered.

"Are you Indian? Mexican? One of those island girls?"

Oh. *That* question. "I'm half-black," I said with a resigned shrug.

Now the eyes canvassing my body sent a different warning through me. One I couldn't do a damn thing about but wait for a chance to run. A crack of thunder rumbling above our heads gave me the opportunity I needed. "Can I please go inside? I'm afraid of getting sick, got a huge final coming up."

"College kid, huh? I mean, you look young enough you could be in high school. But..." The officer closed his tablet and waved a hand off. "Fine. We're done for now. But you need to stop by the precinct and give them your fingerprints. To rule you out when they dust the dumpster."

Gritting my teeth, I assembled a smile and nodded. "Thank you. Thanks..."

I glanced in the direction of the incubus who still seemed to be entertaining the cops meant to question him. He swore that as part of that bond we had he couldn't drain anyone else. But my teeth set on edge as I watched him with exaggerated arms tell a hilarious story that charmed the officers. I should stop that before it got out of hand.

"What are you doing here?"

The words echoed in my ear from my brain outward. I knew I hadn't heard them—there was no one close enough to talk over the splashing of puddles. But I spun around in the direction of the same phrase I'd shouted at Ink before the dead body.

Beside a parking sign stood Cal without his coat. The wind rippled his sweater, sending the cream wool twisting around his body. He was entirely focused on another man I'd never seen before. A half a head taller, the stranger had the same white-blond hair, but his features were broader. Next to Calvin's trim waist and wide shoulders, the man looked like a monolith.

The three semesters I'd known Cal, he'd always been light-hearted and calm. Watching his forehead furrow and his focus flit around the area drew my curiosity. I strained to try to listen to whatever they were saying.

"I couldn't keep—"

"Hey!" A slurred voice shouted, obliterating my eardrums from eavesdropping. Through the piles of forensics and cops stumbled one of the frat guys. "You here about those fucking dogs?"

"Sir." The cop interested in my ethnicity moved to intercede. "This is a crime scene."

"They wouldn't stop howling…"

The concerns of the drunken college student faded into the background while I walked crisply to Calvin. His sharp gaze shifted from his friend and caught me. For a second, my foot froze as if I shouldn't join him.

Stupid. Shaking off the tension sparking through the whole parking lot, I walked over to Cal. He nodded to the man. "We'll talk later."

Before I reached them, the stranger slipped away down a back alley. I craned my head to follow, only for a hand to cup my shoulder. A spike of fear stabbed through my heart, causing me to whip my gaze back.

"Cal," I whispered as if I recognized him in the middle of a mob. At his name, he released me, his hand fumbling to the side.

"Are you —?"

"I wanted to say —"

A laugh of awkwardness slipped from both of us at talking over the other. Absently, I swiped at my forehead, smearing off the beaded humidity. "Look, I...I wanted to explain."

He quirked his head to the side. "Explain?"

"About, the whole Ink thing and..."

He sucked in a breath through his teeth, flaring his nostrils as if he took one long sniff of the world and hated what he smelled. "It's not...it shouldn't— It's your life."

The sting of his dismissal smacked across my cheek. Maybe I read all that flirting the wrong way. Probably. "I was thinking — me, and Dana and Fariah, to make up for all this lost time, we should get together to study at my place."

"Yeah. Sure. Sounds good," Cal said, rocking up on his toes. He lifted his head and stared in the direction his friend had vanished.

"So...tonight, my apartment. You could bring the chips?"

Cal didn't even look at me, his body twisting to the right. "I've got to go," he announced, taking a step away.

Trying to ignore the hurt ping-ponging through me, I put on a smile and watched him dash off through a fence. "See you then," I shouted to a shadow fading into darkness.

Chapter Five

Damn it, Ink!

"I told you to keep them busy!" I shouted. The incubus, as naked as the day he was…however demons were made, twisted around to stare at me. My leg lay extended on the table while I struggled to reach for the lost mark I'd been trying to draw behind my thigh.

He folded up a fist and smashed it straight through the chest of a scrounger. Teeth burst out like an uncooked bag of popcorn. I bit on my tongue to keep the bile down and returned to drawing the witch's ward. The first time I'd met Ink, these creatures that fed off magical energy had attacked us both.

Okay, fine, they'd attacked me and Ink had been kind enough to kick and punch a good chunk of them until I'd figured out how to use my spell book. Now, if I didn't keep the same ward on my body at all times, the walking flesh sacs made of organs and teeth would attack. A single touch of their waggling fat tongues paralyzed my limbs. Also, they stank like a tumor off an elephant.

"Have you yet finished your spell, my bond?"

"Almost... Fuck!" A tongue lashed through the outside wall.

"This has turned into an almost fuck," Ink said as I grabbed my open spell book and smacked it into the purple leech. The creature shrieked, sucking its tongue back into place, and I finished the last of the ward.

Magic pulsed out, banishing the scroungers to whatever demented realm they came from. I dropped my marker to the table, exhausted from the constant fight. "This is getting ridiculous," I said with a groan.

"Perhaps learning the incantation would be wise—" Ink began from the living room.

Shit! A cramp rampaged up my leg, and I hurled my foot to the ground. "Or a tattoo...that way I don't have to recite all the gobbledygook every time I enter a place." *There's also the fact I can't read all the gobbledygook thanks to my brain playing puzzles with my eyes.* I shrugged off the disapproving look of the naked incubus in my apartment and started to cap my marker when a knock came at the door.

Oh no. I took a great step forward, just for the cramp to return with a vengeance. My knee sank and I hissed in pain. From outside, I heard Dana shout, "Layla, you in there?"

"Yeah, just give me a second!" Dropping my voice, I jerked my chin at Ink. "Get in the bedroom?"

His smile turned from entertained to lascivious so fast it was a wonder it didn't smoke. "Excellent. I shall bring the chocolate sauce—"

"No, I have to study and you are...freaking naked. Go!"

Ink's smile slipped, but he bowed his head. "As you like."

He vanished from sight as I got to my feet and threw open the door. "Guys!" I shouted. "You're early."

"Took you long enough," Dana said, storming into the room and hurling her bag on the couch. "What were you doing? Or should I ask who?"

Fuck. Don't blush, Layla. "Please, make yourself at... uh, sit down. I ordered pizza. Should get here in ten minutes or so. Don't worry, I got you cheese, Fariah."

"Thank you," she said, prodding her foot at something on the floor. *Oh shit, the teeth.* I bent down as if I just had to do some stretches and tried to scoop the scrounger's lost molars into my hand. All the while, my friends set up as usual. As if everything in our world was fine.

Glancing down the building hallway, I realized how empty it was. "Where's Cal? Did he...text either of you? I invited him to the make-up study session. Seems weird for him to ditch."

"Does it, really?" Dana asked, her head tipping to the side. At my glare of confusion, she jerked her chin in the direction of my bedroom.

Ah, fuck! I spun around only to find the door still closed. And I just made myself look incredibly guilty. Trying to shake it off, I focused on Dana, but it was Fariah who spoke up, "He doesn't come out at night."

"What?"

She tried to ease past Dana and drop her bag on my couch. "Some medical condition that worsens without daylight. It's also tied with hypoglycemia, which is why he's always eating candy bars."

Why didn't he tell me?

Layla, you have an incubus in your closet, a spell book on your kitchen table and a midterm looming over your head. This is not the time to pout over a guy keeping his shit to himself.

"Maybe I should give him a call. Just to check," I said. Fariah was already cracking her books, but Dana gave me a cluck of her tongue as if I was chained to his cock.

Walking away, I pressed the phone to my ear. It rang through twice, leaving me to wonder why I didn't try texting first. *Because you want to hear his voice.* Cal could never hide anything when he talked. *Yeah, that's the only reason.*

"This is Calvin Rollin. I'm unavailable at the moment, so please leave a message."

Weird. I hung up without leaving a voicemail. *So he's busy. I mean, sure, we've got a huge test coming up. We always study together, quiz each other, cool down when our brains are too full. Get food and go for a walk to stretch our legs.*

What changed?

"Layla..." Dana's slow voice tugged me away from my kitchen. I peered around the wall to find Ink in his *full* incubus glory.

"For fuck's sake," I shouted, rushing for the naked demon trotting out of the bedroom without a care in the world.

"Don't look up, Fariah," Dana said.

I didn't have a blanket to cover him, so I tried to use my body while I shoved on his chest. "What are you doing?" I snapped, my feet sliding on the floor so my hips could at least block his full package. For the most part.

Ink danced back on his heels like they were cloven hooves. "I am…" he started while I kept pushing him back into the bedroom I'd ordered him into. Only the light of the street and my alleyway neighbors cut through the dark room. He could have at least turned a lamp on.

"What in the hell is wrong with you?" I shouted, feeling more homicidal with each minute.

"Hell has little say in my decisions," Ink responded, infuriating me more.

"I expected you to get dressed!"

He crinkled his nose and glanced to the pile of clothing on the floor. "While I can appreciate the costume for the dance, when the steps are finished, it's rather restricting."

"I don't know what kind of kinky whorehouses you've visited in the past, but people wear clothes now. In public. All the time."

Ink furrowed his brows, his sharp face tipping. "But a woman's boudoir is hardly public. I dare say, it's more pubic than public."

A groan at his terrible pun rattled in my chest and a headache grew. Digging into my temples, I glared at his feet. Anger in me had a way of twisting into, well, exactly what Ink wanted…all the time. *Stay calm.*

"My living room is public when people are over. Understand?"

He sighed, raising his pillowed pecs and the new tattoo across them. Made of five lines, the black ink curled around where his heart would be until it formed a single dark hole in the middle. Accurate. But I shouldn't get used to it—his demon body was always changing his tats.

"You need to stay in here tonight. Be as naked as you want!"

"That's hardly any fun without you to join me," Ink said smoothly, caressing the tips of his fingers up my arm. It was almost enough to make me laugh and forgive him, until he added, "Or we could add more to the party, if you so desired."

Gah! "Just...stay here. Do a puzzle! Watch more of your infomercials. I don't care. I have to study. That's what I truly desire."

The incubus snorted, but bowed his head to me. I turned back for the door handle, praying the turmoil in my brain would stop, only to have him say, "Incidentally, when do you intend to hunt the monster?"

"What?"

"The deceased woman you found. When shall you be putting an end to the creature that did her in?"

What in the hell was he talking about? "I'm not. It's not. What creature? Monster? Whatever!"

"A woman found mutilated with what appeared to be multiple claw and fang wounds. Seems that's the work of a creature either crossed from the nether plane or worse."

Why was there always worse with him?

I didn't have time for this. "Look, it's not my job to solve crimes."

"Are you not a witch?"

"According to you...and the book."

Ink rose higher, his head gazing far above me, "Then you are tasked by birth to protect this realm from the happenstance of monsters humans are incapable of, or too terrified to acknowledge."

Where was that coming from? I was learning wards to shield myself from the random monsters who ate magic and witches. Now I was supposed to protect everyone else too?

"No, my task is to pass my midterm. The cops will find whatever sick fuck chopped a woman up and tossed her into a dumpster. That's their job." I'd had enough and wrenched open the door.

Before I slipped back to my studying, Ink said, "I pray you are correct."

* * * *

The box containing a thousand twinkling lights tried to make a break for it. After the long night studying, and handful of hours sleeping, my reflexes were on par with a snail sliding into first base. I felt the "No!" screaming in slow motion as my fingers tasted air.

Suddenly, sturdy hands launched under the falling box. Bewildered at this turn of events, my foggy head turned to find a pair of bright blue eyes shining up at me. "That was close," Calvin said. He nearly collapsed to the floor to keep the box from breaking who knew how many strands of cheap Christmas lights out of China.

"Here," I said, holding a hand out for him to take.

His gaze darted to it, then my face. "Um, Layla." He jangled the box straining in his grip to make the point.

"Ah, shit," I muttered, then blanched and hunted around. Luckily there weren't a lot of customers pawing through the holiday tree section at ten a.m. on a Sunday. Most people walked through anyone in the green polo as if we were thick air impeding their coupon scores.

Cal steadied the box beside the other dozens I'd started to unpack. The floor needed to be restocked in anticipation of the coming shopping rush. Yanking out my handy dandy box cutter, I flicked it open with my thumb, and ripped through the tape.

He watched me fill my arms with twenty boxes of the fifty-count twinkling white lights. "You think you can handle that?"

"Black Friday? No. Shoving these in beside the inflatable snowmen? Probably."

The half-moon smile warmed my heart. It was rare for our schedules to cross anymore, and restocking stopped for no one. But I couldn't escape feeling miffed at his having ditched our study date last night.

Not that it was a date. I mean, Dana and Fariah had been there.

As had Ink.

"I tried calling you last night," I said.

Cal paused in shoving the next stack of boxes off the pallet onto the wire rack. He swiveled around to me, then dipped his gaze. "Must have missed it. Sorry."

"Just, we all got together to, ya know, cram cram cram!" Jesus, I sounded like a lovesick teenager going full cheerleader to get a boy to notice me. "But if you had better things to do…"

"Better? Hardly." Calvin's eyes shifted, the backroom's shitty lighting wiping his clear blue eyes to a milk white. But he swept a hand through his hair and the illusion vanished. Caution crawled across his long face and he twisted from me.

In profile, he said, "Besides, I thought you were busy with…someone else."

Damn it. There went that incubus problem again. "Look, I can explain."

45

"You don't have to explain anything. I...I get it. Totally, one hundred percent, no question. Get. It."

But he didn't. Ink wasn't a serious contender, could never be. And Calvin Rollin was...far too good a person to waste his time on someone like me. Even before the whole 'witch with a pet demon' problem. Now I was an even worse catch.

With the reminder of the last arrival of Christmas trying to tumble out of my hands, I turned to Cal. "Do you have any big plans?"

"For what?"

"The holidays. Thanksgiving break, Christmas. Dana keeps talking about some ski resort."

His lips fluttered, not from a breath, but almost like a growl rolled below them. But it vanished so quick I was sure I imagined it. He twisted his head. "What about you?"

"I don't..." Holidays. A time of family, tradition, putting up that childhood tree. Singing those songs learned in grade school. Fighting off relatives who wanted to smother me in love. At least that was how the commercials sold it. I hadn't seen anything like that in a long time.

Trying to not bring the mood crashing down, I said, "Sleep?"

Cal laughed. "That's all I want for Christmas."

"And a hippopotamus," I threw, in expecting a small nod for my stupid joke. But Cal's expression twisted in confusion. "You know, from the song. 'I want a hippopotamus for...' Please don't make me sing."

His face flattened, the life draining from his eyes as he stared through me. I tried to spy over my shoulder to pray there wasn't a naked incubus wandering around, but Ink was nowhere to be seen. What the hell had happened?

A shiver seemed to knock Calvin back to the present. "Right. Of course. If you'll excuse me, I need to get these out." He picked up my stock and began to march for the sliding glass doors, only for our manager to appear.

"These the fifty count?"

We both nodded, though I was tempted to wave my hand over the huge text stamped on the box proclaiming it as such.

"Put 'em back. Seems they're gonna be a 'door-buster' and there's too many out already."

A grumble rolled through my gut at that late bit of information. At least he hadn't told me after I'd already filled the shelves.

"What's the matter, Leeland? Not excited to do your job?"

"No, sir. Absolutely loving it, sir. Couldn't be happier. Sir."

Whatever had overtaken Calvin must have vanished as he tried to hide a chuckle in a cough. Maybe he'd lost someone to a hippo stampede? Did they even do that?

"You're lucky you weren't working last night," our manager kept on. He knew I was in school and loved to get a dig in every few days that he still had the upper hand. For now.

"Why? Did someone ram the forklift into a stack of beanbag chairs again?" I finished shoving the last of the lights back in the box, and Calvin hefted the entire crate up. I hadn't anticipated that, leaving my wayward hand to sweep over the small of his back. And rest it there. Right above his ass. In snug jeans.

"Some girl got chopped up."

All asses were forgotten as I spun on the manager. "You heard about that? Already?" The cops had practically threatened to chuck me into a cell indefinitely if I didn't stay quiet about what I'd seen, especially to reporters.

"Heard? Gena found the body and called it in."

The blood drained from my face straight to my heart. Panic knocked into it, causing me to wrap my hands around the manager's vest. "What do you mean Gena found the body?"

"In a dumpster," he said, his eyes growing wide as he realized I wasn't about to let go.

"Outside Grizzly's?" Maybe she'd heard about it, wanted to make herself the center of attention.

"What? No. Beside the loading docks. Corporate had shit kittens trying to get the police to keep it quiet. We were under orders to hustle the cops through as fast as possible before the church crowd got in."

Fuck. My heart stopped dead and my hands dropped off him. He shrugged like he was the one to free himself from my death grip while I stumbled into the shelving unit.

Ink had warned me. He'd said that there could be monsters in the city. And I'd ignored him because... because I didn't think monsters were real. Now a girl, another girl was dead.

"I have to go," I said, shoving past my manager. "I feel like shit." It wasn't entirely a ruse, the bile rising in my stomach from visions of a chest hacked to pieces until the intestines bulged between cracked ribs. Slapping a hand over my mouth caused my manager to give me a wide berth.

"You don't have any sick leave," he shouted in my wake.

I knew that. But at the moment, making rent seemed less important than the lives of countless women across the city. It wasn't until I reached the door that I realized Calvin had vanished as well.

Chapter Six

Even after putting my car in Park, I kept my foot on the brake and my hand locked around the gear shift. The streetlight flickered the only way it could at two in the morning. I half expected the bulb to blow just as a shadowy figure appeared down the alley.

"This isn't right," I whispered to myself. Despite only ever having visited a church for a single piano recital, I started to form the sign of the cross.

My passenger twisted his head. "Those don't end with a snap. At least they didn't in my day."

I tried to laugh at Ink, but my teeth couldn't stop chattering as I gazed across the once welcoming parking lot of my favorite coffee shop. The cop cars were gone, only a string of crime scene tape remaining. It looked like the dumpster had been taken too, a bright stain in the cement the only mark where a woman'd been brutally disposed.

"Shall we?" Ink asked.

This was stupid.

I released the death grip on my car and stumbled to the cold ground. A splash of the last remnants of November's drizzle crawled into my shoe to drench my sock. Digging into the backseat, I unearthed the book. Almost on instinct, I passed my palm across the cover and a calm shivered through me. Not enough to knock away my growing urge to leap back into my car and peel away, but it helped.

Ink, however, was not. Striding through the crisp air, he didn't even rub his hands together despite being dressed in his only shirt and pants. He was nearly at the crime scene before he glanced back to find me frozen in place.

"Is there a problem?" he asked.

"Aside from the fact we're trespassing where a woman was ripped to pieces?"

Something in my tone must have struck as Ink twisted his head to the space where the dumpster had been, and back to me. "Of course, humans and their innate fear of death."

"I'd say every species capable of awareness isn't a big fan of dying. If not, we'd all be leaping straight off a cliff for fun."

The demon chuckled deep in his tempting baritone. God help me, but I couldn't ignore the shiver it set off in me. *Focus, Layla. Dead woman.*

Women.

That brought me back to earth.

Guilt hung around my neck, bowing my head as I sidled next to Ink. He raised the tape, which was already blowing in the wind. Still I hesitated.

"If it is not death's existence, are you yet perturbed from discovering a dead body?"

Darkness clanged at the sides of my vision, my heart plummeting. With my back to Ink, I ducked under the tape. "No," I said, focusing on my spell book to try to avoid the past. "It wasn't the first dead body I've found."

That intrigued Ink, his head twisting as if he wanted more, but I was in no mood. Instead, I kicked away a soggy bag and placed the spell book on the ground. An intense dislike came over me, drawing my eyes to the book. It had no face—thank god—but I always felt like it was alive and judging me.

"Sorry," I said to an inanimate object and dug into my pocket for the rest of my monster fighting equipment. A small candle, vanilla scented, and an old lighter were what Ink said I'd need. "What do I do first? Light it?"

He nodded, and I put puny fire to the small wick. It took a few seconds to take, the wind trying to whip the flame away. I had to protect it while I turned to Ink.

"What's next? The bell?"

Bell, book and candle. He told me to pack all three for the mission. I didn't question it until I stood in a back alley in the middle of the night with a tumbler puffing out a whiff of vanilla.

"Do I need to put the candle somewhere?" I asked while trying to jostle out the bell. That had been even harder to find. Not a lot of call for hand bells anymore. I twisted the candle around to stare at the label. "What do witches use this for?"

"To read the book."

He had to be joking.

Ink blinked slowly and pointed to my book. "Being able to read the spells is vital for magic casting."

"Are you kidding me?" I shouted. The echo of my voice pinging off the ventilation ducts caused me to wince into my hoodie. "The candle's just to—I have a flashlight on my phone!" I raised up the light and beamed it at Ink's face.

He didn't shy away from it, but for a moment his eyes went completely black. "I see. Well, that would be more prudent than a candle, yes." Pursing his lips, he blew out the flame.

"And the bell?" I jangled the cheap bike bell I'd picked up at a sporting's good store. It had taken me nearly the whole day to find it.

Ink smiled. "The coven would use it to warn others of any hunters during spell casting."

"For fuck's... Here!" I tossed the bell at him. "You're my coven now. You look out for anyone."

"I cannot do much against hunters."

"I'm worried about cops patrolling the area, or nosy neighbors who wonder why people are lighting candles at a murder scene." Bending my knees, I picked up the book and aimed my phone's flashlight at it. My fingers pried it open to a random page—not that it mattered. The spell book wasn't just an ordinary tome containing magical incantations and was hopefully not made from human skin. It was created only for me. No one else could read it. And no one else could get it to, well...this part was kinda weird.

"What creature can rip apart an adult human?" I spoke aloud as if asking Siri.

In an instant, the pages started to rifle under my fingers. They landed upon an image of a monster with a skull for a head and a pair of antlers jutting from the top. I cricked my head, trying to read the squiggly handwriting. "What's a wendigo?"

"Did the corpse still have her liver?" Ink asked. I stared askance at him and he shrugged. "If so, it probably wasn't a wendigo."

Before I could get to the first sentence, the book began flipping again. This time it landed on an entry on a manticore. I started to read that, only for the pages to fly backward. "Yac—" And it was off again.

I extended the book away, the pages flying erratically like it had developed ADHD. "This isn't helping."

"I'd suggest trying 'stop.'"

A sneer rose on my lips, but I said, "Stop," and the possessed librarian inside my book froze. "How many creatures with claws and fangs are in here? Not a question for you, book!" I said quickly. Still, one page curled up as if it was about to flip itself. Or maybe flip me off.

What was I supposed to do? Anything could be stalking these women, mutilating them. Maybe it was that wen-thing. Not like I checked for a liver before slamming the lid shut.

"May I ask a question?" Ink sidled in beside me. He held a hand under mine splayed against the book and peered down despite the fact that it was blank to him. "Why are you not revisiting the moment of the murder?"

"I can do that?" Would I want to do that? "Wait, like, walking up to the murder in the middle of his killing and try to stop it?"

"No, no." Ink laughed as if I suggested I could fly to the roof. "Time alterations are…not for the novice. Or even the experienced. Some liches panic at the thought. I refer to the shadow memory."

"Shadow memory?" Despite being the witch born for this, it was like walking up to that job councilor the GED program had and declaring I wanted to be a nurse all over again. She wouldn't stop quizzing me on the spot about anatomy terms, as if I should already know everything a nurse did. A potent cocktail of shame and anger boiled inside me.

Thankfully, Ink didn't roll his eyes or sigh in exasperation. "Every living being leaves behind a shadow, and that shadow is recorded in the middle lands."

"Middle lands?"

"The area of existence between this realm and the nether planes."

"But the middle lands. That name is so…"

My demon shrugged. "It's simply a negative space from one existence to another, hardly worthy of a naming committee. But it can be tapped into and explored."

"And I can do that? Rewind or reveal these shadow memories?"

Ink pointed at my book with a smile rising. Pulling in a breath, I asked, "How do I reveal shadow memories?"

The spell unfolded across a page and a half. The creator of it had had to scribble notes in the margins. I tried to focus on the mechanics but when it mentioned 'unraveling the fibers within fibers of the nether realm', my eyes started to cross. "I see a drawable symbol here," I said, metaphorically wiping the sweat from my brow.

Normal English could give my dyslexia a challenge, scientific Latin was a headache, but this magic stuff was impossible. Every time I tried to read through the incantation, the letters shifted six times. Not that I had any idea how to properly pronounce it in the first place.

"Good thing I brought this," I said, fishing out the sidewalk chalk from my pocket. I'd taken to carrying it and a stash of Sharpies with me everywhere I went. While I hadn't found much reason to cast a spell during my typical day, the fear of scrounger attacks kept me always patting my pockets to check.

The spell's ward design was simple enough. I crouched down and struck the cement with the pink chalk. "Do they all involve circles?" I asked while waddling around on my haunches. The chalk line crossed from the garbage-sticky alley right to where the dumpster had been.

Some instinct told me to hold my breath as I drew where the dead woman fell. With the circle finished, I inspected the book resting on my open palm. "Two wavy lines, an eye, and... What's this?"

I raised the book to Ink who only quirked up an eyebrow. Sighing, I scratched the symbol on the ground below the eye. "Omega," he said. "The end."

"Of what?" I asked, smearing the pink dust across my pants. I'd feared people would worry satanic cults were doing unspeakable sacrifices whenever they spotted my wards. But this looked more like a bored kid with no imagination had tried to kill some time.

A hand swept across my shoulders, drawing my gaze to the demon. As Ink stepped into the circle, a dark haze formed off his back. It rose outward, creating a smokey version of his black wings. Impenetrable night curled across his eyes, and in a bone-quaking voice he said, "Everything."

I tried to shake my head in the hopes it would purge the crackling red and black skin crawling across Ink.

But the longer he remained beside me, the more his demon flesh emerged. I settled on twisting my head to the side so I couldn't see him.

"Okay," I answered noncommittally to a potential apocalypse and juggled the book. The next part looked surprisingly easy. With a finger to mark my place, I closed the book and raised my other palm. "Show me the events that led to a woman's death." Bending over, I placed my hand on the eye.

Light burst out of the circle, blinding me to nothing but the sharp pain throbbing in my head. I stumbled back to escape the silent explosion, only for my back to smack into an invisible wall. *What the…?* Spinning, I clawed at nothing inside of nothing.

What happened? What went wrong?

What if I couldn't leave?

Cold circled my feet, the edge of my vision darkening. I clasped two fingers to my neck out of a fear I was about to pass out. But as I turned, black smoke twisted and blew across the endless blank whiteness. It crested upward and held, almost solidifying into a wall. A wall with an edge at the side and a…wheel.

The dumpster.

A shadow of someone's hand threaded through the whiteness. I stared at it, waiting for the actual body to follow. The longer it remained, the more solid it grew, though never fully opaque. Each time the hand shifted, the edges of it spun off in little whirlpools of smoke.

"What do you see, my bond?" Ink's voice boomed through the play of shadow on light.

So this was working. Probably. "Nothing yet," I began, when the shadow woman stepped into view. She wasn't an entire silhouette, the smoke lessening where highlights would hit. A hint of cheekbones, a forehead, the slender bones of her hand. Clutched to her chest was a rectangle of pure white.

I started to lean closer, my eyes drawn to this book or piece of paper, when smoke stabbed through my chest. The shadow woman's mouth opened, her white-gray teeth screaming in agony. The killer didn't pause, slicing twice more with a strange knife. White smoke poured from the woman's chest, splashing on the ground. Whenever the knife stabbed through my chest, a chill snapped from my spine and traced down to the hand bringing death.

Even without being able to see the stranger's face, I felt her terror. I knew her panic, and I heard a misplaced thought that she could survive this. That help had to be coming. That she couldn't die in this shitty town. Her body collapsed to the ground and the knife rose higher. I wrapped my hands around the wrist, trying to collapse the smoke and disarm it. But my palms slapped together and the knife slashed through me as if I wasn't even there.

Because I hadn't been.

Nothing more than a shadow memory, Layla. Remember. She's gone.

At least one good thing came of this. "It's not a monster," I said. It wasn't my fault.

"You're certain?" Ink sounded less than impressed with me. *Maybe I should invite him to cast this spell instead?*

"Do you know any creatures that use knives?"

"It's not without precedent, but you make a valid point."

I wished I could see whoever did it, but turning over my shoulder only revealed a looming shadow. A human silhouette, but without any features to go off, I was stuck.

It's not your job to solve a murder. That's why we have cops.

Still, as the shadow man walked through my body, anger percolated inside. Without a second's pause, he hefted up the body of the slain woman and hurled her into the dumpster. The rattle of it bouncing against the wall and the crunch of bags from her weight burst through my ears.

I tried to shrink away, wishing to collapse the vision and run home. But the murderer paused with his back to me and gazed down at the dead woman. The longer he stared, the sharper his body came into focus. Lines formed, revealing a baggy sweatshirt or coat. Short hair cut close to the uncovered head. And jeans.

Would any of that help the cops? How could I even tell them?

Maybe an anonymous note? That might work. It was in their hands if they'd even read it.

Set on my path, I tried to step back in the hopes the spell's wall would break down, when the murderer turned.

Eyes so blue they were nearly white glared death at me. The long face, ears prodding out from below the shadowed hair, a wide nose ending in a near point. *No.*

The murderer twisted his head to the side and dashed away, his form vanishing in a puff of smoke.

It couldn't be.

A hand wrapped around my arm. I slammed my elbow back, denting deep into a stomach, only for Ink to laugh. All traces of his demon form were wiped away until only a hot man without visible breath stared down at me. I stumbled, realizing that I could see the orange of his eyes and the solid curve of his pecs. Glancing down, I found I'd smudged through the circle of my ward with my shoe, evaporating the white world of the shadows.

"Not bad for your first shadow memory. It might take you a few hours to adjust to low levels of light and the color red," Ink said while I stared hard at the alley.

There was so much trash. The wind ripped open bags and sent the contents flying. My heart stuck in my throat. A candy bar wrapper was caught in the debris above the sewer grate.

"Layla?"

Shit.

"If it is not a creature run rampant, then why are we lingering?"

"Because," I said, twisting around the half of a wrapper to a Whooseit. The only person I knew who ate those was Calvin Rollin. "I think I know who did it."

Chapter Seven

For one week, a three-year-old child with congestive heart failure has been receiving digoxin. What is an early sign of digitalis toxicity a parent should look out for?

It can't be. Not Calvin. I'd believe Fariah was stalking the streets as some murderous banshee before Cal. *He's so… He's too nice.*

Wasn't that what they always said about serial killers? *'Oh, but he was so nice.'*

"Ms. Leeland." Professor LeRoux shattered the tension of scratching pencils. "If a patient walks into your clinic, would they continue to accept the word of a nurse who cannot keep her eyes off another RN?"

Shit. "No, sir," I muttered, trying to lock my focus on my test. Three weeks ago, this had been the main source of stress in my life. Now, I filled in bubbles haphazardly while my eyes kept darting to the man I thought was my friend. The man who could have already killed two women, and more if I didn't stop him.

61

Cal sat ahead and to the left of me. No matter how many times I snuck a gaze at him, he remained head bent over his test. Except for once, when I tried to shake off the brick in my gut to focus. I caught him in my peripheral vision, and those same blue-white eyes were burning at me.

By the time I finished my test, my brain was unable to remember a single question. I stumbled out of the lecture hall needing to talk to Ink again. *I should read through my spell book. Maybe I got the incantation wrong.* Or the shadow memory could have been corrupted. *DNA tests can give false positives, why not the memory of shadows?*

I sounded more insane with each passing day.

"Layla?"

Oh shit. The brick in my stomach hatched the entire wall of China. Sidling through the group of bleary-eyed students came my problem. If Cal noticed my leaning away, he gave no sign.

He crested a hand over his hair as if to shake away a late shower. "Whew. How'd you do?"

"I..." Damn it, my hands were trembling. I stuffed both into my pockets and knocked into the sidewalk chalk sitting inside. "I don't know."

"LeRoux's known for being a right bastard with midterms, but that... Did we even study chorea?"

Cal wore an easy smile despite his concerns. He'd left his coat open, revealing a striped T-shirt. With its blue and white motif, his damp hair clinging to his forehead and the overhead lights striking his oceanic eyes, Calvin looked like he was about to sell cologne to yachters. I stared at his fingers. Strong, yes, but capable of swinging a knife hard enough through a person's guts that her intestines exploded?

"Was that on the test?" I muttered, my brain fighting with my body. One knew he couldn't be the murderer, and the other kept screaming it knew what it had seen. The trouble was, I couldn't tell who came down on which side.

Cal reached for me and I was so deep in my mind that I forgot to jump. He brushed his palm over my forehead. I wanted to lean into the cool touch attempting to soothe my rising panic.

"Are you okay, Layla? You look a little peaked."

"Going up to girls telling them they look awful? How do you see that working out?" Ah, there was that Leeland sarcasm I knew well. *Cling to it so tight it pops when shit hits the fan. Just like my...my mother.*

Calvin's million-dollar smile somehow brightened more. He brushed his shoulder against mine and my entire body jerked. "An excuse to keep you in my bed all day? Sounds like a win to me." His voice dropped to a whisper, his eyes not playing around. He drifted them down my body like he'd already picked off all my clothes before dabbing away my fever with his tongue.

Fucking hell. I'd wanted this for months. For the sophisticated man who'd danced around me since before nursing school started to prove he was into me. He wanted me. And now he could be a mass-murdering psychopath. *Great.*

"Or..." Calvin faded back, his hand falling from my face until both slapped onto his thighs. "You already have someone for that. Of course. Don't know how I forgot."

"Ink's not a—"

Raising a hand, he ripped his gaze from me as if he couldn't control himself. "I really don't care. Your life. Your choices. Do with them as you will." The once tender voice tipped to a snarl, Cal's nostrils flaring as he loomed over me.

"Holy shit, that test!" Dana shouted. She locked both arms around me for support and pretended she'd collapse to the floor for dramatic emphasis. The silence ticked on a beat too long, causing Dana to glance from me to Cal. "Did I walk in on something?"

"No," I said, my back snapping straight.

Cal snorted and shook his head. "Hardly."

"Kay, kay. So, we gonna head to the cantina for lunch?" Dana didn't miss a beat. I watched Cal trying to not stare at me. He didn't raise a hand to hood his eyes, but he tipped his head low and shuffled back through the other students filling the hallway.

"Why the cantina?" I asked, then remembered the date. The fifteenth meant... "Strawberries and ice cream day."

Dana gave a little shake of excitement as if the college putting out fresh strawberries for the soft serve once a month was the equivalent of champagne and caviar.

"I have something else to do," Calvin said. "Later." With his shoulders hunched, he slipped into the crowd, never glancing back.

A hand slid around my shoulders—Dana pulling herself so close that her cheek touched mine. "What crawled up his butt?"

I couldn't let him leave. What if he was planning another murder? "Sorry, Dana, I just remembered I have to...do something too," I said, slapping my hands together in both prayer and forgiveness. The former was for me tracking a serial killer. Gripping tighter to my backpack and the red leather book inside, I wormed through the crowds without taking my eyes off Calvin.

Dana shouted for everyone to hear, "If you two plan to fuck, you should just say."

Cal led me away from the campus and into the crumbling neighborhoods circling the university's manicured greens. Luckily for me, he didn't get in his car, or I'd have lost him in an instant. I watched from across the street as he undid the latch on a tetanus-strewn chain-link gate and slipped into someone's overgrown backyard. At the distance, I could only make out Calvin yelling until the patio door slid open.

"Are we to be spies now?"

Jumping out of my socks, I spun around to face Ink who stood with a hand on my back. When did he put that there? His lips rose in a cheeky smile, and I swallowed my shiver.

"I followed him after the test," I said, focusing on the blond man I thought I knew and the black-haired one I didn't. "I can't let him kill someone else. No matter what." Despite my oath, acid gurgled in my stomach at the idea I'd have to stop him.

"Have you entertained the possibility that he could be a hunter?"

My brain scratched at the idea and I glared at him.

"Both attacks occurred in places you are known to regularly visit."

That was ludicrous. The café was near the rundown frat guy part of town, and everyone went to Bellpeppers. It was the biggest grocery store by the campus, as sad as that was. "That doesn't make any sense. Your imaginary witch hunter killed innocent people to, what, send a message?"

"They've done far worse for less reasons." A cold demeanor swept over Ink, leaving me to try to tamp down a shiver in my soul. Steadying myself, I watched

Cal and his stranger friend fall deep in conversation. Through the gaps in the gate I could see half of Cal's face and a quarter of the stranger. The dark-haired man looked like a late addition a cheap drama would bring on to spice up the ratings. All tattered hair, permanent shit-smelling sneer and too much leather in this damp weather.

Ink pressed his chest to my back, dipping his chin down to land it on my shoulder. Slowly, he stroked his jaw in thought before turning to me. "What dastardly deed do you think is occurring?"

The chances of Cal openly talking about any murders he might have committed and the reasons why seemed highly unlikely. But I'd never seen him so agitated before, both here and while talking to me earlier. I never thought he'd be capable of killing someone before either. "I'm not sure." I wrinkled my nose. "I wish I could hear them."

"Why don't you?"

Snorting, I twisted my head and nearly knocked into Ink's nose. "Because if I get any closer, they'd see me and stop talking."

"My bond." Ink chuckled. He rustled through my bag and raised the spell book. "When will you learn that you are a witch?"

Listening in on a friend's private conversation would be considered a big no-no, a 'reading a person's diary' kind of faux pas. I took the book and asked it to find me a spell for eavesdropping.

Instead of the paragraphs of text, it only required a single sentence I managed to read and... "Damn it, I don't have anything of Cal's."

"What about this?" Ink asked, drawing a finger down the collar of my coat. A blush burned across my cheeks at the single strand of white-blond hair he found. "I don't believe this is your color."

"It must have fallen off of him when..." *Stop apologizing to the sex demon. You have bigger problems.* Rubbing my fingers over the hair, I closed my eyes and recited the words in the book.

A *pop* bounced through my ears like a shattered balloon echoing in a cavern. I reached up to try to massage away the pain, when a voice rose.

"...don't like this." That was Calvin. Could I also hear whoever he was talking to?

Silence passed, answering the question for me. Maybe the one half of the conversation would be enough to piece this together.

"I know he's here," Cal snarled. "You're not the only one who'd like to rip his throat out."

Shit. My face drained from the vitriol I'd never thought possible from Cal. That didn't sound like a euphemism, but a vow from someone prepared to remove a man's trachea with a corkscrew.

I waited for Cal to say a 'but' or insist that he would never harm another person, except all that came was more silence. Whoever he was with must have been doing all the talking, as it felt like a lifetime before Calvin spoke again.

"Where were you last night, Mark?"

Last night? I leaned over to Ink. "Have there been any other deaths?" What if it wasn't Cal I saw, but this Mark fellow? Which would mean Calvin had been in that alley trying to cover up Mark's kill. It wasn't looking much better, but at least it didn't make him a murderer.

Ink shrugged. "I am not the town crier. Also, you don't need to whisper," he said in such a soft tone I leaned closer. "They can't hear us!" he suddenly bellowed, causing me to rear back.

The demon chuckled at his unfunny joke, while I held a hand over my ear to protect it.

"What about me?" Cal said, twisting me back to staring across the yard. "You think I'd let myself get mixed up in that shit again? Don't say that. Please. Not… Look, just don't do anything yet. Let me call the pa—"

"The pa—what?" I shouted, wiggling my ear as if I could tune it to the All Calvin station.

Ink jerked a finger to my stationary hand and the empty fingers. "The hair's been drained to dust by the spell."

"Damn it." The curse charged through me, sending me dashing around in a circle. I didn't have any proof one way or the other. Only more questions with this Mark character added to the pile. Best-case scenario, Calvin was covering up the murders for his friend. And the worst case…?

You always did have terrible taste in men, Layla.

I glanced to the demon chained to my soul and sighed from the bottom of it. Positively abysmal tastes.

Movement across the street sent my head whipping around. Ink locked on to my waist and tugged me down just as two bodies walked through the open gate. With the tips of my fingers, I peeled away the shrubbery to notice Mark dressed like he was late to star in the *Matrix* remake. Black trench coat over black thigh-high boots covered in buckles. All he needed was a pair of sunglasses to complete the look.

He tugged on the collar like he wasn't certain he wanted to even be out of the house. Then he turned to the man in a chunky fisherman sweater behind him.

They clasped hands, but not in an amicable handshake. Mark grabbed Cal up the forearm and they came together for that half-hug and shoulder slug that men do.

"I miss the double-kiss greeting," Ink mused behind me.

"On the cheeks?" I asked without a thought. Mark turned to the left while Calvin lingered by the gate. Did he know I was following him?

"Only after the trousers are lost," Ink whispered, forever delighted in himself.

Seemingly satisfied, Cal turned on his heel and followed the street to the right. Two suspects, both possible murderers...not just murderers, but eviscerators of women. Who should I follow? The stranger in a black trench coat and goth boots? Or the stranger I'd sat and studied beside for a year?

"Ink, follow that man," I said, pointing in Mark's direction.

"I'm sorry, did I put on a pair of pointed slippers today or are you confusing an incubus for a djinn?"

"Just...I would desire you tracking the man who could be killing women. Okay?"

He snickered and licked his teeth. "What you really desire is...heading due south. But I'll play along, this time." With that, he vanished, hopefully doing what I asked.

I tried to not glance at Cal, but the guilt sent my eyes that way. Desire him? A potential murderer and liar? A guy that could rip me to pieces for shits and giggles?

I hated when Ink was right.

Rising to my feet, I gave chase to a man who could kill me if I was right.

Chapter Eight

What are you doing, Layla?

Just hiding in the bushes outside my friend's house while he eats microwaved mac and cheese in the living room. Completely normal behavior, not at all a sign your faculties slipped off the pan and into the fire. It was justified. Because I thought I saw him visiting a murder scene.

It wasn't like I saw *him* do the murder, more a shadowy figure without any discernible features except for his eyes.

Was this what it felt like to lose one's mind?

Maybe the entire witch-and-demon thing was nothing more than a psychotic breakdown when I stumbled across a dead body. Inventing a reason to fix it, to find sense in the senseless sounded like an explanation that a psychologist would have told me. In order to claim control, I went so wildly nuts I mashed half my face into a bush of thorns to stalk my friend.

It's all in my head.

"So far he has consumed a midday meal consisting of a bagel and that bitter beverage there are a multitude of shrines devoted to."

My last shred of sanity flittered away on the wind as I turned to find Ink standing beside me. He absently rolled two pennies across his knuckles as though he'd swiped them from the ferryman. There a good chance the demon had done just that.

He paused his dexterity trick and stared at me. "Do you require any other information?"

"A full name would be nice." *Better than the contents of his stomach, at least.*

Ink jerked his head up. "Why don't you ask that man forever at your elbow?"

I yanked my head back through the small hole in the bush, trying to weigh if that was jealousy in the incubus' voice. The words sure sounded like it, but the tone was as flippant as always.

Standing upon the rickety porch was Calvin, the skeletal trees casting shadows of claws over his face. After locking the door, he bundled a scarf around his neck while he stared up and down the street. Was it guilt causing him to keep checking his sights? Was he afraid of someone watching him?

Someone is *watching him, Layla.*

I abandoned the bush and turned to Ink. "Get back to that Mark character. Keep following him to see where he lives."

"If you wish me to determine his guilt or innocence, I only need ten minutes in a backroom—"

"No!" I shouted, locking my hands around Ink's shirt and tugging him closer. The demon didn't put up any fight, but he stared down to where I grabbed him. "Keep a distance. We don't want him to spot you."

He snickered, brushing his hot lips against my ear. "Is that truly the only reason you wish to keep me caged...or do you have other plans for my body?"

Fight the shiver. I couldn't feel him poking around in my mind, but I knew he was reading my desires and picking what he wanted. "Just...get going."

"Very well. One demon spy at your beck and call." He took a step back and vanished from my sight. It was as if he hadn't even been there, which didn't help with my psychosis theory.

Focus, Layla. Either you've completely lost your mind or magic's real and your friend could be a murderer. Sitting in place waiting for someone else to handle this mess wasn't an option. If one more girl died because of me...

I flinched, the stench of bile rising from my memory and up through my sinuses. *Nope. Not the time.* With a quick glance over the street for both cars and Cal, I wedged my way out of the bush and dashed for his house. The city was a patchwork quilt of neighborhoods, each more or less burnished with the same architecture from when it was built.

I lived in the stodgy cement-brick apartments from the seventies. Dana had a nice ranch home out of the late nineties. But Cal's house looked like a gothic manor ripped from the hills of Scotland had been dropped one street over from a Kum & Go. If the rest of the street hadn't got that *Addams Family* meets *Jane Eyre* esthetic, I'd probably have had shivers crawling up my spine.

The gate, overrun with dying vines because a working student didn't have time to garden, squeaked at my entrance. I whipped my head around, certain that'd have given me away. But no neighbors peeked through the hedges that were more stick than bush. An archway and what should have been a medieval door with a half-circle at the top formed the entrance. But that stained-glass window had been long since bricked up, leaving only a cheap rectangular door behind. Once a brash burgundy, the sun had faded the color to an unassuming pink, except for the indents. Along the edges, it looked like blood had run through the pink lands.

I tried the knob and it turned. Amazing how often people wouldn't bother to lock up. Twisting it, I pushed inward, and was stopped by the deadbolt. *Of course, Layla. You saw him locking it.*

A part of me hoped he hadn't, so I could explain being in his place as a simple misunderstanding. *I thought you were in here. Oops. Silly me.*

I could force it. *Crowbar maybe. Wait.* There was a back door. I remembered it from the cookout. Though his backyard looked more like a garden for a widow whose husbands all died from mysterious illnesses. We'd razzed Cal for it, who'd laughed along with us while he turned hot dogs.

At the time it seemed funny, Cal growing poisons to dispatch his enemies in his backyard. Now, I was careful to keep my hands away from the towering plants straining out of their plots. Razor-sharp leaves brushed over the cobblestones, making me glad I was in pants as I approached the back door.

Windows loomed beside it, revealing a peek into the dark entryway for his kitchen. I tried to peer closer, but dust had left the entire house in a haze. Not that being able to see inside would help me, unless he left an "I killed two women" sign hanging from the chandelier above the counters.

"Damn it," I cursed, tugging on the back door which was more locked than the front. There wasn't even a hint of give. Sometimes the lock could be overpowered with enough force.

Gritting my teeth, I wrapped both hands around the long handle and pulled. My capillaries were about to explode from the strain, but the door didn't budge.

Now what?

I stumbled back to take in my nemesis while wiping my forehead. No sign of any windows open on the second floor. Not that I could get up there without learning parkour. *Wait, what about…?*

Recessed behind a small retention wall, I spotted a gap. Dahlias' paper-like petals stuck to my pants as I eased toward the hole, then heads of the desiccated flowers ripped off as I reached through the open window.

Yes!

A grown woman whose last year had been spent downing pizza while deep into lymphatic systems instead of running marathons would not have an easy time fitting through a small rectangular window. Most would probably call it foolish for her to try. And they'd be right.

I folded my hands together like I was about to dive into a pool and did just that through the gap. It took two seconds for my jeans and the ass contained within to snag on the ledge.

Damn it! Suck it in, Leeland.

That worked to free my stomach, not so much my ass. "Shit!" I cried through clenched teeth. In my shifting, the window pinched into my lower belly like the worst cramps. *Ow, ow, ow…!* I tugged on the strap around my shoulder and yanked the damn bag with my spell book through the window.

It dangled into the dark basement, softly bouncing against the wall as I pulled in a breath. Slapping my hands to the cold, dented walls, I slithered through the micro-gap I'd managed. Just as the last of my ass made it from outside to in, I remembered the first rule of gravity.

"Fu—" I shouted, my face tumbling for the floor. At the last second, I rolled my body forward, slicing my legs against the window ledge. But it kept me from breaking my nose. I tucked in and splattered my back on the ground instead.

As I stared up at a ceiling barely visible in the shadows, I felt a presence glaring at me. Not Cal or any of his new friends. Not Ink laughing at me in the corner. No, this judgment came from beside my head.

Sitting up, only to have fetid basement air knock about in my flattened lungs, I tugged out the spell book. That did nothing to lessen the criticism radiating from its binding. "What? I got in, didn't I? Not like you could help me to..."

The pages cracked apart, flying under my fingers until they landed on an entry devoted to *Breaking into vaults*.

"Well, now you tell me," I said, snapping the book closed. If it were possible for something without lips, a tongue or a larynx to growl, the book managed. Stuffing its rumbling body under my arm, I rose to my feet to find...a dark space.

I'd have to turn on a light or risk snapping my neck on the stairs. Slapping a hand to the wall—which felt like cold stone with massive divots crafted into it—I traced along the floor. To think, I used to do this shit all the time when I was younger.

The single shaft of sunlight penetrating through the weeds and dingy window could only highlight a swipe of floor. It looked like dirt, but I felt solid cement under my feet. Maybe Cal was in the middle of finishing the basement?

My foot slid out and a clank echoed off the stone ground. Absently, I pawed at the piece of metal with my toe, as if that would help me figure out what it was.

Yes, Layla. Very metallic. Much help.

What I needed was… The book grew heavier in my arm. Of course! I pulled out my phone and let there be light.

"What the fuck!"

Dungeon. Torture dungeon. Chains for towing ships lay scattered across the floor with massive manacles that could clamp around my thighs dangling from the ends. Dirt and mud clung to the floor, as if small feet had trampled it down from unending pacing.

I shifted my phone to try to find the stairs, my heart screaming at me to get out.

"Holy shit!" A bone dangled off a black chain suspended in the middle of the room. Pieces of tattered flesh lingered on the ends, but the ball joint was missing as if… *Oh fuck.* As if someone had eaten it.

This wasn't right. This wasn't good. I had to call the cops. *You're trespassing! In a murder basement.* I had to get out of here, then call the cops.

Jesus Christ, how could he…why would he do this? In my panic, I took deeper breaths and a strange thought rolled down my spine. There was no blood. I'd done anatomy, I knew what a dead body decomposing in a room smelled like. This wasn't it.

If anything, I'd say it smelled like a, a vet clinic?

Not the time, Layla. Get out of here and...what? Turn over Cal just like that?

Yes. Just like that. Guys with murder basements aren't worth your time.

But another urge overtook me. I had to know why. All that time together, all those long study sessions shoulder to shoulder, all those meals, and he'd never once seemed creepy. Never given even a hint that he'd...keep bones in his basement. Why did he do this?

"Book, I need a spell. A spell to—" What? Explain the psyche of a serial killer? "To help me reveal a person's darkest secret."

To my surprise, the pages turned rapidly until they landed on a page titled *Arcana Revealed*. "Great, it's all in Latin," I muttered, struggling to balance the book and my phone to read it. I knew enough to spot some familiar bases of words thanks to my nursing studies, but nothing on the page made sense.

"How is this supposed to be helpful?" I gritted my teeth, tempted to throw the book at the wall. *Wait.* The other spell, the one I knew I worked. I could track Calvin's shadow memory. It was worth a shot.

When I asked for the shadow memory passage again, the passive-aggressive book barely turned one page, then another. "I'm sorry I didn't ask you to help me break in. I will next time."

Now, it flipped quickly to the same passage. Using the side of my shoe, I swiped at the ground to try to clear away the dirt. A jangle of the chains sent my teeth rattling deep in their sockets, but I clenched my eyes and shook it off. There was witchcraft to do.

With my trusty sidewalk chalk, I drew the same ward as before, but this time in pale green. Okay, now to give it the date I needed replayed. *The night of the first murder*, I thought and placed my hand to the middle.

Nothing happened.

Hello? Night of the first murder. I slapped that damn eye three times, smudging my work and having to put down new connecting lines.

My leg bounced in frustration, rattling the book. For all I knew, the owner of this dungeon was on his way to make more lamps out of human skin. Maybe there was a limit to how far back this thing could go, like a CCTV recording—after a few days, the shadow memory got wiped. It sounded stupid, but anything was possible.

I needed another date, another time to see what Calvin had been up to while a girl was killed. The night the woman had been found behind Bellpeppers. With the date in my mind, I slapped my hand to the ward, and whiteness engulfed me.

It didn't take long for the shadows to emerge, particles of black rolling across the ground like a dust storm. I watched them against the blank canvas, gritting my teeth for what I feared I'd have to see. As I stared forward, a chain appeared, dangling off the ceiling. There was no bone in it, but a hand of shadows appeared. It gripped the great link, tugging the chain to it.

Oh, god. I wanted to curl into a ball and scream that none of this was happening, but I couldn't look away either. The shadowy form moved into my circle and, as I stared, its wispy edges formed the definite shape of Calvin Rollin. His blue eyes burned in the black depths of his sockets, reminding me more of a demon than Ink ever did.

I slapped a hand over my mouth, watching the shadow of Cal yank the chain farther down. It rattled through a loop in the ceiling, reaching for him.

He was going to lock it to some poor woman. Chain her up and do…the worst things imaginable. I knew it in my head just as much I knew in my heart it wasn't possible

Suddenly, the shadow of Cal jerked and he swung his head to the window. I followed and spotted a small black ball among the white sky resting above our heads. His speed increasing, Calvin kicked away the other chains as he…clamped the big one to his neck?

What?

It dangled off another loop locked around his throat and Cal went almost as limp as the chain's slack. The only burst of color in the shadow form vanished, like he had to steady himself. I felt my own breath holding, my body waiting on the edge for something terrifying about to happen.

His hands thrashed through the air, the shadows twirling off his body. Cal's head tipped back and the shadow's form began to shift. The fingers shrunk into his palm, then the entire arm started to tug inward. All the while, his feet sprang up onto the tips of his toes. The ankle elongated to over a foot and kept going.

White swept across Cal's face, or where his face should be. The shadows grew darker, leaving only the silhouette of a man with a jaw extending out in a V shape. Suddenly, the twisted creature collapsed forward onto all fours. The chain followed, letting him stretch the last few feet in the basement as he kept transforming into—

Darkness snapped against my eyes. I shook my head, prepared to move to the side, when I felt a hand locked to my arm. Ink was never going to believe what I saw.

I turned to tell my incubus and met blue eyes blazing instead.

Shit!

"What are you doing here?!" Cal shouted. I tried to flex my biceps to get out of his hold, but I couldn't even shift a pinkie.

"I...I was..." *Fuck, Layla. Why didn't you think of an excuse before coming down here?*

Because I didn't expect any of this!

Cal's entire body shook with barely held rage and his head swiveled down. Suddenly, his fingers opened as if in shock, letting me tug my arm back. I massaged where he'd clung to me with the strength of a beast.

"You..." he stuttered, pointing first at me, then down at the floor. "You're a witch?"

I swiped at the ward with my foot, clearing a line straight through it. "And you're a werewolf."

Chapter Nine

Werewolf.

The word held power over Cal—his body froze in place the moment I spoke it. Out of my peripheral vision, I caught yellow light beaming down above me. That had to be the stairs.

In an instant, the spell broke, Cal's eyes narrowing just as I spun on my feet and dashed for freedom. Creaking burst under me, my heart certain the entire staircase would blow out and send me tumbling back to the werewolf. But I managed to make it to the landing and had to batter my way through a pile of hanging coats. Shoving them aside and kicking fast, I leapt out of what I'd thought was just a closet into the living room.

The same spot where we'd watched cheap movies together after studying. Once, midway through a flick, he'd fallen asleep until his head almost landed on my shoulder. And the whole time he'd been…he was a…

"Layla, wait!" Fingers reached for my arm, the nails snagging over my bare skin and raking. I jerked at the touch, one foot wanting to kick away while the other wanted to run. They tried to do both, sending me flying to the floor.

I caught myself before the end, slapping my hands to the ground and pushing myself back to my feet. There was the door — just a few more steps to freedom. I caught the handle and started to tug, only for a man's hand to slam into the door.

Calvin's body loomed an inch from mine, his chest expanding with every jagged breath and the hand that'd sliced into me dangling at his side. His legs that'd sprinted up the stairs widened for another chase. And his eyes... Sharper than a razor, they tracked me like I was a rabbit on the lawn.

What spell did I know to subdue a rampaging werewolf? Oh, none, because until two minutes ago I didn't think werewolves were real. Why didn't I study my spell book better?

Focus.

His head tipped and the long nose I once thought of as intriguing sniffed deep. "Magic," Cal grunted.

Did werewolves and witches hate each other? Fight in some never-ending war I knew nothing about?

I stumbled back, wishing I had anything other than a half-broken piece of chalk in my pocket. "Calvin, I can..."

My leg knocked into a hard edge and I teetered. The werewolf's wound-up legs sprung, launching him forward to wrap a hand around my face. He hooked his thumb and forefinger along my chin and up my cheeks, and he held me so tight I had no chance of escaping.

"Please," I whispered, praying there was a single note of compassion remaining inside the animal.

The icy gaze darted behind me. "You almost fell," he said, drawing me to find the stack of crates I'd nearly crashed onto.

I wished that reassured me, that I wasn't still staring deep into the eyes of a potential crazed animal, but he didn't release his hold on my face. Cal raised his other hand, the fingers extended as if he expected claws to be on them. The palm drifted closer, my heart thundering for fear of where it was heading. To pierce my ribcage? Pry out my heart? Rip off an arm?

When it settled on my hip, I felt a macabre sense of disappointment. Until Calvin, always sweet but distant Calvin, brushed the full pad of his palm over my ass. A deep rumble rolled from his chest, which kept rising higher.

"Let me leave," I whispered.

That killed his growl, his head shooting up and the eyes opening in surprise. But as he circled his lips with his tongue—which I'd never noticed was so long before—Calvin flexed his hold on me.

Oh god! I stumbled backward, my hands flying to find anything to grab. One latched on to his forearm, the arm with the fingers attached to my face. I could dig my own claws in, see if that shook him off.

But I'd found his den, sussed out his secret. No chance he'd let me walk away now.

"Ah!" I gasped, my back striking the wall. A picture frame jabbed into me, but I wasn't in a position to complain. Cal pressed closer, first almost shoving his chest into mine, then his hips. His hand remained clamped over my chin. I kept picturing it sliding down to my throat to cut off my air. But he didn't move it even while leaning nearer until he grazed the edge of my jaw with his teeth.

Shit. My legs wouldn't stop trembling, my body wanting to fall to the ground and scamper away. But not all of it. Even as I hung on to his arm, my fingers toyed with the hard muscle clinging to me. With every swipe of his hips, the undeniable surge in his pants grew.

"Layla." Calvin whispered my name as though he recognized me from across the street. I turned to him and he plunged his famished mouth over mine. Inescapable heat pulsed through me, Cal's lips a hard snarl aching to own me. But the longer he kissed me, the softer they became. Almost tender and gentle, he slipped his tongue into my mouth. I answered back with mine. My body hummed with anticipation, my mind pleading for more. For me to taste all of him.

Loss. It flooded my senses and I opened my eyes to watch Calvin break off the kiss. His hand slipped from my face, though the other remained cradling my ass. Slowly, he licked his lips, causing a smile to twist across them. But he shook it off and said in a ragged voice, "You can go."

"What?" I lost all focus, my head whipping to the side to see he'd kissed me right next to the door. He'd brought me to the door.

Calvin pulled in a slow breath and his smile turned winsome. "You asked to leave."

Yes. I needed to get out. He could be a murderer. Except he'd been here that night…literally chained up. He'd chained himself up? To keep others safe? My heart fluttered at the idea and Calvin slunk back. He swiped at his neck like it was tough for him to breathe after our kiss. It tugged the sweater down, revealing a handful of blond chest hair begging to be freed.

He's a werewolf.

Well, nobody's perfect.

I fisted his hair, tugging his lips to mine while flattening my body against his. Cal grabbed on to my shirt and lifted it. But I wouldn't stop kissing him, my lips craving his, my hands needing to run the length of his terrain. I worked under his sweater and swept my palm up his stomach. Abs, a tuft of soft hair, and…

Cal grabbed my arms by the wrists and raised them above my head. Our kiss broke, leaving me staring across the narrow gap into his burning ice eyes. He pulled in a breath, straining the knit weave of his sweater across his flexing muscles.

Locking my wrists together in one palm, he yanked my shirt up to my elbows. Only that blur of cotton broke our stare. Electricity crackled in the space between us. I watched Cal pull in air in anticipation of a marathon.

He unleashed my wrists, letting them drop to my sides as my shirt flew into the circular staircase. The energy was building, every micro-shift in my body zapping a strike from me to him, or vice versa. I felt them not as pain, but a shiver across my skin that I'd never known before.

"Gonna show me the goods, wolfman?" I asked, placing a hand to my hip.

Cal's hungry stare that'd been drowning in my cleavage snapped up. His lips whuffled as if he swallowed a growl. Tugging on the neck at the back, he lifted his sweater to reveal…

"Holy shit!" I shouted aloud and slapped a hand to my mouth.

Take Brad Pitt at his peak, then photoshop in even more ab definition. Doing that would probably break a holy covenant with god, but it'd also give a close representation of Calvin's body. The blond hair was so fine he almost looked waxed, but as I trailed the fur to a small tuft right above his hidden dick, I started to squirm.

"When? How..." I stuttered, my head undulating from his face to his impossible body. "What workout do you do to look like this?"

Cal snickered and his cheeks burned pink. He shifted his stance and wadded up the useless sweater as he tried to hide away that adorable moment of embarrassment. Fuck, it made me want to kiss him even harder.

But I was held up by his magic marvel body, my brain fearful that if I touched him, I'd curse myself for a hundred years. Though, a hundred years would probably be worth it.

Fire burned in his ice eyes. Launching off the balls of his feet, Calvin wrapped his hands around me. He licked and sucked up my neck while tugging apart the hooks of my bra. "A moon-based workout," he whispered before nipping my earlobe. "Very exclusive."

I couldn't contain myself anymore and went straight for his jeans. Calvin buried his face against my neck, but he chuckled on the skin. Certain that was a blessing, I undid the button.

Nails scratched down my back, sending my world spinning. "I think she likes that," Cal said, his voice deep and treacherous. He switched sides and clawed awake my right side. "I'd say she likes it a lot."

Sweeping his palms around my chest, he cupped his thumbs right below my bra and under my breasts. "Damn," I moaned. I hooked my hands to his hips for stability as he upended my world.

Cal flattened his hands at the top of my chest and kneaded with the heels into my breasts. Fuck me, why did that feel so good? Sinking my thumbs into his hips' V, I reached around to pad the sides of his ass. They were that sheer cliff of men who did a thousand squats a day.

"Is that all you can do?" I asked, my voice catching from trying to breathe between the panting.

He smiled brightly, but the eyes were hungry and his palms didn't still. "Layla, the things I've imagined doing to you… I worry they might scare you."

I chuckled at the tremble in his voice, at the raw lust buried in his concern. Wrapping my palm over his bulge, I savored in Cal gasping with animalistic need. "Try me," I ordered.

In a frenzy, he tossed away my bra and tried to work off my jeans. I moved to help by tugging them down, when Cal wrapped his hands around me and in one fast toss hurled me onto his couch.

I sank into the old settee. Hooking my hand around the tall part of the swooping back, I tugged myself up and Calvin reached my boots.

Before I could wonder if he had a foot thing, he tugged both away, then worked my pants off via the ankles. *Clever.*

"You have me, in just my panties and purple socks." I wiggled my toes, causing him to chuckle. "Reclining on your Victorian fainting couch." I pressed my head back like I was about to succumb to the vapors and laughed. Leaning up, I hooked my thumbs in his belt loops, tugging that perfect body closer. "What do you want to do with me?"

Calvin unzipped his jeans, unveiling the million-dollar question and leaving me curling my toes in those purple socks. *Wow. Wide. Can-of-pop wide.* I kept trying to take in the rest of the scenery, but I couldn't look away at the massive breadth he'd somehow kept contained in jeans. I worried my eyes might be bigger than my vagina.

What did you get yourself into, Layla?

Bending over, Calvin locked one hand to the back of the couch while he kissed me, the same 'I need to fuck you' kiss when he pressed me against the wall. I held on to his hair, my body pleading for his touch. It shivered as Cal slipped from my lips. He tipped back my chin and planted a single kiss to my throat. Another swept across my collar bone and back. The next...

"Yes, god, yes!" I screamed, arching my back when he pressed his lips around my nipple. Every swirl of his tongue sent me spinning, my panties a deluge at the thought of his lips reaching that far. I tugged and relaxed on his hair, wanting more of his kiss, but also needing him elsewhere.

When Cal slid his hand down to the lowest curve of the couch's back, a squeak burst from the frame. Would he shatter his old sofa to fuck me? There wasn't even a moment's hesitation from him. His hair slipped from my grip as he pressed kisses from my sternum down to my belly button.

Cal bent to a knee behind my ass, hooking a single finger into my panties. He slid it back and forth, worrying the ripping elastic while I squirmed.

"Are you trying to torture me?" I sputtered. Holding on to my underwear myself, I contorted my legs until the wretched things were kicked to the dormant fireplace.

Cal drew his hands down the backs of my thighs, his nails scratching in a soothing pattern while I tried to calm my rampant heartbeat. "You're the one that's tortured me for years," he said.

Confused, I tried to sit up, when Cal pushed on the back of my thighs, sending my legs dangling above my head. He pushed my lower body farther off the couch until my weight rested on my shoulders and all I could see were those purple socks.

The nails that I'd watched transform into claws raked down the sides of my legs. He started at my ankles and worked his way past my knee, up my thigh and around my ass. I gulped, uncertain if I could last long, when Cal tugged my back to his chest.

His massive cock pushed against the length of my spine while he wound his hands under my thighs. A warm whisper curled across my soaked labia, sending a shiver chasing through me. Cal spread me farther apart, and dove into me tongue-first.

"Fuck!" I whimpered, my hips trying to grind into the face pressing them farther apart so his lips could control me. Teetering on only my shoulders, I struggled to keep my legs extended above me without collapsing. Cal was making that exceptionally difficult.

He licked and sucked as if he were trying to get the last dollop of ice cream out of the carton. A rumble rippled his lips, the growl increasing until it vibrated across the whole of me. He grabbed my hips and pressed me closer to him. My ass flattened against his pecs, the tightening of his muscles reverberating through my entire lower half. I slipped farther down the couch, my head tumbling back to the cushion.

"Oh god!" All the blood that'd been pooling in my brain suddenly found its way straight down my circulatory highway to the clit. Cal jerked his hips, rubbing his cock along my back until I felt his foreskin tug.

Air shot from his nose, the beast panting with fury. I needed to hear more. I ached to hear him beg. Reaching with my fingers, I scraped my nails along his spread legs. I could only reach the outside one, but it was enough. Digging in, I pulled him to me and thrust my back down.

"Fuck, Layla," Cal gurgled. Before I could feel smug, he dove back, lapping that long, thick tongue quickly over the hood of my clit.

My need jumped tracks, my body screaming for more of that hot sucking. I must have dug my nails in too hard, as Cal yelped. He grabbed my offending hand, tugging it off the leg I'd probably dented with half-moon marks.

At first, he twisted my hand around until our fingers folded together. Eating me out with wild abandon, he held my hand almost sweetly. Innocently. My moans of appreciation increased, and I kept crying out for more. That caused Calvin to buck his hips, his massive cock sweeping over my back.

A slow chuckle rolled off his tongue and against my clit. I tried to move with it, my mind slipping further from me with every lick. He broke apart our cute handhold and guided my palm to wrap around his cock.

Holy shit. My fingers strained to the breaking point trying to reach, and there was still more of his rock-hard flesh to hold.

"What's wrong?" It wasn't the question that drew my attention but his having to stop sucking on me.

Wild, I struggled to tilt my chin far enough to find his focused eyes staring at me. "I can't..." A blush burned up my chest and I gulped, "I can't reach."

Cal full-throated laughed, his blond-white hair shaking. "Here." He cupped his hand across from mine, the two of us able to fully envelop his cock. "I'll help."

I expected him to begin pumping, but he left the speed and tug up to me. Locking my palm in place, his fingers barely pressing into my hand, I glided up his cock. When I swept the bulging crown over my knuckle pads, Cal dug his nails in.

"Tighter," he said. Increasing my grip, he did the same. Together we started to jerk him off. The whole time Cal caressed the back of my hand with his pinkie while I worked his cock hard.

The grunting and panting from the man caught in my pleasing hand sent off another pleasure bomb through my system. His licking over the whole of my clit increased when he released his grip from my legs. Purple flashed before my eyes, but I didn't care.

I prepared for his fingers or thumb to thrust inside me. When a palm locked over my stomach, my certainty shattered. Flexing against my meager muscles, Calvin hoisted me closer to his mouth.

My body lifted off the couch. Soon, the top of my head skimmed over the cushions while Cal latched his lips around my clit and sucked. Hard.

"Holy shit!" I screamed. The orgasm started slowly, like thunder in the distance, but it picked up steam fast, arcing up my pelvis and into my chest. I gasped when the electricity struck my lungs. I tried to clamp down, to cling to the pleasure not so much frolicking as rolling out an entire armada of tanks.

"Yes, Layla," Calvin moaned. He massaged his smooth chin against my throbbing clit, kicking off aftershocks about on par with the main event. "Tell me. Talk to me."

"I...I...*fuck*, Cal." My head continued to dangle above the couch, all sense obliterated. The only thing I knew beside the bone-quaking orgasm was my hand gliding up and down his cock. With each pass, my grip strained further the harder he grew.

Calvin groaned. His teeth grazed the back of my thigh, right over my ass, and he pleaded, "Keep going. Tell me you liked it."

"It was..." How did I reassure a guy nearing his climax that I'd obviously enjoyed myself? A hundred compliments flashed before my eyes, but I couldn't catch a one. His grunting stopped and his gaze focused on me. In a cool voice, I ordered, "Bite me again."

Opening his mouth wide, Cal clamped the full spread of his teeth over my thigh. A joke, but the touch of him caused me to gasp. And he bit harder with his incisors.

"Your tongue is so fucking amazing. I want to feel it twirl over my brain."

Total nonsense there, Layla.

"Yes," Cal grunted. He released from his cock, letting me take total control.

I slid my grip down to brush my fingers over his balls and grind the side of my palm against his base. He practically cooed at that, leaning back and taking me with him.

"And," I said, swiping my hand up his cock and rolling my palm over the head endlessly, "even though your monster-sized dick scares me, I'm ravenous to ride it."

"Yes, Layla!" he screamed, his cock pulsing as the full spread of his cum splattered all the way up to my tailbone. "Yes," Cal kept repeating, each word softer than the one before. Slowly, he released me back to the couch and took the seat at the end. Right where he'd always sit when we watched movies.

I clawed my way up, my legs flopping over his lap while Cal let his cock finish with abandon. He was exhausted, his arms draped over the back of the settee. Sweat dripped down the middle of his pecs, the droplets racing each other as they bobbed over the ample hills of abs.

"I have…" He panted, his eyes softening with joy and satisfaction as he turned to me. Without pause, he caressed my shoulder and tugged me to him. Pressing his lips to the back of my head, Cal finished with, "I've wanted to do that for so long."

So had I. Parting my hand down his near-white chest hair I asked, "Why didn't you?"

Calvin laughed. He drew a hand down himself. "I come with a bit of baggage, to put it mildly. Not many girls wouldn't run screaming at the thought of a werewolf eating them out."

I have a literal sex demon that's bound to my soul living on my couch.

Scrunching Ink away into the smallest box possible, I leaned against Cal. He tucked me in safer, our rapid hearts calming to find the same beat. "I'm…" The stupid idea of saying I wasn't like other girls faded. Obviously, most girls weren't witches with spell books and demons. Brushing a finger over his parted lips, I said, "You're worth it."

Chapter Ten

Not even a blanket covered our bodies nestled together on the couch. Cal's reassuring breaths raised and lowered my cheek nuzzled against his chest. He'd pulled me on top of him and we both drifted in and out of sleep. On occasion, I'd feel him shift, the movement plucking me from my REM cycle. But a comforting palm massaging the small of my back would lull me under his spell and I was gone.

"Don't you know what they say about lying with dogs?"

Holy shit! I shot up, shoving on Calvin's chest, until I stared into an amused grin. "Though," Ink said, crossing one leg before the other and scratching his chin, "I'm not against giving you a good flea dip."

"What are you doing here?!" I snarled, snapping Cal fully awake. He craned his head to the stranger leering in his house and bolted...with me still on top.

Panic caused me to push on Cal, who did the same, both of us scrambling for our clothing. Like that'd fix everything.

"You need not rush on my account. The afterglow can be rather delightful, assuming one doesn't suffer a cramp." Ink didn't sound angry. Or jealous. Not even a bit miffed. All I heard in his voice was the same joyful laughter as when he'd discovered Tinder.

Hunched over, Cal tried to scramble away with jeans in hand, but he had to rise to put them on. Which let Ink leer even more. "Is this that jealousy emotion your kind go on about? Or a mortal's fear of failing to measure up? Though, I must say, unless tiny penises are favorited again, you need not fret."

"What?" I slipped my shirt on, which barely reached past my belly, and turned on the jolly incubus.

He didn't uncross his stance, but Ink interjected his words with a finger point as he said, "I thought with all this talk of republics and democracies that the male body of the ancient Greeks would be back in fashion. Beautiful lips, tight firm buttocks and teeny tiny *mentulas.*"

A low growl raised the hair on my neck. *Intercede before you learn if a werewolf can damage a demon. Or vice versa.* In trying to dodge around the couch, I slammed my leg into the armrest—hard. But I gritted off the no-doubt deep bruise to wrap a hand around Ink's arm.

"This isn't…"

Layla, this is exactly what it looks like. And, judging by the rising smirk, Ink thought the same. "I'm sorry."

"Whatever for?" My live-in incubus, who needed sex with me to survive, laughed. "Do not tell me your misplaced concerns are embedded in the monogamy tradition. You humans. I thought you'd have worked that one out of your system by now. My bond." Ink clasped both my hands together in the most patronizing fashion. He even started to pat one while saying, "I do not care if you want to rut around on the rug with a flea-ridden dog for your fun. My intentions haven't changed beyond our original arrangement."

"What arrangement? What's he talking about, Layla? And how did he even get in here?" Cal roared. He raised his head and his nostrils flared. Suddenly, his eyes opened wide and he sputtered, "Brimstone, charcoal dust, the unending torment of corporal punishment. You're a demon?"

"At your pleasure, werewolf," Ink said, touching his forelock.

"You knew he was a werewolf?" I snarled at the incubus. All Ink could do was shrug. "Why didn't you tell me?"

"I assumed you knew, or didn't care enough to inquire. Some put no weight in who they lie with."

"I didn't even know werewolves were real," I tried to shout in a whisper.

"Hm, I'd say you've proven they're quite tangible in the...worshipping Hades position?"

I knew he was enjoying getting a rise out of both of us, but I couldn't stop my entire body blushing. And neither could Calvin, who dipped his head down without making eye contact.

Ink walked past me to Cal and paused so close that if Cal breathed deep his chest would brush Ink's. "You know..." He studied Calvin up and down and cupped his chin in thought. "I don't believe I've ever taken a werewolf before."

"And you're not going to either!" I shouted, rushing to slip in between the two men. As I did so, Ink placed a hand to my naked hip while Cal wrapped his fingers around mine.

Winking at me, Ink peered around me to ask Cal, "Does she keep you on as short of a leash as she prefers me?"

"I'd heard stories of witches and their familiars," Cal said, "but I had no idea you could keep a demon as one."

"I am not a familiar." Lighting struck in Ink's tone, his face darkening and his body lengthening to loom above both of us. The cold swipe of invisible feathers curled from his back through me. In a blink of an eye, he faded back down to normal. "I am her bond. What are you?"

"Someone who chooses to be with her. Layla, why would you chain such a creature to you?"

"That's...um, there's a kinda long story to it." Because I hadn't. I'd woken up one night to find a naked man in my living room, and it'd been one continuous fuck-up ever since. For some reason, I expected Ink to barge in with the truth, but he finally kept his trap shut. "Look, can we all agree that this is really awkward? Three of us, supernatural beings, exchanging bodily fluids and I am just making it worse."

Hanging my head, I turned to face Cal—though Ink kept his hand wrapped around my hip. "He's teaching me witchcraft. I need to learn it to protect people, and in exchange I...feed him."

"So he's a pet? Your demonic hamster," Cal said.

"Oooh," Ink exclaimed, "your bite's much worse than your bark."

For fuck's sake, could they stow the egos for two minutes?

Layla, they're men and you're the post they both want to piss on.

Great. Just the place I wanted to be.

"Ink, why are you here?"

"Because I did as you asked. I trailed the man in question..."

"And what? He got McDonald's then stopped to scratch his ass?" I snapped.

Calmly folding his hands together, Ink said, "There is to be a clandestine meeting. I assumed that would be of interest to you and came to pass the knowledge along."

Cal ran a hand along my shoulder, pivoting me back to him. "A meeting? Tracking someone? Layla, this doesn't sound safe. Can you handle this?"

I snuck into a werewolf's house, didn't I? Okay, if he hadn't been so...amenable it wouldn't have gone well for me. But I didn't have a choice. Girls were dying and Calvin couldn't be the killer. Though he could be friends with the one who is.

Nodding slowly, I pulled in a breath. "I do. It's my job as a witch to protect people."

Wrapping a hand around the back of my head, Cal pulled me closer until our foreheads touched. He drew a thumb over my cheek, both of us breathing in the strong scent from our bodies rolling together. "Here I thought I was gifted with an impossible burden. I should...should I come with? To protect you?"

I began to shake my head, when Ink piped up. "It'd probably save us all a trip since you know him."

Cal's soft face tightened into a rictus and he spun away to glare at Ink. "What are you talking about?" He focused his anger on me. "Who were you stalking?"

"That Mark man you seemed enraptured with earlier."

Damn it, Ink.

"Get the hell out of my house!" Calvin roared. He ripped his hands off me to run at Ink. For a moment, I feared he might transform and attack, but Cal remained human and reached to lock on to Ink's throat. The demon chuckled and evaporated before our eyes, only to reappear next to the door.

"You too!" Cal turned on me. He kicked my pants at my feet. While I struggled to slip them on, he started to pace. "What gives you the right to spy on, to trail, to try and control people?"

Control?

"I can't believe I ever— *GET OUT!*"

Shit. My heart jumped in fear and I broke. All the pain I thought I'd swallowed cracked at once. Calvin glared down at me, his face stone. I had to get out of there. Even with Ink, he might...he could... But Cal would never.

I took a step for the door, and my earlier ramming into the couch rolled my leg. Crying in surprise, I felt myself falling. Warm hands rushed around me, but they came from the demon who'd been on the other side of the room. "Thanks," I whispered to Ink, who didn't say anything.

In spinning around, I caught Cal's face. I feared to see only hatred, but—at least for a second—concern swept through him. *Damn it.*

I abandoned him, locking an arm over Ink's shoulders as we hobbled to the door.

"Thank you ever so much for your hospitality," the demon said to get one last jab in. Prying open the door,

I began to slip out with Ink. Just before I left, I looked one last time to Cal.

"I never want to see you again," he growled. Leaping forward, he slammed the door shut behind us.

Standing on the stoop in shock, I heard the locks rattle into place and the sound of something heavy hitting the floor. Fuck, what did I do?

"Why did you do that?" I shouted, turning all my anger on the only one remaining.

Ink shrugged. "Demons cannot lie."

"You didn't have to tell the full truth either."

His smile twisted about a sickening grin. "You're right. I didn't."

"Just...get me out of here." I said, taking the stairs two steps at a time.

With all the sarcasm at his disposal, Ink said, "As you wish, my bond."

* * * *

Damn it, damn it, damn it!

My foot flailed in agony thanks to the bruise already coating my thigh. I heard a flush from the toilet two stalls down and bent tighter over my seat to try to disguise the book. It wasn't as though light or magic runes poured out of it, but I feared that people could sense it the same way I did.

Smudging back the tear of pain building in my eye, I tried to peer closer to the healing spell. It was right there in black and white, but every time I began to read it, the letters shivered out of place. I wanted to scream in the McDonald's bathroom.

But that'd probably have sent the police to investigate and drag me out with my pants around my ankles. Also, I wasn't alone.

"How much longer do we intend to remain here?" Ink asked. He stood with one foot on top of the trashcan for sanitary napkins, like some kind of tampon pirate.

"Until I can fix my fucking leg, okay?" I shouted through a clenched jaw.

"Is everything okay in there?" a friendly voice called from the sinks. *Shit.*

"Yep, just fine," I tried to respond in the same singsong voice. Everything was great.

I didn't just implode my one chance with Calvin. Climb off him from having the best…

I caught sight of Ink and I had to amend that.

Some of the best sex of my life. Then I turn around and he hurls me out of his house. Well, I'm sorry that I had a vision of you, or your friend, or someone like you murdering people. But there it was.

And why didn't I tell him that? Explain that we were only following, tracking really, him and his friend to try to solve murders?

Because you're a fucking idiot, Layla. You can barely read without taking two hours to get down a page. Everyone knows it.

Scowling, I yanked the Sharpie from the pocket down around my ankles and began to draw the healing symbol over the bruise. In my haste, I jabbed too deep, causing my eyes to well up in pain. But I didn't pause in connecting the final line. A soft light rose from the symbol, which I tried to clamp my hands over, and the ache that'd ensnared my thigh finally abated.

Thank god. I collapsed back at the balm of relief, only to remember there was a metal flusher ready to jab into me. Hooking onto my pants, I began to stand, when Ink asked far too loudly for being in the ladies' room, "How long do you intend to rely upon that form of magic?"

"It's what the book has," I said, turning my spell book over. I asked for healing and that was what it gave me.

Ink pursed his lips. Ninety-eight percent of the time he was in his sex god mode, like if one of the background dancers from a music video followed me around the grocery store. But this was one of those times when he stopped playing at being the coy Dom. He snapped so far into his gruff anger that he stopped being sexy and became pedantic.

"You know I refer to your constant reliance upon ink and other drawing materials for your spells. Most witches have a favorite form, but they can all recite incantations or brew up a potion. A lack of diversification is the sign of an uncultured witch."

Standing, with one hand holding on to the pants that'd been tossed at my face twenty minutes earlier, incandescent rage throbbed through me. I dug my nails into my thigh, right around the healing symbol that'd faded to a faint line. What right did he have to keep questioning me? I was doing the best I could to survive. But there was that damn incubus swooping in uninvited and ruining everything in my life with a cocky smirk and a shrug of his shoulders.

"What do you know about witchcraft? You can't even read this," I shouted, lifting up the book that was blank to his eyes.

Ink hooked a claw over the binding and pushed it down. "I know enough. Far more than you, as is obvious."

"You're a demon, not a witch. You have no idea how to cast magic or read a spell. I'm doing the best I fucking can with this...this problem that dropped on my head. And all you can do is criticize. Tell me that I'm wrong. I'm not a good enough witch after just two weeks. Demon, what gives you the right to preach at me about witchcraft?"

He didn't snarl or stomp, which was good as it'd have cracked the waste bin off the wall. Instead, Ink took in a slow breath and laughed. A chuckle rumbled so low it'd strike terror in the hearts of villagers living at the foot of a volcano. He thought me standing up for myself was funny.

Scowling, I flipped the complicated pages back and forth, unseeing the words. "How does a demon even know about magic?" I whispered to myself.

In an instant, Ink's fun vanished. He stood taller, raising his head so high his black hair blotted out the light. "I've known witches in my days."

"How many witches happily consort with demons?" Why hadn't I asked that question before? *Do other witches call forth demons of lust to do their bidding?* Cal had seemed surprised by it and he didn't claim to be a magic expert. And how had an incubus wound up bound to me in the first place?

"Enough," Ink declared. "I am not your plucky minion here to answer to your bidding. Since you believe you have no more need of me, I will take my leave. I've grown exhausted of this confined latrine."

"So what? That's it? You're just going to cut and run?"

"Yes," he said. His gaze drifted from my burning face to my hand, the Sharpie still locked in it. "What will you do when time is of the essence and your pen cannot work?"

Before I could answer him, he vanished the same way he'd entered. "Joke's on you," I shouted to the ether. "Sharpies can write on anything!"

A fist knocked on the bathroom stall, wrenching me around to face it. What was next? Zombie minotaurs? An entire flock of flesh-eating pixies? In my mood, I'd take them all on.

"Ma'am, are you in that stall with someone?"

"No," I called, my voice withering down to my toes. After buckling on my pants, I stuffed my book into my bag.

"People heard two voices coming from the bathroom. This is a family establishment…"

They thought I was fucking him. Okay, I was, but not here. Even an incubus had standards. My hair curled from the waves of embarrassment rising off my body. It was a full-on swamp of guilt and hormones.

Turning around, I pressed the flusher. The whirlpool sound of water accompanied me as I opened the door. A manager gripped the side of the stall's wall and peered in. His arm kept me trapped in place as he looked around, finding absolutely no one else in there.

"Can I leave?"

Shock crashed over his face, replacing the grit of disgust. "You…you, yes. Thank you," he said, his body folding away as I hustled out of there. I paused at the bathroom door and watched the manager shove open every other stall in the hope he'd catch that phantom man.

Forget Ink. At least he'd been good enough to tell me that Mark would be at the abandoned roller rink tonight. I needed to prepare for that.

In reaching for my phone, my fingers jostled a textbook and a candy bar wrapper I'd used for a bookmark. He'd handed it to me with an earnest smile when we were in the library together.

Forget Calvin too.

All that matters is saving these women. Even if I destroy my own life in the process, it'll be worth it.

With that lie in place, I headed out for the Roll-O-Rama.

Chapter Eleven

I didn't need Ink.

Or even my spell book. It was hardly breaking and entering to slip into the abandoned roller rink. The single chain bolting the crumbling door shut had been left slack enough an elephant could get through.

Graffiti in neon spray paint greeted me, every local tag painted across the half walls that circled the cracking cement rink. I felt both ancient tutting at the vandalism and also a teenager again. A kid angry at any and everything, happy to take it out on an old claw machine left to rot in the back.

Most of the shattered glass had been swept away over the years, probably by other kids who needed any outlet they could find, like I had. Nearly all the padded booths had been ripped out when the place closed, but one remained. I'd rounded third base on that even with a spring prodding into my thigh.

It was a wonder I hadn't gotten tetanus...or other diseases that required a z-pack. "What would that say about a young Layla Leeland?" I said in a soft, raspy voice mimicking our psychology professor.

"That she was a fucking horny teenager just like everyone else trapped in that hormone stew," I answered myself, shoving away the fallen ceiling tiles to reveal the service door. It led to the behind-the-scenes area, which was the perfect place for me to wait for Mark and whatever this secret meeting was.

The knob was long stripped away, leaving only a hole to fit my hand through to open it. Once inside, I pushed the door closed as best as I could. While the ceiling tiles over the rink itself had been tagged with every bored doodle spray paint could make, the maintenance hall looked almost preserved.

Cobwebs dangled off the exposed pipes, their eight-legged owners scurrying about above my head. I paid it no mind, clutching my bag closer to my chest. The entire back area was cement, but not the same smooth finish as the rink. It dipped and swelled on the floor. While the outer wall was brick, the one looking in on the rink was drywall. Cheap drywall.

Muffled voices called from the roller rink's door and I dashed for the secret lookout spot. The maintenance hall swept a hundred and eighty degrees around the rink and midway through was an alcove. Someone years back had punched a hole into the thin wall.

Thanks to the shadows in the rink, it was impossible to see the hole unless a person knew where to look. Dropping to my knees, I hunched lower. I pressed my hand around the hole to act as a barrier because I wasn't risking spiders climbing in my eye. *Time to play the spy game.*

A single shaft of light from the apartment buildings behind pierced through the hole in the roof. I focused on that while ignoring a shake trembling up my knee.

"You are here," a masculine voice boomed, its echo rebounding off the pipes and casting dust into my hair. I didn't move, clinging to my spot, even as he said, "You cannot fool me."

Shit. Did he see me?

A blur shifted before my eye, a dark blue or black jacket stopping just in front of my spying hole. "Brother Mark," the voice shouted like it'd seen a long lost relative. "Come forward and speak to your family."

Damn it. I couldn't see anything. What if I zapped whoever was standing in the way? Nothing strong, a quick jolt that could be passed off as static electricity or faulty wiring. I reached for the book, the binding falling open to the spell I'd learned a week ago, when my blockade shifted.

A goddamn wizard stood in the middle of the ceiling-induced spotlight. Okay, he was a middle-aged wizard with a short salt-and-pepper beard. He didn't have the pointy hat or slippers, nor was there a big stick or wand. But he had a robe on. White as snow, it didn't compliment his tallow skin color a lick. Silver threads caught on the glinting yellow light, symbols of astrology glittering off his cloak as he shifted.

He wasn't alone either. Two men of that hire-a-body-to-pull-out-a-stump type lurked just behind him. They weren't in the silver robes but ragged hoodies. Though, they wore the same color, a dingy blue-gray with a circular patch over the breast. I couldn't make out what was on the patch.

"Father…" the one who'd blocked my sight said. The wizard's wide-open arms twitched, and the blocker added in a softer voice, "Lucien."

"Come to me," this Father Lucien commanded, waving his hands and causing the robes' silver flaps to undulate.

It took a moment, the man Lucien wanted to embrace bobbing so he'd half block my view. But as he kept waffling, the two men behind Lucien crossed their arms. That sent the man skidding to the embrace of the man in the robe, his sneakers setting off an ear-rattling squeak as he went.

When Father Lucien wrapped his arms around the man, I spotted the same black hair and steel blue eyes in the stranger. *Mark.* A pain jangled through my nerves. It sang of betrayal against Cal, my friend. My…coulda been more.

Too late now. Hardly the first bridge you've set on fire, Layla.

Squaring my knees for a long haul made me slip my eye from the hole while Lucien broke off his hug. I'd just lined back up as the man wound his hand back and struck Mark clear across the face.

What the shit?

The ringing slap echoed off the walls to a deafening degree. Mark stood there, his shoulders slumped, without even touching the red welt in surprise.

"You fool!" Lucien cried. "Do you not know what you've done to your brothers and sisters?"

"I'm…" Mark's voice strangled in his throat, the tears swallowed. "I did what I could."

"Obviously not enough," Lucien hollered before pivoting his tone so fast it gave me whiplash. "My son," he said in the dulcet tones of a golf commentator.

Folding his hands together as if in prayer, while also raising them up to Mark's eye level, Lucien continued, "We, your family, need you in this hour. Our way of life is being threatened. Can you not see the enemy at the gates?"

"Yes, Father," Mark mewled.

"Do you not carry their blood on your hands?"

Yes, I knew I wasn't chasing ghosts!

Mark raised his palms and stared at them, as if he expected to still find the blood of those women he'd murdered clogged in his pores. "I...I do," he sputtered, his head bobbing.

Clasping a hand to his murderer's shoulder, Lucien said, "Then you must do whatever is necessary to put an end to this Mr. White and his heathen army."

"Even if...?" Mark's head shot up, the hands falling from his face. He held on to Lucien's elbow. Was it to save himself from another slap?

I gritted my teeth in fear of the same, watching Lucien raise his hand in slow-motion. When it landed on Mark's head, I breathed a sigh of relief. "If the crop is rotten, is it better to burn the entire field or the single bad fruit?"

"The...the fruit," Mark said.

"It is not an easy decision to arrive at, my son. But I think you will find it the correct one, in time." Lucien folded his arms together, locking them under the robes' sleeves. Jerking his head, Lucien directed his muscle to start heading out. After watching Mark with his head bent in obedience, Lucien finally turned to leave.

He made it a few steps before Mark cried out, "When can I return?"

Lucien froze, his spine rigid. I knew that stance and so did Mark. I felt myself curling lower to try to make my body as small as possible. But the father didn't lash out. His face spread with a beatific smile. "When you have proven yourself to the pack. Come."

With that, he turned, leaving Mark alone in the roller rink staring at his blood-stained hands. I sank away, pressing my back against the cold bricks of the other wall. *What was all of that?*

In my vision, I saw someone who looked like Cal but all in shadow. Maybe that man had dark hair and the same sharp blue eyes. Like Mark. Who was killing people because another man in silver robes ordered him to.

And what was that about a Mr. White?

My brain instantly slotted in a placeholder of a bald man with a goatee and a fedora. But something told me this Mr. White wasn't just cooking meth in an RV. That was another problem. For now I had to figure out where Mark was headed next.

A snap like a knife slicing through taut leather rebounded from the rink. Leaping forward, I pressed my eye to the hole. Fur rippled across the naked skin of a man pitching forward onto his hands. It grew in random tufts between his twitching muscles before sprouting into a full hide. All the while, snapping and crunching sounds echoed around the stripped building. My guts tried to upend themselves from the horrifying echo, but I held on as Mark shook the deep brown and black fur coating his werewolf body.

Oh shit, that meant—

Before I could even rise, the second werewolf of the day loped into a run I had no hope of following. *Damn it.* I leapt to my feet, dashed down the maintenance hall, kicked open the door and found myself completely alone.

"You're doing a great job at protecting innocents from werewolves," I snarled at myself. "Just imagine how fantastic this would go it if was a zombie outbreak. Only eighty-five percent of the population turned into mindless ghouls hungering for flesh. Congrats!"

The bag around my shoulder grew heavier, and I peeked inside. "You wouldn't happen to have a tracking spell that works on wolves, would you?"

A sense of both pride and smugness radiated off my spell book. Hauling it out, I let the pages flip to the right spell. "Just so you know, I haven't ruled out that I lost my mind on Halloween from a toxic cocktail mix-in and this has all been a delusion. A difficult to explain delusion that includes bathroom breaks."

There it was. Tracking. Seemed simple enough. I had to put down the symbol where my prey first set off. Kinda funny to think of me hunting the big bad wolf. A soggy jean jacket would have to suffice in place of a red hood.

I took one last glance around the rink, listening for the howl of a wolf running down the streets. Nothing. *Can't ever be that easy for you, Layla*. With that, I set off onto the rink. Even after the years of settling, the ground was still dangerously smooth. My body jerked wildly in an attempt to remain upright, so I had to settle for sliding out like a penguin on ice.

Pausing in the center with the hole's light above me, I dug out my chalk and bent down. Hm, this was one of the more complicated runes. It wasn't a circle but a series of curly non-English letters. They looked elven, even more so as I drew them by streetlight with yellow chalk.

With one hand open flat to hold the spell book, and the other sketching on the ground, I kept my back to the door. The only way for anyone to get into the rink. My ears picked up a low rumble churning from the door while I wrote. A light breeze must have wound its way in through the broken bricks. The next letter looked like an *e* merged into an *m*. Looping around the *m* caused the chalk in my fingers to squeak.

I gritted my teeth at the sharp noise, and a low growl answered.

Whipping around, I came face to face with a massive wolf prowling in the shadows. Its sharp ears stood straight up on the long, narrow head and focused on me. The thing looked impossibly gigantic. Standing four feet tall, the length of its body was easily six and a half or more feet. And the paws…! They dug into the rink, the toes just in the halo of the light.

Each claw looked longer than my finger, all four of them cracking through the cement floor. The wolf growled again and it took a step closer. It wasn't black fur spiking off the back but white. Angelic, pure as snow white. And the eyes…!

Bright blue, they pierced through my brain as the wolf kept its head pointed directly at me. White hair, blue eyes? It had to be—

"Cal?" I said.

The growling stopped, the wolf's deliberate stalking frozen mid-step.

"I'm glad you're here. I need your help to find…"

Those lips that I'd kissed not even twenty-four hours earlier rippled with a snarl. The wolf tugged them higher, revealing fangs sharper than any knife. What was he doing? Was he still angry at me for coming here? For trailing Mark? Well, too bad. His friend had admitted to killing people!

Cal's back legs shifted, taking the full weight of a werewolf. He couldn't possibly be planning to... "It's me, Layla," I said.

Those icy eyes burned with intelligence, but the lips couldn't form words. Even if they did, I doubt it'd be anything kind. The wolf snapped its jaws instead, telling me everything I needed to know.

Whatever he was now, he couldn't be reached or reasoned with. He was only the wolf.

And he hated me.

Shit!

All the compacted weight of the wolf burst from his back legs, launching the murderous jaws into the air. His white forelegs caught the light, claws of pure black extended to rip through my chest. There was no time for a ward, or a spell, or anything.

The wolf landed, its jaws spiting fetid heat against my skin. He reared up, aiming to wrap the whole of his mouth around my neck and bite down. I launched my arm up even as the entirety of the wolf filled my vision. The sharp prick of his first fang pressed into my throat when I slammed my spell book into his skull.

Twisting mid-air, the wolf flew back. And, god help me, but when a whimper burst from him, my heart wept. *I'm sorry, Calvin. I don't know what...*

"Fuck!"

The wolf didn't wait for my sympathy, lashing out its massive paw. Its claws slashed into my inner thigh, slicing a hole through my jeans and deep into my muscle. Its momentum tossed me back, my ass striking the cement with a teeth-chattering blow.

There was no time to check the damage, to crawl away. The wolf opened its jaws, the teeth stained red with my blood, and broke into a run to finish me off.

"Ma golea dau'n taro r I gyd!" I shrieked, lightning erupting from my hands. The sparks weren't much, about on par with a Taser on low. But when all ten bolts struck the wolf, he yelped. His front leg faltered, causing his face to smash into the ground. A fang broke free, the tooth flying across the rink and striking my foot.

Numb, I picked up the tooth and slipped it in my pocket even while I kept a hand trained on the wolf. On Calvin.

For fuck's sake. Calvin was trying to kill me, and I'd give him the same if he didn't stop.

But as the wolf lapped its pink tongue around the hole where his fang had been, he started to scatter back. His paws flew like a dog's on ice, Cal turning to flee from the witch ready to barbecue his ass.

Thank, god. I breathed a sigh of relief at the shadow of the wolf loping over the wall and vanishing into the night.

Layla, you're bleeding.

Oh, fuck. Wet, sticky blood pooled under me. I tried to clamp my hands over the deep wounds, but the bleeding wouldn't stop.

He hit your femoral artery. You're going to die if you don't cut it off.

I struggled to rip open my bag, the strap's buckle winding around my hair and ripping it out at the scalp. *No time to worry.* I dug through my handful of belongings, trying to find anything to act as a tourniquet. Why didn't I carry one with me? A simple rubber strap I could tighten?

Even a goddamn string!

You're a witch, stupid.

The healing spell! Blood smeared all over my hips and jacket from my fingers struggling to dig out the Sharpie. Biting so hard on the cap I got my tongue, I yanked out the pen. *This symbol you know by heart.*

I heard the book flipping open to help, but it sounded distant. Like it was in another room. I had to draw the ward over the wound or it wouldn't work. It'd take too long to fix the tear in my body. I'd bleed out on the floor of an abandoned roller rink where no one would find me for weeks until I was a bloated corpse picked apart by alley cats.

Tears welled up in my eyes, pain thundering from my leg up to my head. An ache cracked in my chest, my heart pounding harder to dump more blood on the rink. *Shake it off or you will die.* A chill crawled across the ground, winding up my legs and down my arms. *Close the circle, Layla.*

Close the...

Why wasn't it drawing? I ran the felt tip back around, ramming it deep into the flayed apart flesh even as my body screamed in pain. But nothing came out.

Oh no. The Sharpie, it couldn't...

A single laugh rolled off my tongue as I stared at the tip of the pen ruined by my unstoppable blood. *They don't work when they're wet.*

Tremors shot through me, sending the pen flying out of my hand. My body crumpled to the floor, smearing my bleeding leg into the other, but I couldn't stop.

Shock. You're going into shock.

That's bad.

I couldn't do anything. I couldn't cast a spell. I couldn't stop the bleeding. I was going to die a worthless witch alone and forgotten without anyone caring I ever existed.

The light above me began to dim, shadows pressing in from all sides. I lashed out with my hand, trying to reach for the phone that fell out of my bag. One finger knocked into the case, then another, when my body gave out. As my face crashed to the ground, a great howl echoed from the city streets.

Chapter Twelve

Did it work?

A sip of oxygen clanged down my body, setting off a racking pain that knotted from my neck down to my toes. I peeled open my eyelids only a sliver and light stabbed into my aching pupils. Another breath attempted the labyrinthian trail to my lungs, this one twisting through my chest.

If I'd gotten the healing spell right, none of this should be happening.

So where was I?

The blood that somehow refilled my veins ebbed from my ears and a familiar sound invaded my unclogged ears. A *chung-chung* told me I was exactly where I didn't want to be—the hospital. Groaning, I rolled a hand to the bars around the bed. One down. I glared at my left hand tucked under the blanket refusing to put in the work. *Come on already!*

With my jaw locked, I forced my hand out and bounced it against the cold metal. Warmth caressed the top of it, and I whipped my head around. Or tried to. I could only manage a slow wobble, but my vision acted like I'd spun my head at mach five.

"Ink?"

My incubus raised the edge of his tight lips. He must have found me bleeding out on the floor. Taken me to a hospital. Saved my life. I spent all my energy focusing on Ink, the teal accents of the room spinning like a top behind him. I'd yelled at him, told him I had it all under control, and the demon had saved me.

The gentle roll of his palm over my knuckles swept both guilt and assurance through me. He continued the rhythmic movement while staring me dead in the eye, "You are safe."

It sounded like an order, but I didn't have the energy to fight him. Or anyone else for that matter. My bones softened to butter in a skillet, causing me to slump back into the bed.

I'd never felt more exhausted in my life. And it was all because of… Biting off the thought I couldn't face, I tried to kick at the thick blankets wrapping me up burrito style.

"What are you attempting?" Ink asked. He didn't rise from the chair pivoted to face the small TV playing through a *Law & Order* marathon. But Ink sat up higher, his long arms extending down my chest while I kept tugging on the blanket with my toes.

"I have to see how bad it is. How much…"

"Layla, stop." Ink's soft inflection hardened to flint, freezing my movements. Numb, I flopped my head to the side and a tear slid over my nose. The demon drew his thumb against the bump at the tip to wipe away the wetness. "My bond." His voice dipped back to his soft roll though the spine. "Worry about it later. For now, you must remain warm to stimulate the blood of virgins inside you."

"Virgins?" I stared at him. *What did he do?* "Did you attack someone and take their blood?"

"Me? Of course not. This healing facility had it stored in their ghoulish ice boxes. But they whispered that much was required to fill your veins."

He was worried about me, about how close I'd nearly come to pouring all my witch blood out on the floor.

Pulling in a cleansing breath, I lay back. "What did you mean about them being virgins?"

"It's a matter of semantics. Everyone is technically a virgin, as no one lives long enough to participate in every potential sex act."

I chuckled at the thought, and Ink—with eyes of amber softening to a comforting brown—smiled at me. He rose to tuck the edge of the wayward blanket back into place and I watched him. A demon that saved me. That could be so stubborn one minute and tender the next.

"Not you," I said, watching him fall back to his chair.

"Pardon?"

"There's no way you can be a virgin by any definition."

"No," Ink said, his gaze focusing on the TV show where the blood was made out of ketchup. "I am not."

"You were right," I admitted, needing to get it out before it grew too awkward. "About the marker, and how it didn't work when I needed it to."

I gritted my teeth for an *I told you so*, which he'd probably earned. But Ink only smiled with an *of course I was* look on his face. That seemed to be enough for the demon who'd lived long enough to watch countless cities rise from the dirt and fall to ash. Leaning back, I closed my eyes for another sleep that'd probably bring more pain than less.

"I'm glad you're here," I said. "Though I'm surprised the nurses let you in." He was hardly family, not that I had any to speak of.

Ink snorted as if the wrath of an RN was nothing to fear. He brushed the tips of his fingers back over my hair. "Sleep, Layla. You will come to no harm as long as I am here."

"What in the hell are you doing back?" A woman in scrubs with dancing turkeys on them burst into the room. She waved her arms at Ink. "You're not supposed to be here! No visitors!"

With a sigh, Ink rose to his feet. "So you keep insisting."

"How in the nine hells do you keep sneaking back into this room?"

"Old Scratch himself, your ladyship," Ink said with a deep bow. The nurse shooed him like he was an obstinate goat standing on her shrubbery. He barely paused from turning and walking out. All the while, she kept an eye on him, and called up the admin desk to ban a man with Ink's appearance.

I settled back, letting her fuss with the equipment, change my IV and lower the bars on the bed. "The doctor will be checking on you in an hour or two. Try to get some rest in the meantime," she said, then flicked off the light.

The second the door closed, a hand brushed over my forehead. Ink crossed his legs as he sat back in the chair for a long night ahead of us.

* * * *

With an unceremonious crash, my ass hit the bed. The massive wad of bandages wrapped around my thigh had sent me teetering to the left. *That's what happens when a leg is split open like a baked potato in a microwave.*

"Hang on, dear," Judith said, her hand racing to catch me. But she was interrupted by the demon that wouldn't leave my side. The hospital took a "Don't ask, don't tell" approach with Ink. As long as he kept to himself and didn't get in the way, they'd let him stay. Probably because they couldn't keep him out without an exorcist on staff.

After a day and a half of my sleeping, lounging and slumbering in a bed, I was nearing release time. The first step was getting the catheter out. My flailing pride overrode my fear, and I had to order Ink to stay out in the hall. Despite his constant cat-and-mouse game with the nurses, he listened to me without question.

Judith had helped me to the bathroom for the most painful piss I've ever taken. In there, she'd given me the sly 'is your partner a domestic abuser' quiz. I'd answered truthfully, but chuckled and admitted I was in school to be a nurse.

"Put your head down," Judith said. She slipped on the finger clamp heart monitor and jotted down the numbers. "Should I quiz you on those?"

I glanced over to the constant whirring companion I'd tried to ignore. While I recognized a good sign that I would get out of here soon, I still said, "Only if you want me to relapse."

Laughing, Judith said, "I hear that." She gave me one last smile and a quick nod to Ink, who returned it.

As the door closed, he leaned over me to ask, "I am at a loss for why you have not healed yourself?"

I paused in running through the gamut of daytime TV, letting the clicker fall to the bed. "Because the last thing I need is a doctor reading a chart that says a patient lost five pints of blood, had her adductor longus muscle shredded to hamburger and fifty stitches in her thigh—only for him to look up and realize she's just peachy and thinking of going for a jog later."

"You run for pleasure?"

I snorted at the idea that seemed preposterous even before a wolf tried to eviscerate me. Though, maybe I should take it up in case of other...

"Hey, where's my favorite patient?"

My smile cracked wide as Dana charged into the room. Fariah walked behind, the notes I'd missed in her hand. Without pause, Dana ran to the monitors, eyeing up the numbers.

"How are you, Layla?" Fariah asked. She sat quietly on the side of the bed beside my feet.

I let out a weary sigh and admitted, "Tired. But I can at least sit up. Ah, fuck!" In doing so, I strained my thigh. My veins pulsed with a dash of morphine, but it wasn't enough to tamp down the pain always a slight shift away.

"What in the ever-loving shit happened to you?" Dana asked, her arms crossed as she glared down at me.

I'd only given the bare facts, loss of blood, nerve and muscle damage. The truth seemed harder to explain. "There was a..."

My jaw dropped with the arrival of the last man I ever thought to see again. He held a vase crammed with sunflowers, daisies, pink roses, orange lilies and more.

Only those frightening blue eyes pierced above the soft flowers, setting my teeth on edge.

"A what?" Dana said.

I focused on her, my face twisted in confusion.

"You said there was a…then trailed off, like that."

Calvin placed the vase on the table and I watched him the way a rabbit does its predator. What the fuck was he doing here? "There was a wolf," I said loudly, waiting for him to react. To shiver, to sneer, to do anything but keep fussing over the fucking flowers.

"A wolf?" Fariah gasped.

"Yeah, a giant one. Charged at me out of nowhere, no reason whatsoever to attack." *There.* Calvin twitched. It was only for a second, but I saw it. "I tried to get it to stop, but…" Waving my hand to the weeping bandages under my blue patient gown, I said, "It sliced me up good."

"Jesus," Dana gasped. "A goddamn wolf? In the middle of the city?"

"What are the chances?" I said in a dead voice.

While my friends flocked around my injury, I glared at Calvin. He wouldn't meet my eyes, pawing at his elbows while he fidgeted.

"Well," Fariah said. "I hope you've contacted the authorities to deal with such a dangerous animal."

"That's the idea," I said, still glaring at Cal, waiting for him to say something. To declare that it was him. To laugh manically and run out of the room. Do anything but stand there acting like he had no idea what was going on.

It was Ink who swung down, his touch startling me from my mission. I glanced to him just when he whispered in my ear, "I would advise against that."

"What? Why?"

"Authorities are more likely to become cannon fodder when...wolves are involved." We both stared at Calvin, who—for the first time—looked me dead in the eye. A hand rubbed my shoulder reassuringly and I clung to Ink's forearm for strength. I was going to need it.

"Um..." Dana interrupted. "We should probably get going. Let you rest up before you're ready to be discharged. Do you need a ride when that happens?"

"No, Ink can... Ink will help."

Shrewd eyes sized up the man whose entire body had been created to scream danger. "Isn't that *nice*," Dana declared, a hand pressing into her hip.

"I believe that is the first time I've ever been called such." He gave her a full toothy grin, his face contorted as if such a move brought him pain. *Ink...*

Dana snorted once at the display, then brushed Fariah's arm. "Let's go already. You coming, Cal?"

"Actually..." He twisted on his feet, his voice soft as he spoke to Dana. "I...I'd like to stay a little longer. If that's okay."

She shrugged and jerked a finger to me. A blush crawled up Cal's cheeks and he dipped his head. "See you later," he called, leaving Dana and Fariah to walk out of the door.

Anger boiled through me. I wanted to rip his throat out, to claw apart his leg and leave him bleeding on the floor terrified of death. To kick and punch his face in over and over until...

"Layla." He gazed at me with those haunting eyes and my heart stopped. I clung tighter to Ink's arm, squeezing the biceps. All that precious blood drained from my face and I started to tremble in the bed.

I didn't want to die.

"Stay back!" I shrieked, wagging a finger at him.

Cal reared in shock, his mouth opening as if I'd, what, welcome the man that had tried to murder me the night before last? His lips moved through words he didn't speak and he bent his head. "You blame me for the attack."

"Of fucking course I do! You tried to kill me!"

"What?" Cal gasped like he'd been kicked in the solar plexus. "What are you talking about?" he asked, moving closer.

"Don't you take one more fucking step or I'll...I'll let Ink kill you!"

The incubus bent closer to whisper, "You are aware that I only kill via se—"

"Shut up!"

He closed his eyes and leaned back, but the smirk remained in place. I didn't care. This might be the last chance I had to ever confront Calvin. And I was taking it. "I was attacked by a wolf in the city—the only fucking thing that could be is a werewolf."

"I know," he moaned as if he knew how it felt to have his hot blood pool on the floor. "I tried to warn you away. To keep you from—"

I wouldn't let him try to guilt me. He didn't warn me—he threw a fit, then stalked and attacked me. "A wolf with eyes as blue as ice."

Calvin's head shot up.

"Your eyes."

"That can't be. That isn't..." He slapped his hands together in prayer and pressed them to his lips.

"You did it. You followed me, you stalked me and you tried to kill me!"

"Layla." He began to move, and I jabbed my finger at him. There was no magic, but Calvin was rooted to the spot, a hand reaching out for me. "It wasn't me. I swear to god."

"Bullshit." I wanted to spit on him, to crush him under my foot. To…to not feel pain in my belly because of his cracking eyes. To stop my heart from fluttering with anything other than fear in his presence. He tried to kill me. There was no coming back from that.

"He is correct," Ink said, whipping me fully around in the bed to him. "Actually."

"What? No. The wolf was white—"

"How white?" the traitor asked, but I ignored him.

"And I…I knocked out a tooth!" I shouted about my memento. Wanting proof, I patted at my hips before remembering all my clothes were elsewhere.

Ink raised a finger and pointed to Calvin, who had the same half-moon smile he always did. There was no gap to damn him. But he could have had it replaced.

In a day and a half?

"Once I realized you were attacked by a werewolf, while the healers attended to your wounds, I dropped in on the only one in residence I was aware of." Ink folded his arms, but jerked his elbow in the direction of Calvin, like I didn't know who we were talking about. "He was in his basement that night. Chained to the wall."

He could have…

"Layla?" Pain and betrayal rattled in Cal's voice. He rubbed his palm along his jaw, brushing the rare stubble while staring at me. "You thought it was me? You thought I could ever…? Of course you would. I shouted at you, ordered you out of my house."

It wasn't him.

That's a good thing. I could look at him again. Be near him. Trust him.

So why wouldn't my hands unclench from my blanket? Why did they keep twisting it into knots with every word from his mouth?

Calvin folded his hand into a fist and knocked it against his head. "Tell me, the wolf that you saw...that, god, I can't believe they'd try to hurt you. What was his coat color?"

"Like I said, white."

"From snout to tail?"

I nodded and Cal's entire face crumbled. He looked about to collapse to his knees, when Ink was just there. Gripping Cal's shoulder, Ink kept him upright. For a beat, the werewolf turned to the incubus and nodded his thanks.

"Are you saying there's another werewolf out there? One that's...that's killing people? Stalking them and ripping them to pieces?"

Mark. Shit, in all my anger at Cal I forgot about that weird meeting he had with some guy named Father Lucien. He was a werewolf too, but with dark brown and black hair.

How many were there?

Calvin shook his head. "I cannot believe that another would... You, you deserve the truth. All of it."

I leaned back, waiting, but Cal seemed to have given up on being forthright. "Well?" I prompted.

He snorted once and said, "Not here. Do you know the old bridge outside Autumnbrook woods?"

Not really, but that was what Google was for. I nodded slowly.

"Meet me there, Friday night, and I'll...I will try to explain everything I can. Some of it is still impossible to believe."

That was rich coming from a real-life werewolf. I crossed my arms, not giving him an answer. Cal hunched his shoulders higher and he started to turn. "For what little it matters, I prayed for you to pull through."

I ground my teeth, a sharp smack of "For what little it helped" clinging to my tongue. But I swallowed it, not wanting to kick him while he looked about to drop himself.

With a slow shuffle, Calvin drifted for the door.

"Just so you know," I shouted, raising my head, "I won't be coming alone." In case he didn't get it, I jerked my head to Ink.

Cal sighed in resignation. "I wouldn't expect anything less."

Chapter Thirteen

The second the marker finished its twirling loop to end the symbol, relief flooded through my leg. I'd tried to not stare too closely at the bruised and puckered flesh they'd stapled together. But it was hard to look anywhere else while drawing my spell.

"Oh fucking god," I cried, straining my wounded leg into the air. As the magical balm swirled around my inner thigh, the massive knot in my entire body finally released. Going from unavoidable agony to endless bliss was more intoxicating than any orgasm. My body slumped back onto the couch, only for Ink to catch me.

I stared up into his distractingly handsome face in awe. "How didn't the nurses throw themselves at your feet?" slipped from my softening lips and I reached up to touch his.

Ink chuckled, catching my fingers before I could bat at his too stupidly perfect mouth. He wrapped my hands safe in his, massaging over the knuckles while saying, "My charms do not work on everyone."

That idea sobered me up. Okay, not entirely as I kept staring agog at him. "There are people immune to incubuses? Incubi? Sex gods?"

His laugh rolled down the chest that'd been trapped in clothing for three whole days. He had to be chafing under there. With a smile, Ink placed my fingertips to his lips and gave a soft kiss. "You'd be surprised how many do not glance twice at me." He moved to kissing my knuckles, each touch warm and soft. "Cast me aside because their hearts are already wound up with another, be it a person, place, or fervid interest."

"That doesn't bother you? Make you want to chase them more?"

"Why ever would I? Do you prefer the steak that's presented to you cooked, or would you rather jump out of a car and pursue a steer on foot?"

It's not about feelings or even a challenge with him. It's just food. Delectable, mouth-watering, impossibly attractive food. The entire time in the hospital I was dead from the waist down, metaphorically speaking. But the second I'm back in my apartment resting on Ink's lap while he seductively licks my fingers, I want nothing more than to rip his clothes off.

Does that make me the steak?

Another burst of relief shivered through me. The entire muscle the werewolf had shredded to kibble knit back together below my skin. I rode out the wave of pleasure, curling my toes and tipping farther back until my head rested on Ink's thighs. He wasted no time in perking up, the mountain in his pants nearly pressing to my cheek.

He did save me. Found me where no one else could. Stayed by my side night and day until we were safe behind closed doors. Would I do the same for a sandwich, even one I really enjoyed eating?

"Thank you," I whispered.

My words so surprised him that he stopped his tender kisses around my wrists. I placed my hand against his chest and undid the buttons. They all but fell apart with a single touch, the tips of my fingers dancing through the demonic chest hair below.

At Ink's continual stare of confusion, I said, "You didn't have to stay with me in the hospital."

Snickering, he said, "Where else would I have gone? The meager gift shop did not even have an herbalism section."

"Uh-huh." I shifted, pulling myself up until I sat in his lap. Ink always managed to get his hand right over my ass in any situation, and this was no different. I leaned closer to him. The fire in his eyes burst to life and my body responded in anticipation.

"What would you have gotten me, if there was a pile of herbs instead of balloons with get-well messages?"

He caressed his other hand over the cheap T-shirt Dana had lent me. Starting at my belly, he swept his fingers back and forth over my skin in delicious torture. Leaning forward until his nose bumped into mine, Ink whispered, "Wolfsbane."

I kissed him with every sinful thought perched on my tongue. How I wanted his hands to pinch and knead every inch of my skin. His teeth to nip and nibble over my breasts. His cheek to rub against my inner thigh without worrying about a sharp pain.

Until I wanted that too.

Suddenly, Ink tossed me into the air. I crashed back down with my legs splayed right over his crotch. His laugh rolled like thunder cracking through the gates of hell, and I loved it.

"Are you comfortable in this delectable position?" he asked, darting his gaze to my naked thigh. A pair of panties kept him parted from what he wanted most, but it didn't last long. He tugged on the inseam elastic with his thumb, causing me to squirm and bite my lip for more.

"No problem," I said, sweeping my arms over his shoulders until I could wind my fingers through his hair. Tugging his head back, I pressed my thighs together, trapping his hand right where I needed it.

"What about you?"

Ink scoffed. "My stamina is in question?" Even with that wound to his ego, he slipped his fingers farther into my panties. Only the barest whisper caressed over my soaked lips.

Nuzzling his cheek with my nose, I moaned. "You're trapped in those dreaded pants and can't get free with me in your lap."

"I am a sin of lust," he thundered, nipping up my jaw until he swirled his tongue over my ear. "Trousers are no challenge at all."

Yes! I rolled my hand down the non-challenging pants, pressing my palm to his cock that never slept. Ink nibbled his way down my throat while he kept teasing me with his finger swirl. I reached for his zipper to—

"Ow!" I cried. Something sharp struck my inner thigh, the one the werewolf didn't rip to shreds. "Shit." Another one hit and I flipped around, my ass falling to Ink's side. Yanking open my legs, but not for fun reasons, I watched in macabre fascination. One of the two dozen staples the doctors had put in my skin shivered.

It danced within my flesh like an excited chihuahua that had to pee. Just as I leaned closer, it pinged out of my thigh and struck the wall. Left behind was skin practically baby smooth without a single scar in place. I trailed my finger down it, getting no jolt of pain, when the next staple did the same.

They were going to take a while to dislodge. With a sigh, I leaned back against the armrest. Ink massaged my knee and up my thigh. "How am I going to explain that to the doctor? Oh, those staples you put in me? Don't worry about removing them—they removed themselves just fine."

One more problem with being a witch. I thought I had it all figured out. Wait until they released me, heal myself then limp around in public for a few weeks. God knew work wasn't going to give me an inch. After receiving the news that I'd got my leg ripped to shreds by a wild animal, they'd told me to buy a pair of crutches and get back in before the week was over.

I forgot about the follow-up visit where a doctor would discover a damn near miracle had occurred right by my crotch.

The man who tried his damnedest to create more miracles brushed back my oily hair. With his nose burrowing into the hollow behind my ear, he said, "Would you have preferred the alternative?"

Lying around in pain, guzzling down ibuprofen by the kidney-destroying boatload and gritting to get through every day on my feet? Not a chance. Too bad I didn't have a 'make everyone forget that even happened' spell.

"I did wish to tell you," Ink said, his voice shifting so fast out of its sex loop it nearly caused my head to spin, "you impressed me."

"How?" I'd gotten my ass handed to me by a werewolf on my first mission. Nothing about it was impressive.

"You damn near tore the head off that man even after the truth was revealed."

I clenched my fists. One was in an anger that wouldn't stop throbbing through me no matter how much time passed. And the other was guilt, because I jumped right to the worst conclusion and couldn't let it go. "Why is that impressive?" I asked. He might have not done it, but Cal knew something, and keeping that from me put me in danger.

Ink dug his bottom teeth into my neck and slowly scraped the top down to join them. A moan rolled up from my staple-freeing thighs and I clung to his arms for support.

"It's been my impression that most humans will comport themselves to appease a mortal they take to bed."

He thought that just because I'd slept with Cal once, he owned me? "I don't work like that," I said.

Ink's smile rose into the full smirk I came to expect. "And that is what impresses me."

"Would that even work? Ripping off a werewolf's head? Could it kill one?" I needed to do research, prepare myself, learn the damn spells already. But Ink's body was so warm and his hands so damn skilled.

"I daresay removal of the head is deadly to most species." Even with the staples still pinging out of my skin, Ink massaged my other thigh. My head filled with needs for what he could do with his fingers. With his tongue. And my incubus heard them all.

Before he could ply me apart, I asked, "What about demons?"

The wandering hands froze. His tongue stopped toying with my earlobe. "Why do you wish to know?" The voice was cold and careful.

"In case any ever threaten the citizens of this city I'm destined to protect."

Ink chuckled, his thumb brushing straight through the center of my panties. I barely caught my breath before he answered, "You need not worry, because I will slay them for you."

I tried to sit up, to look him in the eye, but Ink weaved his magic that put me right under his spell. I didn't intend to come up for hours.

Chapter Fourteen

Bitter winds creaked through a rickety bridge arced over a thin creek. A trampled path led across the faded gray planks to the other side, but it'd be almost impossible to find in summer. I was only able to stumble upon the bridge thanks to most of the trees having shed their leaves.

"I hope he gets here soon," I said, blowing my breath into single, barely visible puffs. Ink said nothing, but he stood up straighter with his hands locked behind his back. If I didn't know any better, I'd swear that was his battle stance. Though anything outside of thrusting hips was probably a battle stance for incubi.

Why'd Cal even want to meet here? To unleash the rest of his werewolf pack upon me? Silence the witness then total world domination.

A crack loud enough to tell me it was purposeful caused me and Ink to turn around. Cal stood on the twig he'd sacrificed to get our attention. He'd been smart enough to dress for the woods in late November.

The jacket was open, but ready to be zipped up when his fleece-lined flannel wasn't strong enough. His stubble was nearing on beard territory, not a good look for the blond. Though to feel it was…

"Hi," he said, shuffling a foot through the crackling leaves.

"Hi," I repeated. At the earnest look in his eyes, the concerned waving of his foot like he didn't know what to say and the hands stuffed in his pockets, I melted. I transformed back to the newest hire who'd found her pudding 'accidentally' stolen by a cute coworker. He'd bought me an entire pallet's worth to make up for it, the dork.

Who's also a werewolf and is probably good friends with the one that tried to kill you.

Focus, Layla.

"You said you had something to tell me." The gloves were off. I raised my head higher and focused only on his eyes. Forget the rest of the body, though, god, was that a hard order. Shit, he had that vein, the one right beside his hips that traveled straight to the—

"You brought company," Calvin interrupted, swiveling his head to take in my escort. "Funny, I didn't think demons answered to another's bidding."

"I am a confounding creature of sin," Ink said and took a bow.

In no mood for a pissing match, I stepped between them. Ink snapped up rod straight, and Cal stepped back. That stung, but I shook it off. "You know why Ink's here."

"Do I? Do even you know why he's here?"

I crossed my arms tight to my chest. "To keep me safe. It's more than you've done."

Calvin swallowed and shook his head. "Layla, I was only… No, you're right. And I won't fight you on your incubus. Come on. It's this way." He jerked his head and walked across the rickety bridge.

I waited on the other side, clinging to the rotting handrails. Even though the stream was at best a foot deep, even though I'd just watched Cal cross it, I froze. Ink's unnatural body heat coalesced behind me.

Cal watched me dig my fingers deeper into the wood and risk splinters. "You never told me you have a fear of heights."

"What?"

"The bridge, it's almost two feet off the ground. A dangerous height. If you'd like, I could carry you across. And you can keep your eyes shut the entire time."

It was a joke, I knew that. But the way he said it sounded genuine. As if, should I honestly fear walking over a tiny bridge, he'd sweep me off my feet and carry me the minor distance.

If you cross that bridge, and he says or does something unforgivable, there's no coming back.

Shaking my head, I walked up onto the planks. Cal dropped his arms like he'd really wanted an excuse to cart me around. I stepped onto the other side of the creek beside him, when Ink's hands massaged down my shoulders.

"How delightful. What shall be next? Gathering small berries for jams? Foraging for twigs? Oh, I know, collecting leaves to press into books."

Cal chuckled slowly. "If we take too long, it'll be chasing squirrels." He turned and led us onto an even less visible path. But he knew exactly which branches to pick up and where to duck. How often did he walk this?

To my surprise, Ink jogged up beside him. "How much do you share with the common wolf? Do you howl?"

Shit. My face burned as Cal glanced up and a smile rose. "Yes. But only for good reason."

"Interesting," Ink kept on. "Do you find yourself capable of licking your—"

"Okay!" I interjected fast, wrapping both my hands around Ink's biceps to tug him back. I'd been worried about the two ripping each other's throats out. Why did the pair of them getting on strike me as more dangerous? "If you don't mind, I have a few questions to ask myself too."

Ink extended his hand and faded back, leaving me and Cal to walk awkwardly side by side. At that moment, the path narrowed. Trees and thorny shrubs pressed in around us. I tried to turn my body and walk partially sideways, but it left me staring at Cal's face. Even in the cold, dark woods, his half-smile made my lips twitch in response.

We stumbled together in a silence that grew fatter with each step. The tension had practically flattened us both to the ground in awkwardness, when my shoe slipped on the wet terrain. I felt my ass heading for a muddy night, until Cal had me in his arms.

"Whoa," he exclaimed, his hands wrapped around my elbows, his chest pressing tight to my back. My skin turned extra crispy at my near ass-planting into the dirt, then the feel of him. His muscles didn't just press—they cuddled me. Cal's fingers slipped forward, circling my wrists and almost reaching for my palms.

A shiver trembled up my spine and I danced forward out of his hold. "That's…it's fine. I've got it now."

"Good. Wonderful, I…" Absently, Cal swept through his hair then scratched at the beard hiding away his jaw. "You had something you needed to ask?"

"Yes, I was wondering, if…if I need to cast a spell or make a potion."

He quirked his head. "I won't stop you if you do, if that's your concern."

"No, because. I mean, a werewolf, you know attacked me. Not so much bite, more clawed, but still. Isn't that how…you make more werewolves?"

A laugh of pure glee broke from Calvin. It felt like it was at my expense. "No, not at all. You don't need to worry about becoming a werewolf. Not from a claw wound or a bite. I haven't heard that one in a long time. Whew." He wiped at his eye as if a tear were there, then moved on, pushing away the branches for me.

I gave chase, my consternation growing. *That's how the movies all say it works. Werewolf bites someone, boom, they grow hair the next full moon.*

Layla. Don't be stupid.

"How…how do you, ya know, make more werewolves then?" I asked.

Cal held up a fallen branch, but he turned to beam his shocking ice-blue eyes on me. "The same way humans do."

"Oh, that's…" Jesus Christ, could witches spontaneously combust from too much embarrassment? Ink remained disquietingly quiet.

We're all adults here. We all know how…babies are made. God knows you've tried with both of them. That doused my flaming face with cold water. Ink was easy—demons couldn't carry any STDs because they weren't really alive. Nor would I ever have to worry about a possible pregnancy for the same reason.

But Cal was mortal.

And why did I even care? We'd slept together once. Nothing was done to worry about...a litter appearing. The chances of us fucking again seemed remote at this point. Leading me into the freezing cold woods to talk wasn't exactly an aphrodisiac.

Unaware of my sudden lecherous turn, Calvin launched into an exposition mode. "The truth is that werewolves can only mate with other werewolves."

"So, what we did in your living room was, what? Werewolf macramé?"

His snort was annoyingly adorable and he brushed back his hair. "Sorry, we can, um, do what we did and...far more." The wistful voice pinged through my heart, trying to drag me to rush into his arms. But the water seeping up my pants legs stopped me dead. "There simply won't be any children produced."

"Really?"

Holy shit, Layla. You do not want babies. Not now. Maybe not ever. Do not start mourning the lack of blue and brown eyed children with olive skin and blonde hair.

Calvin shrugged and ducked to walk under a massive fallen tree. "I could explain it in detail, but I don't think that's why you came here."

I followed after him, asking, "Why am I...?" Rising through the gnarled trees sat six buildings. They towered above the old growth in the forest, all sides painted green except one. That was black with a circle of silver-white in the middle. Had we stumbled into some backwoods training ground for the Marines, or a militia's artillery stash they'd get rather pissed about sharing?

"Cal," I gulped. The sunlight was nearly gone, rendering all but the tips of the trees and the sharp points of the four corner roofs in darkness. I couldn't make out any people moving along the bridges strung across the raised buildings, but my gut told me they were there. *Watching.*

"This is where I…" He stopped nervously scratching his ear and turned to face the compound. His nostrils flared and he sneered. "Where I was born."

What? He'd told me he came here from New Mexico for school. Even gave me a tiny cactus from there, which I smashed to bits fighting off a tumor monster. Exhausted with his endless lies I'd never questioned, I reached for the fallen vines to dive through them. A hand lashed to my wrist, stopping me dead.

"Wait," Cal said. He kicked at the vines, sending golden leaves tumbling to the ground. It revealed a massive barbed-wire fence hidden beneath the forest's foliage.

"Holy shit," slipped from me. I stood frozen in place and Cal gave a quick twang to the wire. The sharp line danced down the tree line, far beyond what I could see. An inescapable shiver crawled up my legs, and I didn't realize I was reaching for the first safe body until I nearly had Cal's arms wrapped around me.

"This is charming." Ink's sharp voice knocked sense into me. I didn't leap out of Cal's arms for fear I'd tangle myself in the barbed wire, but I huddled away and watched the incubus swing his head up. "Haven't seen a forest fortress since my days with the Vicomte de Lautrec. Haven't eaten so much boar off bare buttocks since then either."

A groan rolled inside my brain, which I barely managed to hide. In doing so, I caught Cal grimacing. We both cracked a small smile together. Damn it. I shook my head and stared along the fence instead. My heart needed to remember this wasn't adorable Cal who'd translate the harder Latin for me. Not just, anyway.

"What do you mean you were born here?" I asked, trying to make my voice cold and determined. "Where is here?"

Cal's nervous itching carried to his neck, his fingers scratching until red furrows were left behind. "This is the compound for members of the Eternal Moonlight." Even with his body hunched inward and his feet slanted together, his face contorted into rage when the words left his lips.

Through the darkness of the forest, his eyes gleamed whiter than ever and he narrowed them on only me. Cal's shoulders raised and my knees knocked from the growl in his voice. "I was born in a cult."

Chapter Fifteen

"Born and raised in a cult that to the outside world looks like nutty organic farmers." Cal glared up at the towers and I tried to follow. "We all were. Mark, me, Eli."

"Eli? Who's Eli?" I asked because I needed to say something and blurting out 'Holy fucking shit, a real cult? Like drinking Kool-Aid, building a spaceship for your alien overlords, and everything?' wouldn't go over well.

"He's..." Cal shifted and a rueful glance parted over me. He reached as though he wanted to tug me close for a hug, but it landed against his side instead. "He's my brother. In a sense. Our mothers were tricked into joining from college, or out of high school."

"How the hell do you convince someone to move into a compound in the woods covered in barbed wire?"

A grimace crawled over him and he shook his head. "It's surprisingly easy. I spent the first eight years of my life thinking it was normal to be silent all the time. To dig in the fields until my fingernails wouldn't grow back. To pull maggots out of bread and eat what remained."

"Fucking hell," I sputtered. "Is it...is it a werewolf thing?"

Cal turned to me, his eyes narrowing. "You think that only beasts would be so cruel?" I opened my mouth to try to defend myself, but Cal kept going. "There are humans in there too. Probably more humans than werewolves. They delight in watching everyone, spying, tattling, torturing those that disobey. Often more than the beasts that roam the woods."

"I know people can be the goddamn worst," I snarled. "I just wanted to know if there were wolves in the forest right now. Wolves that could try to eat me. Again."

The anger in Cal's angelic eyes vanished and he turned stricken. "Of course you would. No. There aren't many and the ones who are don't prowl outside the compound. I...I'm sorry."

Great. Now I felt bad for making him feel bad.

While we both marinated in our guilt, Ink barged in. "Then what is the large mass moving through the trees at, I'd guess, the speed of a gazelle?"

"What?" Cal raised his head to the cold night air and pulled in a deep breath. "I can't smell anything."

"Not much help then, are you?"

Cal sneered at him. "You passed a hamburger place on the way here. Before leaving the apartment, you ate a pickle and butter sandwich, for whatever reason. And had sex."

Fuck. My cheeks lit up and I glared at my shoes while Ink clapped. "Fascinating. It was a pickle, butter and marshmallow sandwich, incidentally."

Calvin snorted as if he'd save that fact for later. "I cannot smell a werewolf in the forest."

"But there could be one out there?" Why hadn't I read up on how to protect myself from werewolves? *Get a crucifix, or holy water. That's freaking vampires.*

Oh shit, are vampires real too?

Ink peered through the trees with his demon eyes. "Probably more than one."

No, I should have studied how to stop werewolves. Maybe my book had a ward to shield myself. I swung my purse around, the entire weight thrown off by twenty pounds of magic. In doing so, I almost smacked it into Cal's leg. Our hands brushed together, his fingers winding over mine, and we stared into each other's eyes.

"I will go and see what it is," Ink declared. Before I could tell him that was a good idea, he vanished.

The idea threw off Calvin, who tried to find him. "Does he do that a lot?"

"I don't think I've watched him walk farther than a block," I said and dug out my spell book. The weight of it in my hands washed a calm over me, but it couldn't fight against the anxiety streaming from Cal.

Instead of opening the pages, I pressed the book to my heart. "How did you get out? Of the cult? I've heard that it can be…impossible. Deadly."

"It is. And with werewolves involved, it's doubly so." He drummed his fingers on his thighs, causing his knuckles to glance against my legs too. Instead of shifting back, I leaned closer. "I don't know the full of it, only that my mother received 'special treatment' from the asshole in charge. She used that to sneak away not only me, but the werewolf kids from two other women. They couldn't risk running, so they gave up their babies in the hope we'd all have a better life."

My brain hit a brick wall, unable to process that much pain. He stared up at me from under his brow, his head hanging lower with each second I didn't speak. But what could I say? 'Sorry you were in a cult? Good job on getting free. What are we doing outside their fortified compound?'

"I'm sorry," Cal sputtered. When my gaze tried to find his, he began to pace erratically and shuffled both hands through his short hair. "When you said you were tracking Mark, following him...and me, I...I lost it. I overreacted. I knew I did the second you slammed the door. But I swear, if I had any idea a wolf would attack you, I'd never have—" Cal wound himself up so tight his teeth snapped.

He drew his hands up my arms, rolling them around my elbows as more trauma fell from his lips. "We were never alone growing up. Eating, sleeping, even taking a shit, someone was always there. Always watching. And you had no way of knowing what they'd report about you in the truth circle."

I fought to not wince from his fingers tightening. "I had no idea."

A sarcastic laugh snorted from his nostrils and the vise on my arms eased. His chest rose with the anxiety deflating. "I thought I was over it. Over all of it. Kept it in the past. Long gone. And next thing I know I'm panic-shouting at the girl I..." Cal's mouth opened, his lips parting. They called to me, tempted me to kiss him. *Take away all the pain, forget our blow up. Just be.*

"...I go to school with," he whispered, turning from me.

I did the same, hoping the disappointment wasn't palpable on my face. "Why are you here?" I asked instead. "Outside this compound? Risking all that past trauma and bad memories?"

Calvin worried his forehead and he stared daggers at the towers in the trees. His stance hardened. Those arms that had felt so soft and tender when he'd rescued me from the barbed wire turned to granite. Every muscle in his body tensed and flexed, the fight response seeming to take control.

I didn't know what to do. That was a lot to take in. To keep secret and carry without anyone knowing. A snicker slipped from me and Cal's silent vengeance faded to a curious look. "Just thinking how, out of all of us in the group, you seemed the most normal."

"It's not easy — " His face snapping to a snarl, Calvin leapt for me. On instinct, I raised my book to protect myself. When his hands locked around my body, he pulled me down into the brush. "They're outside the perimeter," Cal growled in my ear.

"I take it that's not normal?"

He'd crumpled himself over top of me, nearly all his body exposed to the threat while I hid below. It pushed his cheek against mine, so I felt his jaw move with every word. "Not in the slightest. I know a place we can hide. This way."

Remaining hunched over, Cal locked his fingers around my hand, and pulled us deeper into the woods. There was no easy way through the mess of trees. Saplings slapped at my chest and tore into my hair. We had to squeeze around trees while the sound of feet pounding over the leaves grew closer.

"What are they doing?" he snarled. "No one is allowed outside the compound after dark."

"Maybe they're escaping?" I said.

He didn't respond, but a growl at the foolish idea rumbled up his arm and into mine. The deeper we rushed into the forest, the harder it grew to see. I had to rely on Cal shoving back the branches. But he missed just as many.

"Come on, hurry up," he chided me.

I ducked down, the gnarled branches of the trees scraping over my scalp. He tugged harder on my hand, and I took a big step, only for my head to slam back. "Ow, ow, fuck!" I tried to curse in a whisper, which wasn't working. "The goddamn tree's got my hair." A huge section was going to be ripped out by the roots if I didn't untangle it.

After tugging my hand out of Cal's, I wrapped my grip around my hair and yanked. The whole branch creaked to keep its hold on me. "Let go, you fucking Ent!"

Light swept across the forest we'd trampled through. Even with my tiny human ears, I heard the prickle of voices murmuring over the leaves. *Damn it! Damn it!* I pulled harder, tears starting. Pain burst out of my scalp, but I had to get free.

A blur swept in front of me and I fumbled back. Cal stretched out his palm to catch me, and I felt five sharp pricks poking into my spine. Calvin stuffed his free hand in his pocket. But it wasn't fast enough to hide the claws that'd cut me free.

With branch tips stuck in my hair, we bolted farther into the woods. Another creek formed here, a deeper one. Cal didn't even ask, just hefted me up into his arms. At the water's edge, he leapt, our bodies hurtling three or maybe four feet into the air. Before I could breathe, we landed on the other side.

"Was that necessary?" I asked, despite my libido demanding that it was and he should do it again.

"Water carries scent," was all Cal said. Despite the concern rattling in his voice, he didn't put me down. I clung to his neck, watching us cross an overrun field to the ruins of a half-rotted barn.

At its threshold, he finally opened his arms. As my feet hit the grass, I said, "Here I thought you'd kick the door open and carry me inside."

"Too much noise," he responded, though for a brief second his lips twisted into a smile. Gripping the edge of the plywood, Calvin tugged up the blockade nailed over the doorway.

He didn't need to tell me to slink in, though more of my damn hair caught on the rough side. I made it two steps in before my foot crunched. It was so dark, I couldn't see two inches in front of my face, but my imagination made up a human skull I'd just shoved my shoe through.

"Here." Cal swept me up, practically pulling me over the rotten floorboards with grass and small trees prodding between them. "We need to hide behind this." A lectern that'd once been nailed to the middle of the floor lay on its side. The same vines that'd wrapped around the barbed-wire fence twisted over the top where a teacher's books would have sat.

Cal pressed my back closer to the crumbling wood and I slipped lower until I was hidden from view. I expected him to sit beside me, but he hovered above. His haunches taut, he folded a single fist to the floor right beside my hip and glared at the door.

Who knew what was going to walk through there. Werewolf? Crazy cultist? Armed militia member, which was as good as a crazy cultist? I wanted to turn around to look and prepare myself, but I was trapped between the lectern and Calvin's insanely muscled body.

My face was stuck staring directly down the swoop of his pecs. Even under the baggy flannel, the firm muscle flexed to steel on one side. God, if anyone else knew what he kept under all those loose sweaters...

"This was not how I wanted the night to go," he whispered. His watchful gaze darted down to me only for a second, but my lips slid into a soft smile from it.

"Trapped together in the woods with mad cultists chasing us? All alone in the dark? What guy wouldn't want that?"

He chuckled without making a sound. "I don't know. A hot tub, twenty-four-hour room service and a feather bed sound better to me."

"Weirdo," I said. Cal dipped his head under the lectern, his laugh washing over me. Those damn lips weren't even an inch from mine, taunting me to taste them.

A pain pressed tighter to my hip. I swiveled my head to find my purse— For the love of god, of course! My spell book practically leapt into my fingers and I whispered, "A protection spell."

The sound of its pages flipping drew Cal's attention. "What is that?"

"Witch Google," I said and drew my finger down the page. Oh boy, there were a lot of protection spells. An entire diagram stretched out over two pages. It divided into categories to protect against demons, monsters of the mortal plane, nether creatures. The last box was marked celestials but it had no spell under it.

With my nose nearly pressed into the binding string, I glared at the tiny text. Whoever wrote it must have had hands the size of a porcelain doll. Even without my stupid dyslexia, there was no chance I could read it without a magnifying lens. Or maybe a microscope.

Cal's body tightened and the voices that'd called from around the forest weren't so distant anymore. I heard one ask if those were footprints. *Shit.*

An inhuman growl rose in Cal's throat. His chest expanded, pressing me tighter to the barricade. He swept an arm around the back of me and raised his head higher until his eyes beamed over the top of the lectern. Was he going to turn into a werewolf this second? While he held me?

What if they had guns?

I needed something, a way to fix this... The pages flew under my fingers, potions to cure toothaches written on the back of spells to defang chimeras. None of it helpful, all of it useless in my muddled brain.

Wait!

Yanking out my Sharpie, I flicked the cap away into the darkness. It had to touch both of us. Straining, I embedded my cheek into Cal's chest and reached both my hands around his back. No fur. Not yet, anyway.

Oh, fuck! The sound of wood ripped through its nails echoed about the dilapidated building. I dug my palm into Cal's latissimus dorsi and started to draw. As the line trailed from my skin down to his, the flesh below heated up.

His growl shifted to a snarl, shoving me further from my work. My hand slipped to the side, cutting off the connection. All I could hear in one ear was the rabid anger of a werewolf, and in the other, the splintering of the plywood door. *Ignore it, Layla. Finish the goddamn symbol.*

Leaping off the ground, I wrapped my legs around Cal's waist. It was for leverage, but my body entwining around his must have shocked the man so much that his growl stopped. The burning fever faded under my touch, and he turned his eyes to me in utter surprise.

"Stay quiet," I said and drew the last of the line to connect us.

Did it work?

The plywood flew off the doorway, three circular lights sweeping into the room. I stared in horror at one aiming at the ceiling like a full moon. They couldn't see us yet, but if my spell didn't work, it'd only be a matter of seconds.

I dug my cheek into the side of Cal's neck and buried my lips on his shoulder. An urge to scream and run shivered through me, but Calvin lowered us to the ground. I clung tighter, having to keep my hand in the same spot.

Hard-heeled shoes slammed over the fallen floorboards. The lights increased, swinging rapidly across the back of the schoolhouse. A tattered flag with twenty-three stars dangled from above where not even bored vandals could reach.

"Search for them," a man commanded. Through the blood pounding in my brain, I heard gun barrels slap into open palms. *Shit.*

Quieter than a whisper, a breath from the mouth circling my ear spoke one word. "Layla."

Closing my eyes tight, I enveloped Cal and he surrounded me. All the while, the sounds of men come to kill us drew closer.

I don't want to die. I don't want Cal to die either. Please, don't see us. Turn around.

Leave.

"What's that?" a voice bellowed practically beside my head.

He was just behind the lectern, only the scrap of wood hiding us. But it sent my heart racing and a yelp built in my lungs. I bit down on Calvin, screaming into his body instead.

Light skipped right over the top of my head, piercing through my imposed darkness, and my eyelids opened.

Where the hell is Cal?

My hands clung to nothing. Empty space. His heartbeat thumped beside mine, each reassuring breath whispering across my throat. But he was gone. And so was I.

Holy shit, it worked.

A face thrust itself right over mine. I stared in horror at a rash of red dots clinging to a sunken chin. If he dipped his head an inch lower, he'd knock it into my nose. *Don't scream, Layla. Don't even blink.*

"Well, what is it?" the same voice shouted.

The chin dropped and I retracted my neck as its owner spoke. "Nothing. Some fucking rat's nest is all."

"But he smelled them…" another person, a woman began.

"He's wrong," the first voice declared. "Get back to the perimeter. White could be anywhere."

I clung to my invisible werewolf even after the lights switched off. Even after the sound of their boots clomping against the ground faded to my pounding heartbeat. Even after the chances of them returning became ludicrous.

"Layla," he whispered. His knees pushed together and he raised his hands off the floor in order to wrap them around me. Cradling the nape of my neck, Cal spoke my name in shock and relief. I wanted to scream and laugh at the same time.

He pressed his lips to mine and I gave in without question or qualm. The once hungry, inescapable kiss when we'd ripped our clothes off in his house softened to an ache of forgiveness and need. Cal tipped back, taking me with until I sat on his lap while I dove into his kiss. The hard purse of his lips nipped over mine, his tongue piping his masculine heat through me.

I raked my nails over his back, padding my hands into his muscles. His touch leapt straight down to the back of my pants, Cal trying to pinch both of my ass cheeks in one go. When he placed his middle finger right on the top of my tailbone, I lost it.

I needed him.

Bunching his flannel shirt in my fist, I pulled him to my lips and started to lean back. My legs shifted and I flexed my inner thighs around Cal's waist. In doing so, my ass slipped to caress over his bulging cock.

"Excuse me," a voice shouted from outside.

Fuck!

"May I ask you a question regarding your…? Oh, never mind then."

My panic ebbed as I realized there was only one person who'd deploy that flippant sarcasm in the middle of a freezing forest. While sliding out from under Cal, I was careful to only risk a quick peek over the lectern. Silhouetted by moonlight, Ink leaned against the ripped-open door as if he had all the time in the world.

"What? Finished already?" he asked.

Cal turned to me, his face overwritten with guilt. I took all the shame. Had I really planned to…in here?

Where there were rusty nails, jagged boards and probably hantavirus. I was losing my damn mind.

I struggled to stand, my legs trembling under me. Calvin dodged to the side, giving me a wide berth. Ink didn't shift from his nonchalant, sexy lean, his hands loosely folded over his chest. "There are, in fact, numerous armed guards in the woods tonight."

"Yeah. We noticed," I said and almost rolled my eyes to Cal. Some help the demon was in all of that.

But Cal was turned in on himself, his fingers worrying together as he whispered, "I don't understand."

"Who were you talking to? Before?" I asked the demon. Anyone else and I'd think it was a ruse to warn me of their presence. Ink never cared.

"You didn't see them? Probably a him, but I try to not judge. Some fool yet lingered to the side of this...delightful domicile." He finally moved from the doorway, his eyes brighter than a flashlight in the dark. I stared at them in awe, when Ink took my hand.

"So cold," he whispered and vigorously rubbed my palm between his.

I tried to ignore the incubus to focus on the bigger problem. "Cal, do you think they saw us?"

He wrung out his hair and shook his head. "I don't... None of this makes any sense. Look, I need... I have to figure this out."

"Hey." I reached for him, catching his wandering fingers and wrapping them safe in my hand. My half of the invisibility spell caressed his palm. "You're not alone in this."

Cal raised his chin, and a half-hearted smile came with. Then he caught sight of Ink, still rubbing life back into my other hand. Turning his head to the side, he tugged his palm free. "I'll tell you when I have an answer. When I find my brothers and get to the bottom of this."

With his head bent, he jogged past me and out of the doorway ripped to pieces by men who had nearly killed us. Before he vanished into the moonlight, Cal said, "I'll see you soon."

"Well, Monday. We have class," I called.

Cal didn't answer. He raised his head to the sky and ran into the forest, leaving me with my demon and more problems than before.

Chapter Sixteen

"Thanks," I said, an automatic smile rising for the clerk ringing through the last of my groceries.

There'd been no sign of Cal for the past four days. School had shut down for fall break, and every time I'd called him, it had gone straight to voicemail. Dana had got through once and said he couldn't make the last study session before everyone vanished to the four winds. Apparently, he was sick.

Which was what had sent me out the day before Thanksgiving to a grocery store. Carts clogged every escapable aisle, parents whole-arm sweeping boxes of stuffing and French-fried onions into their baskets. One bounced off the head of their kid, but there was no time to stop and check for wounds. There was turkey to procure and pies to war over.

Hefting the three bags up, I made a beeline for the door. There hadn't been news about the cult either — at least, no one had shown up at my door in the middle of the night. That wouldn't have gone well for them stumbling into the den of a naked demon.

I had an entire week ahead of me holed up in the apartment with Ink, living off leftover pre-cooked ham and probably fucking through the parades. It should be the vacation I deserved, but my mind wouldn't stop churning back to Cal.

The sick lie couldn't hold up for long. Why did I let him leave to take on his potentially murderous brother alone? What if he didn't want me there to help? Did he choose to lie low to find his brother, or to help him?

A chilly wind whipped through the parking lot. I finished sliding my groceries in and raised my scarf higher up my cheek. Voices carried across the cement jungle, babies screaming in exhaustion, parents whining with hunger. But none of them seemed to feel the cold bite in the air.

Shaking it off, I reached above my head to grab the trunk to close it. A shadow lurched from the side and my first instinct was to sigh at Ink failing to remain at home. But when the hand snatched at my keys instead of my ass, I spun around in shock.

And my heart dropped.

Black hair, a patched trench coat left open to reveal a shirt clinging to a body that cracked skulls like walnuts. Piercing blue-white eyes.

Mark.

"It's you." I sneered, ducking back from the werewolf. With both my hands, I secured my purse tight to my body, though the spell book's radiating calm did little to stop the hair rising along my neck.

He twirled my keys on his finger, keeping them just out of reach, like he wanted me to try for them, leaving me wide open for an attack. I hunched my body tighter to my magic book and glared instead.

"Look, green-skin." Mark snickered, raising his lip in a snarl to reveal a canine so sharp it looked like it belonged to a vampire. I was so focused on that, his shit-talking passed me by. "Whatever game you're playing at stops here."

I shook off the dread crawling up my spine, and the hypnotic twirl of my only means of escape. Sneering, I said, "What the fuck are you talking about?"

Mark laughed, his head tossed back. The longer jet-black hair shook to the side, revealing not only four studs lining his ear but a tattoo on the side of his neck. Three small paw prints led up to his jaw.

A hand lashed out, fingers slamming around my wrist. I tugged back and he twisted, digging his claws into my skin. The rising pain demanded I yelp, but I bit it down and yanked back harder. All it did was scrape my flesh over more on his claws.

"Listen to me, witch," Mark snarled, tugging me across the parking lot until his breath bathed my face. "Keep the fuck away from my brother."

I fished through my purse, trying to find my protection while the damn werewolf watched with his eyebrow cocked. "Let go of me." My voice dropped lower. Why was it doing that? I should be screaming. There were people everywhere and yet no one was looking our way. They had their own mortal lives free of werewolves and demons to get to.

"Your type… Claw don't believe it, but I know you. What do you call 'em? Covens? A pack of disgusting executioners."

"Like you're one to talk." I yanked harder on my arm. His claws didn't stab through my skin, but my hand couldn't move a millimeter. Mark had complete control of me, the fucking bastard. "I know what you are."

"Which is why I ain't scared of you," he said and jerked his chin to my purse. "Or that little book of yours."

My rummaging froze at his noticing. I'd started to retract my fingers slowly from my bag when I felt it. *Yes!*

Mark drew closer, pulling me across the pavement until his teeth glanced over my cheek with every word. "You might have magic but your body's just as fragile as the rest of 'em. I will do anything to protect my brothers. Anything."

His spittle splattered down my cheek and I yanked my head away. Unable to wipe it off, I suffered the slimy chill and stared him up and down. Mark didn't even bat an eye, his teeth gnashing together like he planned to eviscerate me right there in the parking lot. *Just like those other women.*

Meeting him head on, I lifted my chin and dropped the bomb. "Then why are you working with the cult?"

In an instant, his eyes opened wide, his mouth dropped, his nostrils flared, and I attacked. A thick spray of pepper solution erupted from my palm, gushing over his entire face. It shot up his nose, slammed into his eyes and punched down his throat.

Mark howled in agony and started to crumple back as if he could flee from the pain smashing apart his senses. Before he could snatch my keys away, I yanked them out of his hands and kicked him in the knee. Another cry broke from the big, scary wolf. "Fuck the magic—it's me you should be afraid of. I know what you are, and you can't stop me from telling Cal."

Leaping into my car, I tried to shove my keys into the ignition before I even landed in my seat. They scratched all along the steering column, failing to get me to freedom in my panicking state. I reached to slam the door closed, when Mark wrapped a hand around it.

"You have no goddamn idea what you're fucking with," he screamed. The stench of pepper coating his face stung my eyes, making tears drip from my ducts. I raised my foot, prepared to kick him in his balls, when the asshole let go.

I slammed that door closed so hard it made a crunch sound. *Worry about it later. Get out of here.*

Turning over the engine, I barely glanced into the rearview mirror before I rammed the car into reverse. Mark had enough sense to roll out of the way, his back striking a cart return. I pulled back into the parking lot, then kept rolling in reverse. All the while, I stared at the red eyes glaring death at me.

He meant it. If I didn't leave Cal alone, he'd come for me and I'd be another body in a dumpster.

Horns shattered the air, shocking me awake. I shook off the snarling face of the goth werewolf and shoved on the accelerator until he was nothing but a speck in the rearview mirror. It took about five miles until I had to pull over and vomit.

Chapter Seventeen

Thanksgiving morning dawned, and I willingly went to the werewolf's den armed with only a casserole dish of mac and cheese.

"This is stupid, this is so stupid," I muttered, shaking my fingers on Cal's stoop. After his brother's friendly visit the day before, I had to talk to him. "Why didn't I just send him an email? 'Hey, your brother's a psychopath who attacked me in the parking lot, so I pepper sprayed him.'" Yeah, that'd go over well.

There was that other issue too. The reason why Mark had left bruises on my forearm and tried to scare me away from Cal. He was working with the cult and wanted to stop me before I revealed the truth. It all made sense.

Except for the part where girls were being randomly killed and their bodies dumped in the trash. And why a man who'd been out of the cult for nearly a decade wanted back in. Or the whole 'we're also werewolves' part.

But the rest was airtight.

This was why I wanted to be a nurse and not a cop.

Music blasted from behind, and I turned over my shoulder. A family rolled out of their SUV, the radio still cranking through the open doors. The kids dashed for the door of a relative, while the adults stood frozen watching me, the strange brown woman who'd been standing here for ten minutes.

Damn it.

I raised my fist and knocked on the door. When the chain rattled, I wrapped my hands around the dish and hoisted it up. It could be both an excuse and a shield should Mark lunge for me.

The door whooshed open and Cal stood there. He swept his ice-blue gaze down me and his dark blond eyebrows bunched. "Who are you?" he asked in an odd whisper-crackle voice.

"What?" I sputtered, leaning closer, which sent him skittering back. The nose was too lean, his cheekbones a hair too low and the blond mane was longer than I'd ever seen it. "Who are *you*?" I repeated, staring agog at the stranger with nearly Calvin's face.

"I've got the turkey prepped. Who's at the…?" The moment Cal swept in beside the stranger, their variations became apparent. I kept glancing from one blond man to the other like I was trying to solve a spot-the-difference picture puzzle.

Instead of having the clear eyes of the man at the door, Cal's were red-rimmed. The white-blond locks stuck to his forehead, giving him not-unflattering bangs. At the sight of me, he tried to comb them skyward. "Layla?" he asked in a croaky voice.

Bouncing from one man to the other, I shoved my dish forward. "I heard you were sick and wanted to bring you this."

Cal snickered, sweeping his long eyelashes down. Gathering the dish into his hands, he said, "That's sweet."

"It's mac and cheese," I said, my legs shaking. He had been ill, or under the weather enough he worried about getting sicker. And here I was, barging in fearing the worst. "It's not Thanksgiving without the good stuff."

"Oh?" He lifted the lid an inch and took a deep whiff. "Come in, come in." Cal reached over and cupped my elbow. I damn near floated into his house while the stranger dashed so far from me he trampled over the shoe pile beside the stairs. "Layla, this is Eli."

Eli lifted his chin an inch, gazing over my shoulder. A cute blush burned over his cheeks and he gave out a single, quick, "Hi."

"He's my brother," Cal continued.

"Don't you mean twin?" I said. Both men stared at each other, frowns rising.

Shaking his head, Cal responded, "Not really. We look a little alike, but…"

"I'm the cute one," Eli said. From anyone else, I'd write that off as bravado, but Eli spoke in such a plain voice it came across as fact. He wasn't trying to impress anyone, only repeating what he'd been told.

"What's Cal then?" I asked, turning my head to the man shrinking at all the attention.

A whisper of a smile rose on Eli's thinner lips. "The nice one."

"I agree, one hundred percent."

"We shouldn't…we don't need to…" Poor Cal's blush climbed so high his hair turned red. He kept brushing his shoulder over the bottom of his cheek and staring anywhere but at the two of us.

"And Mark's the strong one," Eli chirped out.

The light, joking air imploded. My hackles shot up and I glared at the ground while sweeping through the living room to find a hint of the worst brother. All I could hear was an announcer on TV talking about the parade balloons, but that didn't mean Mark wasn't here and about to attack.

"I should go," I said. *What? You came here to tell Cal what happened.* Even with my declaration, and my body leaning back, my feet froze in place.

"It's Thanksgiving," Cal said, as if I had no idea. "You should stay. I got a two-for-one deal on a turkey and a ham. No way we can eat all that." He turned to Eli who shrugged and picked at his nails.

A real Thanksgiving dinner? I hadn't had one of those in years. "But this is, you know. I wouldn't want to interfere with family time."

"Do you mind her staying, Eli?"

We both turned to the quiet man who wilted at the attention. Only the whites of his eyes were visible, his gaze darting between us, and he flared his nostrils. Was he sniffing me? Eli's eyes closed. "No. I don't mind witches."

"There," Cal said. He slipped the casserole dish into the crook of his arm and wrapped the other around my waist. "It's a very witchy-wolf Thanksgiving."

"But I get the hambones," Eli called, like it was the most important request in the world. Made sense for a werewolf, in a twisted kind of way to have plans for gnawing on the bones later. He brushed a shock of hair behind his ear. "I make stock with them."

Or that.

Cal guided me deeper into the house. While I wanted to savor the comforting touch of his hand caressing the small of my back, my hackles were in no mood to rest. "What about...your other brother? Will he be joining us?" *Smooth, Layla.*

It was obvious I caught Cal off guard, his head whipping to the side in surprise. He opened his mouth, but it was Eli who said, "Mark doesn't do Thanksgiving."

"Or gatherings in general."

But he certainly did family, enough to risk war with a witch for his brothers.

"I better get this somewhere warm before it clumps up," Cal said, raising the dish higher. "And put the turkey in."

"You cook?" I sputtered.

A wolfish grin rose across his lips, the energy of it lighting my libido on fire. "You have no idea," Cal whispered, his voice crackling into a growl.

With our heads nearly pressed together, he pushed on the swinging door to the kitchen. I made it one step inside only for my elbow to clang on a pot. The blur of movement sent me twisting just as a pile of pans tumbled for the floor. I managed to hook a wok's handle on my fingers and catch the tumbling stack of frying pans in the other palm. The rest were lost to the floor, but Cal barely glanced at them as he walked to a double oven painted harvest gold.

Dumbstruck, I stared at the graveyard of swap meets past. Plates of every imaginable pattern and size were stacked on the counter next to a breadbox stuffed to the gills with boxes of candy and protein bars. What counter space wasn't taken up with old-fashioned cookware held food in various stages.

A mass of green beans cut in half lay on a cutting board that jutted over the stove. The burner beside must have been on as something white bubbled up higher over the sides. Cal opened the top oven and added my macaroni to it. I spotted a few other glass dishes resting inside, but couldn't take any guesses before he closed the door.

"Don't tell me you were expecting a galley kitchen in this ancient house." Cal tugged a flour sack towel off a mass of them hanging from a cabinet handle under the sink.

There was barely any room for two people without the stacks of food and messy pots pressing in. I found myself sidling into a corner where a broom and mop waited beside a giant sack of potatoes. "A pot rack might be nice," I said, staring up at the ceiling where a rickety chandelier hung instead. The light barely reached an inch out of the clouded sconces. Most of the visibility was courtesy of the windows beside his back door.

Cal tipped his head up and he laughed. It drew me to his Adam's apple, that knot that gave life to his deep voice which could make me quiver. With each dip, I wanted to drag my tongue across it and nip his earlobe.

"One of those two-foot-deep ceramic sinks?" he said, his tone as pure as snow. Like we were back to the first days of class, just friends.

I tried to shake away the pang bouncing through me. "Maybe a cute herb garden around the window, and some adorable knickknacks filling a butcher-block island."

He snickered and finished knotting the towel around his waist. Aprons could be sexy on the right man and without any disgusting or infuriating puns. But just a towel, thin enough for the shape below to be seen, waving and wrapping around him as he walked, demanded I keep staring at his lower half like a civilized lady who just stumbled upon a wild man in the forest with only a loincloth between them.

Walking across the kitchen as though he didn't see me drooling over him, Cal turned his back, and bent deep at the waist, thrusting his ass out to aid him reaching into the oven. *Don't stare.*

Why not? We did fuck right out in his living room.

But we weren't a thing. *We're friends*, I thought. *Hoped.* Anything more seemed...

It's funny, I always thought Cal was that impossible crush. When a guy's too everything – too hot, too nice, too smart and too perfect. So drooling over him was easy, but dating him would never happen.

Now that sounded trite compared to the real problems between us. *'You might judge me because I dropped out of high school when I was sixteen'* seemed a lot less important compared to *'You're a werewolf and I think your brother wants to kill me.'*

"So," Cal said, rising from the oven. He slipped on an oven mitt shaped like a dog's paw and picked a lid off a pot. Slowly stirring its contents, he stared at me and the light-hearted atmosphere imploded. "You gonna tell me why you're really here?"

"I heard you were sick and...wanted to know if it was true," I admitted.

"Ah. The mac and cheese was a cover."

"A delicious one. There's smoked cheddar in there." In wanting to defend my food, I walked closer to try to jab in its direction. But the kitchen was so small, I could only slip into Cal's personal bubble, the dangerous zone where the vibrancy of his eyes pinned a person to the ground.

Those damn things were like a truth serum. "I was worried. You weren't answering my calls and…"

"Did you think I'd skipped town?" The scraping of the spoon against the bottom of the pan set my teeth on edge.

"Or you were in danger and needed…help." God that sounded stupid. The second I said it aloud, I flinched. He was a werewolf, could probably rip the bad people into pieces. I…had nearly been killed by a werewolf twice now. All I'd do was get in the way.

The hard line in Cal's lips softened. They parted to let a slow breath escape and he paused his stirring. "I'm glad you came to help," he whispered and leaned at the waist. I curled my toes, my eyes drawn to his lips beckoning me to them. Suddenly, Cal froze and he stood higher. "Because I don't think I can prep the potatoes and baste at the same time."

He didn't want me. Or he knew it was too much work. *Demon. Witch. Wolf. Don't be sad, Layla. Do you really want to try that hard to be with someone?*

I buried the answer so deep I couldn't hear it. With a forced laugh, I said, "You think I can cook?" Cal glanced to the oven where he put my mac and cheese and I snorted. "That one don't count."

"Well, you can either peel these potatoes, or watch me do it." He tossed a spud the size of a baseball into the air and caught it. I watched its rise and fall, mesmerized, until he held it out to me.

With a resigned sigh, I accepted the potato and turned for the sink. I reached for the peeler, an old all-metal one, and began to slice off the skin. Warmth blossomed against my neck, then arms swept around my waist. Transfixed, I stared at the hands cresting against the backs of mine. The veins prodding from the back, so blue below his pale skin. His nails chewed to the nubs with cooking grit under them.

Cal slipped his fingers to match with mine and he raised the peeler off the potato. I winced to find a massive gouge in its white flesh. But he didn't say anything, only twisted the spud around and put the sharp edge of the peeler to work.

"What...are you doing?" I asked, my senses flooded with the touch of his chest gliding over my back and his hips pressing against my ass.

A slow laugh puffed against the side of my neck. I strained my head higher, aching for him to put his teeth to the tender skin. But Cal focused only on the potato, leaving me hanging in limbo. "Helping," he said. The half-naked potato spun in his fingers, and he resumed the strokes. Gentle, certain, never wavering, each brush of his hand peeled another section off.

I was so enthralled that when he finished and placed the peeled potato onto the cutting board, I jerked my head to the side. It felt like someone ripped away my toy. But when he picked up another and was about to put the knife to it, he paused and placed the spud in my hand.

The same careful strokes sliced over the potato I held. Even with the sharp edge gliding close to my fingers, I trusted him. His free hand slipped over my belly, holding me tighter to him.

"Cal?" I whispered, my voice husky.

"Hm?" he answered, brushing his lips against my throat and up my jaw. A shudder danced through me, but I clung tight to the spud.

"How many potatoes do we need?"

He laughed and pointed to a bucketful beside the sink. There had to be at least ten in there. I bit my lip. "Maybe we should get more. Just in case."

Dragging his nose against the nape of my neck, Cal whispered, "Sounds…smart."

Chapter Eighteen

Two hours in a tiny kitchen with twin ovens blazing caused me to melt into my boots. The cool clouds just beyond the back door taunted me with freedom. Then Cal would smile and next thing I knew, another fifteen minutes passed with my internal organs baking more than the biscuits. After sliding the gravy to a lower burner, Cal pulled off his ironic oven mitt and swiped his forehead.

"I don't know about you, but I need a break," he confessed.

"Don't know? Look at me?" I said, gesturing to the sweat running down my face.

He swept his palm over the small of my back, his chest almost pressing the side of me. The fire tripled in my veins as Cal leaned closer to whisper, "You're dewy." After tugging the towel off his waist, he brushed it across my forehead. "Like a rose garden after a rainstorm."

While I snickered at him, Calvin hooked onto his sweater and hefted it off. I had to pinch myself to keep from groaning. He wore a shirt underneath, though it was a lot tighter than the pile of wool had been.

But when Cal released a sigh of ecstasy courtesy of the cool breeze, my toes curled and I tugged on my collar for air. That drew him to glance at me and he held out his hand. "We don't stand on much propriety here at Chateau, um, Wolfington?"

Even as I laughed at his joke, I stared down at the flannel shirt I'd slipped on. I only had a thin camisole on underneath. Hardly Thanksgiving-appropriate wear. But the unquenchable hunger in his gaze sent my fingers flying to the buttons. I shrugged the shirt off and he took it without pause, though he let his eyes wander across the lacy embellishments hugging my cleavage.

"I'll go put these somewhere safe," he said while shoving open the kitchen doors. Walking beside him down the narrow hallway I caught sight of the dining room. Whenever we studied at Cal's, most of the banquet table was covered in random junk and laundry. But someone had taken the time to completely clear it, added a tablecloth and set out plates, silverware and glasses.

Here I'd planned to spend the holiday sitting on my couch chewing on the turkey special from a pizza and sandwich place. Were there lit candles? I craned my head back, trying to determine if they'd put down a cornucopia centerpiece.

"Hey," Eli called far closer than I expected. In this old house, only a handful of electric bulbs burned below ancient sconces. It was more shadow than light, which didn't seem to bother the wolves one bit.

Stepping from the living room, Eli hoisted a phone from his ear to Cal. "Mama Cat wants to talk to you."

"I'm a little busy with dinner and…" Calvin said. He extended his arms full of our clothing back to me and I gave a little wave.

Eli's gaze dropped to the ground and in a soft whisper, he added, "She said it's important."

"Oh, all right. This should only take a few minutes," Cal explained to me and took the phone. His face lit up and he all but shouted, "Mom! Happy Thanksgiving to you, too." The conversation faded as Cal eased around the rickety staircase and began to climb.

I watched him vanish until a prickling sensation rose in my gut. Whipping my head, I swore I caught Eli turning to stare at his shoes.

"Do you…um." Scratching at my ear, I strained to find any small talk that didn't involve werewolves or magic. "Do you live around here?"

"No." He shook his head fast and clammed up. Apparently there would be no follow through for that.

"What do you do for a living? I'm studying to be a nurse," I added, hoping my sharing would give Eli the opening he needed.

Darting only a sliver of his gaze to me, Eli rubbed the toe of his shoe against a knot in the floor. It creaked with every press. "I know. Cal told me."

This was going fantastic. Might as well put me on the phone with his mother next.

"I'm a tech service rep for a…an insurance company."

"That sounds…" I began, my will to live draining. I had no idea what any of that meant and was about to pretend it had to be exciting.

To my relief, Eli chuckled almost the same as his brother. "It's not that boring, but pretty close. Lots of spreadsheets and databases. Funny the things people leave in databases."

I nodded along while fully lost. But at least he was talking to me. Another round of dreaded silence landed on us, and I jabbed a finger up to the second floor. "Shame that your mom can't be here."

Eli's body went rigid. He clasped his hands together and tented the fingers until the knuckles turned white. The soft, tenuous voice hardened to a sledgehammer strike. "My mother's dead."

The cautious eyes sharpened and he glared down at me. I knew what he was waiting for. The 'I'm sorry,' or the 'That must be hard.' I met his gaze and said, "So's mine. Since I was a kid."

His head jerked. Was he agreeing with me? Had he lost her in childhood too? I reached out to pat Eli's shoulder. The tossing of his head paused, but he didn't look up from his shoes.

With a resigned sigh, I said, "Holidays are the fucking worst."

A laugh rumbled in his throat and he admitted, "They are. But Mama Cat…Catherine, a joke we'd all… Never mind. She'd make them better. Try to."

"Is that—?" I craned my head back as if I could see Cal through the floor. Calvin's mother, the only one to escape the cult and save the three boys.

Eli followed suit, his head pressing closer to mine. "She doesn't leave New Mexico. Would never come here."

That struck deep and I turned to Eli. "Did you all move away when you escaped the…when you left?"

He pressed his tongue to his top lip like he was trying to keep a secret stuffed inside, but Eli nodded.

"Then why are you all—"

The front door blew open, cloudy light silhouetting the black wolf of the family. "Fine, I came and…" Mark stopped and screamed, "What the shit is she doing here?"

Fuck! And I'd left my purse in the car.

Advancing so hard the chain on his coat jangled, Mark stomped down the hall without closing the front door. He reached a hand out, no doubt to try to claw me again, when the worst thing that could happen did.

Eli got in the way. "She's a friend of—" the sweet, innocent brother said to the dangerous psychopath.

That set Mark off. His eyes widened and he shoved poor Eli to the side.

"What are you…?" I started, reaching to try to catch Eli.

"Get the fuck away from him!" Mark screamed at me. His grip launched not for my helping hand, but my throat.

I reached to slap the fingers away, when another hand beat me to it. Mark's entire arm bent out of the way, and the mysterious hand kept going. It wasn't until it cuffed the werewolf's jacket and hauled him off his feet that I knew who it belonged to.

"If you could move, my bond," Ink said so politely it jarred me into obeying. The moment I shifted to the other side of the hall, the incubus advanced and slammed Mark to the wall with one hand. The werewolf's feet dangled a foot from the floor. Ink reached out and adjusted Mark's coat, swiping away a smudge on the lapel.

"That was bothering me immensely," he said without a care.

"Who the fuck are you?" Mark screamed, his feet waggling in the air.

"Come now, use your little canine brain."

After taking a deep whiff, Mark's eyes widened and he stuttered, "A demon? What—"

"What in the hell are you doing here?" I shouted over Mark. The werewolf against the wall stared at me, but all my focus was on Ink.

He didn't shift his grip on Mark, but Ink glanced over his shoulder to focus only on me. "You are at the mercy of three werewolves. And after my last rescue, I did not think you'd wish me to wait until a hospital was required."

Damn it. Guilt bubbled inside me. I could never really repay him for what he'd done. He didn't have to save me. It probably would have freed him of this magic bond. But he had.

"Ink…" I began, softly caressing his back.

"Fuck off!" Mark hollered and he crammed both sets of claws into Ink's exposed forearm. The demon didn't even blink.

"There is no use struggling, mutt. You are of mortal make and I am…your better."

The fight slammed to a stalemate. Mark wouldn't release his grip, and—despite Ink's assurances—a dark liquid began to weep from the white claws punctured into his skin. The incubus tightened his hold, shoving Mark farther into the wall until I heard a crack in the plaster.

"What's going on down here?" Cal shouted, his steps thudding into the stairs. He hooked on to the banister and turned a sharp corner, just in time to watch Mark swipe a hand at Ink.

The demon didn't move fast enough. Four slash marks tore open his flesh and the same burgundy red liquid dripped across his face. Ink sneered, tugged Mark forward, then slammed his body into the wall. A crack spidered out from where Mark's head hit, but he growled back.

Anger surged through me, my hand raising to send a shock through Mark for what he'd done to Ink. He'd disfigured him without a second... *Wait.* The paper skin the claws had ripped clean open began to mold together. In a matter of seconds, the only sign Ink had even been injured was the lingering liquid crackling on his fresh skin.

"You're going to have to try much harder, dog," Ink said.

"Wait!" Cal dashed to us. He pressed the shrinking Eli farther away and locked his hands around both Ink's and Mark's arms. "What the hell is going on?"

"Your littermate attempted to injure Layla. I stopped it," Ink said, drawing every eye to me.

A fury raced across Cal's features, but I couldn't tell who it was aimed at. He alternated his vengeful glare from me to Mark, then the demon suspending his brother in the air. Not about to be thrown under the bus, Mark called out, "She pepper sprayed me."

I didn't even blink at the horde of men twisting their accusatory stare at me. Stomping closer, I raised up my wrist to reveal the welts Mark left behind. "Because you grabbed me in the parking lot." The pinned werewolf only gave a slow eye roll at the markings he had caused. It was Cal who caught my hand and turned my arm up to reveal the dark green bruises to the light.

Snarling, Cal slammed his hand up through Ink's hold, shattering the demon's grip. But he mangled Mark's jacket and hauled his brother to his face. "Did you hurt her?!" When Mark didn't answer, Cal shook him, bouncing his brother's head against the wall. "Did you hurt her?"

"What do you care? She's a fucking witch." Mark narrowed his eyes and turned them on me. The venom in his words should have shifted their color green.

"Layla is my…" Cal started, when he looked over his shoulder at me. I didn't realize I'd huddled next to Ink, who'd wrapped a protective hand around my waist. A part of me wanted to shift away, but not the part that feared having my face ripped open.

With a low growl crackling the words, Cal said, "She is not to be harmed. Under any circumstance."

"For fuck's sake, Claw. Get your nose out of her pussy for two seconds and think," Mark shrieked. Even after I'd coated his face in pepper, even with a demon about to snap his windpipe, this was what made him plead. When he sounded about to snap out of fear. "Witches can't be trusted. You know that. What they do to us."

Cal snarled, but the back of his neck burned red and he clenched his fist tighter. "You believe those urban legends? We're not kids."

"No." Mark raised his head and glared dead on at his brother. "We're not. You used to want me to help you and now… Now it's all about the bitch instead."

With a sigh, Cal opened his fist and stepped back. Mark tried to mash the lapels of his coat into place, but he kept his hand far from where Ink had held him. Even with the black tee partially obscuring it, I spotted a white mark rising on his skin. Had Ink nearly killed him to protect me?

"I don't need your help, Mar. I don't need your protection. I'm fine!" As Calvin spoke, his words grated into a growling snarl of a Doberman guarding his domain. Goosebumps erupted down my legs and I clung tighter to Ink.

Mark shook his head at the idea and raised his hands to the heavens. "So that's it, then. You're just gonna roll over for a witch's cunt?"

Cal's pupils widened until the entire iris turned black. He wiped a hand over his face to hide them away. "What I'm going to do is eat some fucking turkey. What about you?"

A slow laugh spurted from Mark. He stared at his brothers, Eli sliding closer to join the pack. Then, the glare turned on me and his lip curled into a snarl. "You think I'm gonna sit down to dinner with a witch and her demon?"

"It's Thanksgiving. That's what you do," Calvin grumbled, his voice weary and his body weaving. He massaged his temples and glared at the only bit of the house without people crowding it.

Mark snorted once and shook his head. "Well, I don't." Eyeing up Cal once more, who offered no resistance, Mark stomped for the open door. At the edge, he paused. "One day, she'll use you. Drain your blood, grind up your bones, rip out your teeth — all to feed her spells." He didn't even look at his exhausted brother, but stared right at me as he repeated, "Witches can't be trusted."

The slam of the door rattled through the house, increasing the crack in the wall until plaster dust tumbled free. Ink gave a little swipe of his shoulder and resumed standing nonchalantly. I focused on my demon because I had no idea what to say. Apologize for protecting myself from a man that attacked me? Insist that I didn't even know any spells that required werewolf teeth? Tell him that his brother was working with the cult Calvin feared?

'Witches can't be trusted.' Cal didn't even question that. How many of those urban legends did he believe?

This wasn't the time. I should let everyone cool down. Give it a few days. Then find somewhere public to tell him. At least before Mark tried to silence me for good.

"I should get..." I said.

"Eli, can you set another plate?" Calvin interrupted, turning to look at his brother.

With a quick jerk of his chin to his chest, Eli dashed past Cal. He gave a wide berth to both me and Ink before vanishing into the kitchen. I stared at the swinging doors, fully lost. Did he think Mark was coming back?

"I assume you eat," Cal said to Ink.

He blinked a moment before giving a soft bow of his head.

"Then I hope you like turkey, stuffing, mashed potatoes and yams." He wore a smile, but the wear showed. Cal looked about to collapse from an emotional fight I wasn't so certain that he'd won. Concerned, I brushed his side. For a beat, I feared he'd push me away, but Cal drew his palm over my back and his arm found its place across my shoulders.

"We should go and check on the oven stuff," I said. "Ink, why don't you take a seat and wait?"

"The story of my unending existence," the incubus responded, adding a solemn bow for emphasis.

Eli dashed past, a plate in his hand and silverware crammed into a plastic cup. "'Scuse me," he said and turned to Ink. "Do you like your fork on the left or the right?"

The pair drifted into the dining room, Ink saying, "I don't much mind. Though I am surprised there are utensils at all. I imagined we'd be ripping the bird apart with our bare hands."

However Eli responded was cut off by the kitchen door swinging shut. Away from the others, I turned and whispered so quietly my lips almost touched Calvin's cheek, "You didn't have to do that."

He glanced to me, surprise etched across his face.

"Letting us stay for dinner. I'm sure you have... It was all so... I don't want to mess your life up."

His lips wound into a winsome smile, Cal drew the tips of his fingers around my cheekbone. When he brushed the nape of my neck, I parted my mouth in anticipation of a kiss. "It's... It's Thanksgiving. A mess is to be expected. Family...friends, sharing what they can together. Who could ask for anything more?" With that, his hand dropped and Cal—the friend—drifted to the stove and the pan of burning gravy.

"What about your brother?"

In a huffing snarl, he said, "Mark can shove a yam up his ass."

Chapter Nineteen

My phone said it was one-fifteen when I took a quick peek. Or what I thought was quick—I caught Cal watching me from across the table. A sea of licked-clean dishes stretched between us, all the traditional turkey fixings happily digesting in our stomachs. For a flicker, I wondered what would happen if he swiped the plates off and leapt across the table for me.

Fingers brushed over mine, yanking me from Cal, and Ink whispered in my ear, "You're driving me mad."

What?

He brushed the tip of his nose up my cheek and darted his fiery eyes to the man attempting to look anywhere else. "Suffering with unfulfilled desires is like dangling a scrap of meat in front of a dog. If you don't solve that, I'm liable to snap."

This was not the place for Ink to do what he always did. I shifted to the side, tugging my hand away, but the incubus kept smoldering in his chair. It was a wonder he didn't set off the smoke alarm.

Unaware that the sex demon was trying every trick in his book, Eli rose and began to gather the plates. The strike of a mug bouncing into a fork caused me to jump.

"Are you okay?" the quietest brother asked. He'd opened up a bit more during dinner — at least with Cal's guidance — but this was the first time he'd spoken directly to me without any prompting.

I jerked my head and smiled. "Yes. Just thinking that I should head home." To try to prove to myself that was what I wanted, I rose to my feet and stood awkwardly by the chair. "Got to get ready for my shift."

"When do you go in?" Cal asked. He slipped to his feet. The festive sweater was back on him. In fact, all the men were more dressed than me. Why didn't I ask for my shirt back?

"Uh, five. I get to work the entire sale overnight. Won't break free until daylight."

Cal paused beside me. He drummed his fingers against the back of the tucked-in chair and I nervously picked at the cover on my phone. "That's what I've got scheduled too," he said.

"Oh, we're on the same shift. That's lucky." A small dollop of giddiness surged through my over-dopamined system. Slogging through thousands of belligerent customers wanting to rip our heads off for a ten-dollar discount didn't seem so bad with Cal around. A darker thought struck. "What about your, um, wolf issue?"

And with that, it shattered. For a time, we could pretend that I wasn't a witch who'd pissed off his brother and maybe the whole pack and he wasn't a werewolf born in a cult. Ink remained his usual self with a plate of predominantly mashed potatoes and green beans slathered in honey. Not that I wanted to think about him much.

Scratching his forehead along the furrows, Cal said. "It's...I have it handled. You, um, you probably want your shirt to get home. It's cold out there. Why don't I...?"

"I can get it," I said, starting to move just as Calvin made a break for the stairs. I was in such a scrambled state, my hip bounced against him. His hand flew out, finding the only thing to steady himself was my waist.

Without any resistance, Cal pulled me to him. My palms flattened against his chest and I watched with rapture how his bottom lip puckered out in the middle.

"Ahem." Ink's cough ripped open the awkwardness. I stood in the arms of a man I thought was a friend. Maybe more? Would he even want to be more? Could I afford to be more with him? Why was this so fucking complicated?

I expected my incubus to tug me away, maybe call me his 'bond' a few times. But Ink rose to his feet and picked up the rest of the plates Eli couldn't. "If you will excuse me, these require the tender ministrations of skilled hands."

A groan rattled deep in my chest at Ink's neon innuendo, but he was genuine. He and Eli slipped out of the dining room and down the hallway with the broken wall. Midway down, Ink asked, "When you rut, is it always in human form?"

"Damnit, Ink..."

"My binding rules have not changed. It is mere curiosity," he called and the kitchen door swung shut, trapping Eli in the same room as an incubus.

Shaking my head, I sighed. "Your poor brother."

Cal snickered. "I think Eli can handle it." We started the walk up the stairs, Cal a half a step ahead of me and our hands brushing.

"Against…all of that? I can barely deal with Ink most days and your brother's so shy and innocent."

A low laugh rolled from Cal. We reached the landing and he pointed down the hall to his bedroom. "Innocent? Out of all three of us, Eli got the most tail."

"No? Really?"

Shrugging, Cal flipped on the light. I'd been in his bedroom before. Sharp-sloped ceilings made walking around it awkward unless you were four feet tall. The wrought-iron latticework on the windows increased the gothic manor feel. But the decor had a very 'bought the mid-priced bedroom set at Ikea' ambience.

There, on the bed with a plain black headboard, was my shirt. He'd even taken the time to fold it. My flannel was going to get spoiled, as it spent most of its life tossed into the passenger seat of my car.

"It started in junior high. The girls flocked to Eli. He always had a small gang of them following him around, cooing at him. I think he wound up taking like four different dates to prom because he didn't have the heart to turn anyone down."

"Eli? The man that wouldn't look up from his plate except to ask for the salt? Who said maybe five words in an hour?"

Cal shrugged. He paused beside his bed, but didn't pick up my shirt. I wasn't in a hurry to grab it either.

"It's just that, if I had to pick from the three of you who'd have a dozen girlfriends it'd be…"

"Mark?"

Obvious bad boy with serious authority issues who answered to no one. Leather fetish and he probably wore eyeliner in high school. It'd be catnip to any girl looking for a project.

"It's okay," Calvin said, talking before I could respond. "People always think that."

"I was going to say you, actually. I mean, you're..." *The class president and quarterback rolled into one. The hot debate team leader who was also the adorable dork in Home Ec making brownies.*

Cal wrinkled his nose and stared down at himself. "I'm what?"

"You're so..." *Bright. A beacon of light without being obnoxious about it. A source of calm and hope even on the worst of days.* "Clean."

"Clean?" He raised his arm and sniffed the sweater, his eyebrows knitted in confusion.

"Good. The first time we met, I thought—well, I thought you'd never want to have anything to do with me. I'm still not sure why you..." *What are we?* "Wanted to hang out."

"I'm far from 'clean.' In school they called me Claw because I'd..." The brightness dimmed in his eyes, Cal twisting to stare over my shoulder. "There wasn't anything like school in the cult. We didn't stand still for longer than a handful of minutes or we risked a beating. Being trapped at a desk, told to sit and be quiet...it took some adjusting."

"What happened?"

"I scratched a classmate, with my human fingernails, but it was enough to draw blood. A lot of blood. And Mar, he, uh, bit someone."

That didn't surprise me. "What, did a classmate get too close to his food?"

Cal winced. "It was the teacher, actually. We had to move after that. Mar never adjusted. I don't think he wanted to blend in the way Eli did. The way I tried to. All that shit in the past, it needs to stay there. But Mark…"

He focused on me and I felt the world fading away. "You don't need to hear all of this. It's…you wanted to leave. With your shirt." Cal turned to tug up my flannel and I reached for it the same time. His reflexes were far quicker than mine, and my sluggish body failed to adjust to the lack of anything to pick up. Weary, I sunk to my knees and planted my side on his bed.

"Layla?" He worried his palm over my bare arm.

I moaned, and dug my face deeper into the welcoming embrace of the mattress. "This is so…nice and safe." Rolling my arms, I tugged his bedspread into a lump to form a makeshift pillow. "I want to stay here forever."

Everything hit at once. Midterms, bleeding out on the floor, a demanding sex demon, glaring down an insurmountable hospital bill, being attacked before dinner. The strip of sinew I'd been plucking back and forth to keep going finally snapped. I didn't want to do anything but sleep.

"That can't be comfortable," Cal said.

"You'd be surprised," I muttered into his blanket.

"Your body's half on the floor. Here." When he swept his arms around my waist, I don't know what I expected. For him to help me to my car. For Cal to take me to a guest room or that couch we'd fucked on. The idea of him placing me in his bed and smoothing my hair over his pillows never occurred to me.

Instead of starfishing out, I curled up on my side. My eyelids transfigured into cement, but I didn't need to see. Taking a deep whiff cast a calm over me from Cal's scent. Pecans and the woods after it rained, an oven just before the bread is put in to bake and a warm amber that was somehow bright blue.

"Are you cold?" Cal asked. I tried to shake my head, but it was already burrowed into his pillows. This was the softest bed I'd ever lain on. Or my body was so exhausted I could have passed out on sharp rocks. It didn't matter either way. I was in heaven.

Sleep danced through me, tempting me to its dark embrace. The mattress buckling behind me shot the last bolt of energy. When heat licked against my ear and an arm glanced over my hip, I calmed.

"Come to join me?" I asked, rubbing Cal's hand and guiding it to cup my belly. His entire body pressed to mine, the two of us spooning together without a care in the world.

"You made it look tempting."

I was the one to scoot into him. To feel his chest expand with every breath against my back, to wrap myself in the warmth of his embrace. To tuck my ass right against his crotch. If it weren't for that, I'd have passed out in an instant.

Here was the port I so badly wanted against the storm of my life. A hot guy who could cook, owned his house, was smart enough to become a nurse and could lick his way out of any box. To take an afternoon nap with him beside me and not worry that he would sneak off with my phone or laptop. To know that when I woke, he'd be there.

It was a delightful dream I didn't want to abandon. And I'd have happily played the part for an hour or two in Cal's bed. Except, with every breath of his cresting against my cheek, I felt him stirring.

Did he get woozy whenever that happened? All that blood flow zipping away from his brain to plump his cock. At that size he'd need a lot.

A warm kiss caressed the nape of my neck and Cal's hand swept up my belly. Was he already out? I tried to not move for fear of waking him, but he brushed his wandering palm under my breasts. The slowly inflating cock suddenly sprang to attention and I couldn't bite down the moan that slipped free.

Cal groaned in response, and he started to grind his hips into me. Every thrust of his can-sized cock into my buttock sent me reeling. I hadn't had a chance to ride it before, and because of the mess I'd gotten into after, I didn't think I ever would.

Reaching behind, I swept my palm over Cal's ass. He paused his grinding and dropped the hand that'd been massaging over my shirt to the bed. "Don't stop," I whispered and pulled him tighter to me.

"Fuck, Layla," he groaned. With mad energy, he swept under my shirt and worried below the underwire trap on my bra. When the warmth of his palm circled my breast, I tossed my head back. It struck his chin, but Cal didn't stop. His gyrating hips increased tempo, Calvin's moans of pleasure shivering through my ear and down to my aching core.

I struggled to reach for him, to unbuckle his jeans, to again try to take all of him in my hand. But he was suckered to my body, twirling his free hand against my nipples. I sputtered at the soft touch, almost but not quite sharp enough to send me reeling. In order to encourage him, I tried thrusting my chest out, when he abandoned it entirely.

A pang of loss shuddered through me until Cal tugged on the button of my jeans and undid the zipper.

With only our panting and the light creaking of the bed for ambience, the pull of the zipper sounded like a crack of lightning. And his cock jerked in response.

Yank my pants off. Throw me onto my back. Fuck me so hard I can't walk to my car.

But he slipped his hand away from the V of exposed pink panties and massaged the pad into my hip instead. The bed shifted as he rose onto his elbow. He nuzzled his nose into the hollow behind my ear, then flicked his tongue against my lobe.

"Layla." He breathed my name as if there was nothing in this world but me, him and the buckling bed. Taking my chin, Cal slowly pivoted my head and the rest of my body until I rested on my back. All the wolfish hunger from our first time was gone. I could only see a tender need, his smile cautious and uncertain.

I held on to his arms and tugged him to me. The kiss rolled through me, as slow as a Sunday afternoon in the park, and twice as perfect. I lapped my tongue over his bottom lip, wanting to tug it between my teeth and bite down, when Cal pulled back.

What did he want? With the tips of his fingers, he pushed back a piece of hair off my forehead. Was he having second thoughts? Third regrets? "Well." I shrugged, struggling to bury the rising tide of anger in my voice. "Let's do this." Despite my statement, I didn't reach for his zipper or do anything but stare in concern. Was this when he'd finally realize he could do so much better?

Brushing his palm from my cheek down to my shoulder, Cal said, "Layla...this is going to sound stupid."

I'd been living a whole heaping pile of stupid since I'd found out I was a witch. Unless puppets or small animals were involved, he couldn't freak me out.

The hot werewolf leaned down and, in a whisper I almost couldn't hear, said, "I want to make love to you."

That was it?

He wrapped his fingers in mine and pressed our innocent handhold to the bed. Bending to me, Cal brushed his lips against mine. The touch was that of a single breeze glancing against my skin. A shiver trembled through me and I wanted more. But he leaned back and tugged off his shirt.

That body with muscles so defined he looked like water had chiseled him from a mountain over a millennium wasn't some fever dream. Watching him bundle up his sweater, the trail of biceps, pectorals, abs and lats all flexing in twitching intoxication sent me reeling. Why didn't I have my phone? I needed a video of that. Or a gif that I could watch on an endless loop.

But the werewolf built for hard fucking drew the tips of his fingers across the sliver of my exposed lower belly. The ring finger toyed with my panties, causing me to buck my hips for more. Cal kept trailing, circling back around a touch higher.

"Slow," he said and bent over to place a kiss right above my belly button. "Gentle." He pushed my shirt up, his next kiss on my sternum. "So you can *enjoy* all of me."

"Yes!" I shouted, then tamped down to whisper the same as he had. "Yes, please."

"You don't need to say please with me," he said and lifted my camisole off. While he tugged off my bra, Cal added, "I'm here to please you."

It sounded so much like Ink's desire kink that I frowned. I didn't want to think of the incubus who'd have already taken me from behind, then microwaved a bowl of ice cream on top of popcorn after. This was about Calvin and making love in his bed.

Hooking onto the belt loops of his jeans, I tugged on him so hard he fell forward. His hands splayed beside my head, his entire body helpless in my grip. Working his pants open, I nibbled along his jaw and risked a harder bite to his lobe. Instead of a yelp, a low grumble roared through his chest pinning me deeper into the mattress.

"I want to hear you come. To watch you explode inside me. To have you howl my name," I ordered in his ear. "I want to please you."

When he plunged his soft lips over mine, Cal surprised me. I curled my palm over his straining boxer briefs, and the gasp of delight from his mouth drew a grin of power to mine. He kissed my devious smile away, then trailed his mouth in perfunctory bites down my jaw while working off his jeans.

It was a mad tangle of denim, legs, hands and mouths. Hot, sucking mouths. Famished, dancing fingers. Knees and thighs kneading and caressing. I didn't even realize I was naked until Cal slipped in between my legs and rested his cock in my curlies.

Fuck, that wasn't some magic wand in his pants, but a magic tree. And I'd thought I could handle it?

He must have read my sudden concern. Brushing his knuckles across my cheek, he stared down at me. The dappled light straining through November clouds cast a golden halo in his hair. "Slow," Cal said, bending closer. He placed a kiss to my collar.

"Gentle," he whispered and sucked on my nipple.

I arched my back to him, a whimper chaining down my throat. Trailing his lips across my breasts, Cal spoke against my skin. "Until you beg for me."

We traversed our hands everywhere with no destination in mind. He licked around my ear, nibbled my belly, sucked his way down my arm. I answered him in kind, pressing my teeth tighter to his muscle and sinew until every little gasp from him sent me reeling. Cal tasted me from neck to navel while his rock-hard cock crested against my skin. I reveled in it bouncing down my leg, dipping into my stomach, and always skirting right outside of entering me.

Time ceased to be, the rest of the world evaporating. All I knew was the man above me, kissing and caressing my body. Cal descended closer until he propped himself up on only his elbows. I laughed in glee at how he kept swiping his chest against my hard nipples.

Then he ground his pelvis into me.

The sweet teasing and light tonguing snapped to a puncture of need. It struck through me, demanded I wrap my leg around Cal's thigh and grind back on him. "Oh fuck, Layla," he cried in between kisses.

It wasn't enough. My body buzzed on the edge of the abyss, every cell inside screaming for the last ingredient to pitch us over.

"Cal?" A confounding chill swept through me, as if my body had become so aroused it feared either orgasm or death. He paused in nuzzling my neck and beamed those soft-blue eyes at me. Tracing my fingers from his cheek to his mouth, I tugged on his besotted lip, and said, "I need your cock. Nothing else will do."

His smile would warm my soul for a hundred years. Leaning over, he gave a quick kiss to the tip of my nose and sat up. I was about to follow suit when he pressed me back down to the mattress. He tossed me a square package that was surprisingly navy blue and not brag-worthy black. I didn't need any instructions, already tugging apart the plastic and easing the condom on while he kept leaning over on his treasure hunt.

Cal finished rustling through a box by his bed and returned with a clear bottle. Drenching his fingers in lube, he slicked up his sheathed cock, rolling his wrist to try to reach every far-flung inch. The sound of the bottle's cap snapping shut caused me to jump in anticipation.

But he drew his fingers down my inner thigh. Traced the curvy muscle that made finding jeans a nightmare. *God, yes. Shove them aside. Enter me. Let me pound away on you!*

"Layla," Cal whispered. Hooking his fingers under my knees, he raised my legs to curl around his waist. With one hand locking his cock into position, Cal walked closer. "I need you—"

"Please! Please, Jesus, god!" I shouted over the top of him, and Cal thrust forward. All those hours of teasing sent him slipping in without pause. I became aware of his cock resting inside me, waiting. Risking it, I clenched down and my vagina rebounded fast against the steel filling it to the brink.

A snort of urgency shot from Cal. With his eyes closed, he tugged his hips back and thrust in. Oh holy fuck, I was not ready!

It felt like the whole of a mountain was ripped out, then shoved back inside. But even under the shocking flush of pressure, my need demanded more. It wanted to feel the world move again.

Cupping his chin, I caused Cal's eyes to open. He watched in surprise as I pulled his lips down to mine. "Slow," I whispered against them and ground down onto him. His groan echoed inside my mouth, so I did it again. "Gentle." Scraping my nails over his back, I rounded over his ass and dug in to drive him even deeper.

Sweet fucking hell!

"Until you beg for me!" I screamed to the heavens. My orgasm clenched around him, hugging his cock in an eternal embrace. It reveled in the unending weight pressing and plying every tingling nerve until the whole of my buried clit erupted. G-spot, internal, clit orgasm. They all happened at once, causing me to cry incoherently and tumble to the bed in a fit worthy of possession.

"Lay...la." He panted my name while trailing his fingers across my lips and down my body. Cal caught one arm, then the other. I expected him to hoist them above my head and pin me down, but he wrapped our fingers together. Holding hands, he started to thrust.

Gentle, slow swerves of his hips. Tender, careful jerks of his pelvis. I couldn't stop shivering below him, my body lost to a cycle of orgasm and release. Only the sound of our bodies blending together, our breaths straining in our chests and the squeak of the bed filled the room. I lost all sense of existence, only knowing the throb of his cock pulsing through me.

"Please," Cal whispered, what could have been days later. His skin flushed red and he shook his head. "Please be mi—?" In an instant, his mouth parted and all the tension running the length of his body unwound. His eyelids fluttered and a smile of pure serenity crested his lips before he collapsed on top of me.

Burying my nose in his hair, I breathed in the scent of him. Deep and rich, like an aged whiskey sipped by the fire in a log cabin. His face rose with my breaths, Cal's cheek pressing on my breast while he came back. It took a few seconds before he blinked away the orgasmic haze and turned to look up at me.

A crash of thunder shook outside the house. But I didn't shiver from the oncoming storm. I wrapped around the warmth of the werewolf as we tucked under his blanket — our hands intertwined forever.

Chapter Twenty

Forget the clock. Forget the whole world howling outside the door. Stop time and stay in this moment forever.

"Mmm, don't leave," Calvin groaned, his voice sticky with sleep. He tried to tighten the hands he'd had wrapped around me, but I slipped them to reach for my jeans.

"It's only two," I said, a sigh of relief rattling in my nose. I dropped my phone back into my pants and let them plummet to the ground. But I didn't slide back into bed either.

As if accepting that the warm body he'd curled around to nap with wasn't returning, Cal rose to sit. *Damn.* Would I ever get used to that body? He swiped his thumb into his eye to dig out sleep and the juxtaposition of a body built for sex with the sweet cutie waking up sent me reeling.

"What were you expecting?" he asked. His hands thudded to the bed as if he had no idea what to do with them.

"After all of that, I feared it might be March," I said, bunching my snarled hair in my palm. Cal smiled with pride, looking more the lion than wolf.

We'd vanished for over an hour. What were the chances of Ink and Eli not noticing? One had the senses of a wolf and the other was a sex demon. Negative a billion. Still, I tiptoed closer to the bed and rested my hip on the edge.

I needed to go, for so many reasons. But I couldn't escape the electric pull tugging me back into Cal's arms. He leaned forward to catch my hand in his, the same way he did during sex. Fluttering the tips of his fingers over my palm, Cal set off another fire inside. But this one began in my heart.

"Can I ask you something?"

He glanced down and smiled. "I have absolutely nothing to hide, my shame or otherwise."

"As if you could feel anything approaching shame for..." I looked to his crotch and that source of un-shame jerked awake. A blush burned over my cheeks and I bit down on my lip to keep from reaching to caress it. "The whole slow and gentle thing. Don't get me wrong, it was...holy shit."

"Holy shit just thinking about it makes me want to take another ride? Or holy shit why don't I have a smoke bomb to throw as a distraction? Can I leap out of the window instead?"

I scooted further over the bed and rested on his chest. "You know which one," I said.

Cal shrugged as if he didn't and I slapped him lightly on his pec. "Then again, I suppose witches can probably conjure smoke from their fingers, so..."

My laugh rolled with his, our foreheads pressing closer. I paused from kissing him and asked, "It's just compared to our first time in the living room...?"

"Ah." His self-deprecation stopped and a shroud cut off his emotions.

"It was like night and day."

"Exactly," he said, causing me to spin off his lap to stare at him. Pulling in a deep sigh, Cal stared up at the ceiling. "Werewolves are...bound to the moon in a way humans aren't. We cycle with it."

"Meaning?"

He raised my hand and placed my knuckles to his lips. "When the moon is waxing, I want to nest in a warm bed and make gentle love."

"And if it's full?" Like it had been on the fifteenth.

Cal tugged on me so fast, I yelped in surprise. He held me tight in his arms, pressing his forehead to mine, his eyes filling my sight. "I chase whatever I want and fuck wherever's convenient." A low growl rippled his lips, sending shockwaves down my strained core.

"So if it hadn't been a full moon when I broke into your house...?" I began and Cal winced as if he'd done something wrong. "Well, I'm glad I didn't wait a day."

He smiled, but the worry wouldn't vanish from his eyes. "It's not always so strong. Some months I barely even notice. Most don't sense my change in personality. But lately..."

Picking up his arms, I wrapped myself in his embrace. Cal buried his chin on the top of my head and softly swayed. "Is that why you chain yourself up? Why you're avoiding going out at night?" I asked.

"You're too smart to be this hot. It's not fair."

I saved the compliment for later, but ignored his dodge. There were chains in his basement and I needed to know why before this…whatever this was could go any further.

Wincing, Cal tipped his head down so I couldn't see his face. "Yes. We can control the change, for the most part. Though it's easiest at night when in full moonlight."

The worry radiating off him shifted to shame. "What happened?"

"Nothing. But it could have. I'd been changing late at night, usually taking a quick run to the woods and back. I only need a few hours in wolf form, then I'm good for a day or two. Some of the kids in the neighborhood took notice of the big dog dashing over fences."

A light smile rose and Cal leaned back against his flimsy headboard, taking me with. "They'd leave little treats with notes. Sometimes toys I'd try to hide for them to find later. Toward the end they'd even sneak out to pet me."

He paused in running his fingers over my arm and stared at his hands in shock. "I always had control. It was me, my mind in the animal. Not the other way around."

"Cal…?"

"One of the kids, I don't know how old, little. Kindergarten or something. You know how they are."

Not a clue. I'd tried to avoid kids all of my life so far.

"He tugged too hard on my fur. It happens. I'd done worse to myself trying to slip through automatic doors. But something in me snapped and I…I almost bit him. He cried and I ran, but I couldn't let it happen again. So I've spent my hour or two in the basement on lockdown."

"With a bone?"

His eyebrows folded in confusion. "Oh, the turkey leg. Put off dinner too long from studying. That doesn't usually happen, though I do sometimes leave a ball down there. Or my laptop with YouTube running. Claws are hell on trackpads."

"So you're...becoming more, um...?"

"Feral?" he asked, causing me to flinch. "I don't know. I don't know *why*. It never happened back in New Mexico."

There was another question that kept rattling around in my mind. "Why did you come here? Back to where you were trapped in a cult? Don't get me wrong, I'm glad you did because I doubt I'd have ever visited New Mexico."

"Shame, the adobe pueblos are beautiful." He buried a kiss in my hair, then whispered into the pile of black curls, "I wanted to be a nurse. I needed a school."

"And there weren't any close to the pueblos?"

His voice softened to the point I could barely hear him say, "It's a good school." It sounded like an assurance he'd repeated to himself every day for years. It was a good school, but not worth reopening old traumas for.

Plus, it couldn't be that good. They accepted me.

Warmth ensnared me as Cal wrapped his arms tighter around my body. He drifted his lips to my shoulder, the dew of his breath beading on my skin. "Please, please don't..." A shudder rocked through his frame and down mine. "I wish we could stay in this bed for days."

"Someone has to check out a thousand Karens armed with expired coupons tonight," I said, but my heart jabbed a finger at his idea. *Call in sick. Or quit. Find some other minimum wage job until I graduate and face even worse hours but slightly better pay. Lie beside him, kiss his body until I know every inch of it with my eyes closed. Forget the paranormal shit, the witchy fingers, his wolfy claws.*

"I want it to be you and me," Cal said softly. "And no one else."

There went the boom.

"Cal, I..." I twisted in his arms, causing his embrace to shatter and his hands to fall to the side. "I can't just abandon Ink." Because I had no idea how to banish him and we made a deal. "He saved my life. I owe that to him."

A smile of thorns twisted up Cal's lips. He cupped my cheek, pressing his thumb against the swell. "After I risked it. You deserve...better. Someone better than me."

"That's not true. I'm not..." An angel. The shit I did when I thought my life meant nothing, when the world told me I was worthless would cause him to never look twice at me. "Not that great of a girlfriend," I chickened out, terrified of watching him turn cold. "I always leave the seat down."

Cal laughed. "I suppose that's not an issue with a live-in demon."

"Ink's not permanent," I said sincerely, then puckered at the terrible pun. But hope rose in Cal. "One day, when he's taught me all I need and is ready to move on, then maybe we can...try."

I wanted him so badly I could taste his kiss. I wanted both. Ink to teach me magic and ransack me exactly how I desired. Cal to tussle over school with and make love for hours on his old quilt. I wanted to be selfish and have it all.

"Friends?" Cal said and held his hand out to me.

I stared down at his fingers, picturing them as a gnarl of barbed wire. But what other choice was there? Taking them, I put on a smile. "Friends."

A sullen silence fell between us, two naked people who were nothing more than friends scrambling to slip back on clothing. I turned to face his dresser covered in unpacked boxes while Cal took watch over the south wall. Back to that awkward existence of laughing at each other's jokes, helping when times got tough and keeping all that burning sexual tension buried deep inside.

I hadn't thought of how long it'd take me to get my witchcraft enough up to the speed I'd feel comfortable on my own. Months? Years? Rolling my shirt over my arms, I risked glancing behind at Cal's back. The terrain was just as impressive as the front, but a series of jagged white scars crisscrossing over almost the entirety of it gave me pause.

"We could go together," he said, jumpstarting me from dredging up horrors from his childhood in a cult. A slow smile loped across his mouth. It vanished under his sweater before his whole head popped through. "To work, I mean."

"Oh, um, I should head home first. Shower off…" I waved my hands around like I was trying to land a plane, causing the jeans I held to flap wildly. "And I don't think I could fit into your uniform top anyway," I babbled, trying to wedge myself out of this fast. I lifted my leg to ram my foot into my pants, when Cal's sweeping gaze landed right on my inner thigh.

I don't know what reaction I expected. Maybe a little wolf moan, a pant, a sudden declaration that pretending to be friends was moronic and he'd take me now? Him wincing and turning away wasn't it.

Numb, I raced to button on my pants so fast, I almost missed him whispering, "Does it hurt?" He gestured to my inner thigh which was now hidden behind denim.

"Uh, no. I didn't expect the scar to remain, but…" I shifted haplessly on my legs, wanting to dance out of there before I did what I had to. "There's something I need to tell you, about the night I was attacked." Unable to look at him, I focused on my fingers. "I was trailing Mark…"

Cal coughed, as if he wanted to stop me, but he had to hear the full of it. "Look, Mark can be an ass. Beyond sometimes. But it couldn't have been him that…hurt you. He's a dark wolf and you said it was a white one."

"That's not it. I managed to sneak in on the meeting that Ink overheard your brother mention. Mark was talking to a man. A man in a long robe called Father Lu…" *Shit.* The name fled from my brain. "Lucas? Louis?"

"Lucien." A growl rattled through the name, Cal raising his lips in a full snarl. He gnarled his fingers together and squeezed. Did he picture a neck in them? Lucien's? Mark's?

Mine?

I nodded quickly and scratched along my arm. The movement must have triggered the wolf in Cal. He launched forward and grabbed my hand. Would he try to pin me to the wall? Demand that I tell him everything I saw? Or order me to keep my mouth shut and forget it?

When he started to pet up and down my arm, the tips of his fingers setting a soothing tingle through my body, I stared at him.

"Damn it! I should have fucking known the second you said it was a white wolf. That rotten bastard!"

"What bastard? Who?"

"*The* father," Cal spat, his hackles literally rising. The hair from the top of his head to the back of his neck spiked like a porcupine. "He's a werewolf, a werewolf with a pure white coat. I can't believe that fucking asshole would... No, I completely believe he would. He's done worse for less reasons."

It was the man in the strange robe? I hadn't seen him transform, but he might have in the parking lot. Away from prying eyes. If he'd sensed me watching, then I was a loose end to tie up.

Suddenly, Cal wrapped his arms around me, pulling me to his chest even as he frothed in rage. "I swear to the fucking moon spirits and anyone else watching I will slit him open and dance in his innards."

The leader of the cult was a werewolf. Werewolves could only have children with other werewolves.

Shit.

"Cal?" I tried to lean back, to catch his eye, but he'd clamped the full strength of his body around me. "You can't... He's, is he?"

The word's presence burst through the room, neither of us needing to say it. Cal hardened around me, his chin digging into the top of my head to keep me from looking at his expression. "He's an abusive, murdering rapist. That's all that matters."

But if Lucien was his...

"I wish Mark had finished what he went there for," Cal growled.

"Your brother wasn't meeting with your...the father to kill him." The arms he'd had fastened around me slackened and I felt blazing eyes peering down. "He's working with him. For him."

In an instant, Cal jumped away from me as if my touch burned him. His face knotted in accusations I braced for. "That's not, there's no fucking way…" I waited for him to throw me out just like before. He wrung his hair, looking ready to physically do it himself, when he stared at my thigh and the hidden wound. The anger didn't vanish, but he faced the wall to say, "You don't know Mark."

"I know what I heard and saw. What I risked my life to see."

That caused his jaw to slam shut.

"Your brother was pleading for an opportunity to rejoin the cult. To do whatever Lucien asked of him. And after that, I was attacked."

"You don't…" Cal slapped his palms to his eyes and tried to rub away the truth.

He'd call me a liar. His brother planted that in his head. *Witches always lie, right. And I'm a witch. So if A equals B, then B must equal…?*

The sound of his hands pounding into his thighs caused me to twitch. His shoulders slumped and in a defeated voice, Cal whispered, "I don't know what's going on, what Mark's up to, but he'd never rejoin the cult."

"How can you be so certain? Relapses happen all the time. To have known nothing but that life as a kid, struggled in the outside world, maybe he thinks it's his only answer."

Cal didn't reply. He stepped to the side and pulled his bedroom door open. I got the hint and walked silently out to the stairwell. At the top, I bellowed, "Ink? We're leaving."

The incubus took a few moments to slide out of the living room, his trademark smirk in place. "So no seconds?"

I bit down my scowl and jabbed a finger to the door. "Either you can ride with me or do whatever it is you do." With that, I took to stomping down the stairs two at a time. When he bowed his head and followed me to the door, a sigh of relief rose through me. I didn't want to be alone, even if it meant letting a demon sit beside me.

Eli slid out of the living room, one hand holding tight to the doorway. "Goodbye, Mr. Ink," he said while staring at the floor.

"And to you as well. He's quite a fascinating conversationalist. One word to convey what others would spend entire scenes on," Ink chattered.

I yanked open the front door and started to shove the incubus through. *You just spent your entire Thanksgiving day with these people, stop being an ass.* Working a smile on, I gave a little wave to Eli. "Thank you for your hospitality. It was nice meeting you."

The youngest werewolf responded with a quick shake of his fingers. He raised his head higher and his full smile finally started to appear. But I was too busy pushing Ink the rest of the way out to pay it any attention.

"Layla."

I shouldn't stop. Just keep going to my car, drive home, wash up for work and spend the next ten hours in Black Friday hell stewing in my rage cauldron.

Swinging my head around, I stared up at Calvin. He clung to the bannister, his face a disturbing gray. "When Mark escaped with us, he'd had his leg broken and re-broken so many times, it took him years to learn how to walk without a crutch. He'd never go back."

I gulped at the image of a young child hobbling around on a shattered femur no doctor set, but I knew what I saw that night. Mark all but kissed his father's ring. People changed. Why couldn't Calvin see that?

Without responding, I slipped into the cold November rain.

Chapter Twenty-One

I slammed my car door with more force than I meant. It drew the curious glance of the man who didn't need to follow me to work. I'd asked repeatedly in the car why Ink came with me. Last thing anyone wanted was to be on the other side of the counter on Black Friday, which started on late Thursday afternoon now. All he gave me was his sly smile and a toss of the head. That was demon code for "I don't want to say."

Without any ceremony, Ink fell a step behind me, walking with his head high and gazing across the denizens already frothing at the door. We weren't due to open for an hour, but that didn't faze them. They chattered amongst themselves while blowing hot air on their hands, excited for the Thanksgiving tradition of ransacking and pillaging stores in the name of peace on earth.

I'd left my coat at home, hoping the green and yellow shirt of all Bellpeppers clerks would be enough to keep them from ripping me to shreds for cutting in line. None of the patrons glanced my way, but the wind did a sharp slice through. I shivered, tugging the sleeves down my hands, and turned as if glaring at the wind would stop it.

A halo of blond-white hair shivered in the breeze. Rising from the car like a god emerging out of the sea, Cal let his coat fall open. The wind rippled the fabric, tousled his hair and left me dumbstruck.

"The wolf arrived on time," Ink said, his hand suddenly curled over my shoulder.

I swiveled one eye to him while keeping the other on Cal. There was no envy in his face, no curl of his lips in a domineering snarl. Ink looked as neutral as a demon could. I'd tried to hurry home, certain he'd seduce me into bed to satiate his needs. But Ink had barely given me more than a small kiss before he turned to his favorite channel, QVC. It had left me standing in the shower, my mind churning in confusion, until the water ran cold.

"Is that why you're here?" I asked, spinning from the man I needed to stop watching. Friends didn't mentally peel the clothes off the other, or leave only a scarf on for fun. I'd made my choice and had to live with it.

Ink stared down at me, his lips pursed in confusion. I didn't jab a finger at Cal so he'd know we were talking about him, but I gave a soft toss of my head in his direction. A chuckle, like stones shattering in an earthquake, rose from Ink. "Are you once again determined to set me upon the wolf in a fit of jealousy? Do you wish to watch us rip each other limb from limb for your amusement? Or do you hope I'd take him in a more grunting, panting, feral arrangement?"

Fuck. A full shiver rang from the ear he whispered into all the way to my toes. I tried to lean away in order to blank Ink's accusation from my brain, but it was too late. The idea of them, and me… *Friends. Just friends. Get it together, Layla.*

"No," I shot out, causing Ink to gaze at me patronizingly. He knew what desire he'd flitted into my brain. *Asshole.*

Ink drew his hands down my arms as if to unruffle my feathers. "I have no quarrel with the Claw," he said, jerking his chin in Calvin's direction, "but that Mar character is a threat to you. You still bear his mark from the lot of parking. I will not let him draw near you again."

It was all to protect me. He'd done it twice now without my having to say so, or ask. It felt strange to find that the only person who cared enough to sit by my bedside was a demon. "Thank you," I said, sweeping my fingers through his hair.

Ink caught my wrist. He pulled my hand to his lips and, his amber eyes staring directly into mine, placed a single, fiery kiss on the palm. That was what I'd expected two hours ago. Damn it, I had to be on the clock in twenty minutes. But the piercing demand in his eyes that I rip off all his clothes clanged through me.

I was honestly debating attempting a quickie in my car with hundreds of people standing in the parking lot, when Ink broke his eye contact. He glanced from me to a man standing in a little circle of the crowd. "Greed?" Ink called, raising his hand high and waving.

The guy, a mid-twenties-something man with jet-black hair pulled into a ponytail, turned. His face split open wide, but it wasn't a smile. More a leer combined with a snarl. I shrank at the hunger in his eyes, when Ink tugged me closer.

My heels skittered on the concrete, but I couldn't stop. The crowd parted, leaving the three of us alone in an island.

"Lust," the man said while dipping his head to Ink. "Last I heard you were trapped in…you know."

I expected a scoff from Ink, but his voice crackled and his eyes darkened. "As you can see, I'm no longer a 'house guest' of Lucifer."

"A shame the roaring twenties passed you by while you toiled below."

Ink's shoulders locked in, his entire body tight with tension. But an easy smile swept across his face as if he didn't have a care in the world. "I'd have had more fun in the Victorian era, truth be told. The meal tastes better when it's a challenge to catch."

The man laughed and slapped Ink on the shoulder. "Don't I know it." His head swiveled to me. "And you must be his next dinner. Charmed." When he reached a hand for me, I buried mine deep in my pocket.

"Greed…" Ink warned. He slipped in between us, surprising both me and what had to be another demon in human form. "Forgive me, I should have introduced you. This is Layla, a witch."

"A witch? You do like to live dangerously."

"And Greed is—"

"The sin of greed?" I interrupted. At the rise of surprise on Ink, I sighed. "There had to be more of you demons walking around. Stands to reason." Except I hadn't given any thought to it. Ink had seemed special, a rare sex demon that cared for me. How common were these things?

Greed found my reaction hilarious. The snicker dripped from his lips like yellowed tobacco oozing off a cigar. My head felt weary and pockets empty just standing near him. "In these times, I'm hardly a sin. I dare say most would welcome me into their homes with open arms. It's not as much fun as it used to be."

"Social commentary from a demon? Let me guess, you and the rest like you own Wall Street," I said.

He snorted and shook his head. "Hardly. We dabble, but you humans barely need a push anymore. It's so dull to fill to the point of bursting just from sitting on the board of a company. Here's much more satisfying. A sip, but a hard-fought one."

I stared around the crowd who'd wasted their Thanksgiving away from family and hearth to stand in the cold. Who rubbed their hands for not only warmth but the hope to snag a deal that'd make it all worthwhile. "Are you…tempting them?" I asked, my hackles rising.

Greed raised a single shoulder and smoothed a finger over his wispy mustache. "I think that's enough talking to you," he said, holding a hand up to dismiss me. "Lust, we should hunt together. We haven't since—"

"Borgia's little bacchanal in the Vatican," Ink said, his eyes lit up with rosy nostalgia. "I nearly had three cardinals in my bed that night. At once." He sighed and leaned closer to Greed. "I'm afraid that will have to wait. You see, I am bound to Layla."

Both Ink and Greed turned to me, the latter sizing me up like he intended to run me off so he could have one more demons night out. "Of course," Greed shouted, "that is how you escaped hell. Makes sense."

What did? Ink had slammed his flapping mouth shut.

"I'd heard rumors about your dallying with witches. Always seemed unwise to me, letting yourself be tied to another in such a fashion. They're such fragile creatures. What if she steps on a nail?"

I scoffed at his insinuation. "A nail's not going to kill me."

"No? Well, congratulations. You must be quite proud."

The goosebumps rose along my arms, a combination of shame and rage bursting at once. "Even if a nail could harm me, it doesn't matter. In— Lust will save me."

"Of course he would," Greed said with a chuckle. "He'd be banished otherwise."

"Layla, perhaps we should…" Ink interjected, his fingers clamping onto my arm.

I shook them off, his weakening grip sliding down. "What are you talking about? Banished how?"

"If a demon is bound to a witch, should that witch die without releasing him, the demon is yanked." Greed threw his hand as if he held a ball. "Straight to hell."

He didn't care about me. He didn't tenderly watch over me because he wanted to see me survive. He had to keep me alive so he could keep hunting others.

Greed scratched his cheek. "A dangerous gamble for any demon with you bags of water and meat. You practically festoon your world with ways to expire."

Suddenly, Ink's hand latched around Greed's chin. He didn't raise the demon off his feet, but shadows spread from Ink's back like wings. His skin crackled, fire roiling inside. Greed clung to the wrist of the man pinning him. "You…!" Ink thundered, that single syllable shattering the air like a rifle shot. Ink faded back to human. Releasing Greed, he muttered, "You speak too much."

The other demon didn't even brush off Ink's sudden fury. Greed peered closer to the man and said in a low whisper, "So do you, Lust." Then he popped back up without a care in the world. "Well, enjoy whatever time you have left with your little witch. I have a mob to incite."

He didn't care about me. He'd have left me to bleed out on the floor if I wasn't his meal ticket to stay in this realm. Ice sheered up my gut, massive bergs clipping off the wall to splash in my soul. Numb-legged, I turned for the door.

When a hand clasped to my shoulder, the frozen wastes burned into acid. "My bond..." Ink began, his usual schmooze hitting a brick wall.

I wrenched myself out of his grip. "You!" It wasn't much of a comeback, but my brain slammed into itself until only a handful of words reverberated in my skull. *Traitor. Conman. Liar. Cheat.* "You're using me," I managed to force out.

Ink bent over at the waist until his ear was nearly in range of my mouth. "And...?"

"And who the fu— Damn it!" I slammed on my curse filter as best as I could given the inferno inside. Gnarling my fingers like an old crone's, I imagined plunging them into Ink—not that it'd do anything. "You never said that you need me to stay alive. And so help me god, if your excuse is that I never asked, I will make you sleep outside!"

A slow breath the demon didn't need filled his lungs. He drew his tongue down his teeth, paying special attention to the fang I'd had plunge into me on far too many occasions. "I do not understand the issue.

Our bargain has not changed or been altered. Why does it matter?"

"Because…" *I thought you cared about me. That you liked me enough to risk your own safety for mine. But no. It was all about protecting your hide. Demons are selfish pricks.*

My eyes burned from the tears of anger I kept locked inside. Out of the corner of my eye, I caught the man I'd slept with earlier that day. Cal shuffled quickly into the crowd, who were beginning to converge on the door. But people seemed to have enough sense to stay away from the werewolf, even without him having fur.

I'd given up the chance to be with a wonderful man for a demon.

Everything inside me hurt.

"My bond," Ink began, but I slapped him away. "Don't!"

"Layla, this is a…misunderstanding. Is it not advantageous for you to have a demon so devoted to your safety that dooming you would also doom me? You won't find any mortal man who'd feel the same."

I didn't listen to him. Ink'd always had a direct line to my cunt. One word here, a little touch there, and I'd been happy to leap on him. Now, the doors had slammed shut, the windows bolted and my bedroom was locked off in a bunker ten miles underground. Ink, that charming, sarcastic demon, grew sullen and thoughtful. He knew just how royally fucked he was.

Not caring about the patrons, I pried my hands between two puffy camouflage jackets and said, "Excuse me." They shifted a moment, as if happy to let me through. But the winds changed. Not the cold breath of the North—this was another putrid wind I couldn't feel anywhere except in my brain. It whispered of need, of having to be the first, the winner. That to not answer to my wants was as good as death.

Greed started a stampede.

The shouts began haphazardly. A "Hey" or "Watch it" mixed among the crowd. But when their feet began to stomp, when their hands slapped to the glass doors, causing them to shiver in their frames, the madness took hold.

Two male bodies slammed into both sides of me. Air splattered from my lungs in three spurts, nearly sending me tumbling to my knees. But I heard the increasing thump of feet. If I fell, it'd be a crushing end.

Locking onto the back of another man's winter coat, I yanked myself to my feet. "I'm an emplo—" I shouted, only for a woman to elbow me in the nose. "Fuck!" Pain rang up my sinuses and back into my brain.

"Layla?" a voice shouted from outside the throng.

"Cal?" I tried to call back. Shit. He'd been deep in the throng before this began. What if they trampled him?

Opening my hands wide, I started to recite the spell for lightning. The first three words lanced from my tongue, a charge bouncing between my fingers. From out of nowhere, a foot bashed into my ass, sending me toppling to the pavement.

Legs and feet blurred past, the endless darkness of the Bellpepper parking lot ready to smash me in. I met it face on, so when the cement stopped rushing to me, my mind skipped. Shouldn't it be finishing the job? Someone slotted arms around my waist and plucked me up to my feet.

I turned to find my savior—Ink, pursing his lips in peevishness. "Greed never could control himself," he said.

Annoyance swarmed through me. So he did what he always did. What he had to do to keep himself on earth.

Gratitude swept over the anger. I'd nearly bashed my face in and god knew how many people would've run over me without a second's pause.

"I suppose you expect me to thank you."

Ink tipped his head. "I never expect anyone's praise, gratitude or otherwise. Now, if it's all the same" — he flung a hand out, snatched at a collar and hurled someone away from us — "I'd quite like to leave before we're smashed into wine."

My stomach turned at the imagery. I'd nearly been this year's newest vintage. Ink made a good point. We managed to shove three feet out of the wave of human avarice, when I remembered. "Cal!"

"What of him?"

"He's in there. I have to save him. We have to save him."

Ink sighed as if he had a thousand better things to do. "You are aware he is a wolf of Selene and will most likely survive?" At my glare, he held his hands up. "I can see this is important and will shove my way through, for you."

He's just trying to get on your good side again.

Well, if he saves Cal, it'll work.

The demon gave no fuss into hurling people to the side so he could pass. They flew through the air at his touch, but rebounded off others. Instead of a domino effect, it was more like pinball, sending people crashing back into us. I could already tell this wouldn't work, but I had to find him.

"Cal? Calvin!" I shouted trying to listen over the crushing stomp of feet and people screaming for more.

There! A blond halo appeared in a circle of people. When his eyes, the blue nearly drained to a soul-stomping gray, flashed past, I knew it was him. "Ink, he's over..." I jerked my head to Cal, but something told me to look up.

A strange sensation drew not only me, but the demon and the werewolf to all turn away from the mad throng and stare at the sky. Just as we did, a dark shape plummeted from the top of the building. When it struck the cement, ghastly sounds of splintering branches and exploded water balloons burst through the chilled air. The crowd's rabid lust for cheap merchandise shifted on a dime, their screams echoing to the stars.

A broken man's body lay before them, his blood pooling under the door into the store.

Chapter Twenty-Two

Behind the flat three-story roof of Bellpepper's titular pepper sign rose the half moon. Its Cheshire-cat grin highlighted a silhouette of a man standing in awe at his handiwork exploded on the concrete. Rendered in shadow, the murderer was formless, but I knew who it was by the throb on my arm.

The bastard vanished behind the sign.

"He's gone around the back," Cal shouted and took off for the left. I broke into a run, shoving the people in a blind panic, to take the right.

Pain throbbed up my feet at the pounding I gave them, but I wasn't letting him vanish this time. The side of the store strained past, growing larger with every beat of my heart. How was it so massive? I walked the full floor every day, but now it felt like it stretched to the next county.

Only the hooded floodlights aimed at the ground to catch potential shoplifters cast any illumination. The teetering streetlights couldn't reach through the terrain of buildings. I almost ran past, certain he'd use the back docking bay to escape by jumping onto a truck.

My ears perked at the sound of metal careening off itself. Sparks snapped through the rising dark, twisting my head around to watch a ladder collapse fast to the ground. He didn't wait for the steps to strike the pavement, the murderer leaping off.

His hand almost struck the painted line, the balance lost in his panicked jump. But he managed to right himself, and turned — bathing me in those ice-blue eyes. Mark sneered at me. With an otherworldly flexibility, he launched his body ninety degrees and took off running.

Fuck! He had a good head start, which would only get worse. I tried to dig into my purse to excise the book. Some stupid need to protect Cal and to prove I was on his side kept me from looking. But the second I felt the cover slide free, I shouted, "How to stop werewolves!" The pages shivered, flitting fast, and I jammed a finger in place to whatever it landed on. I had to find the werewolf before I could stop it.

"Ink!" I called. Would he even come? He was only loyal to me in as much as he needed me to stay alive. Would he try to stop me?

The scent of sex and brimstone filled my aching lungs, and I smiled. "Shall I gather up the horses for a proper wolf hunt?" Ink asked. Despite keeping pace with me running all out, he spoke in the same even tone as if we stood in my living room.

With a grim set to my jaw, I nodded. "Get him."

"My pleasure," the demon said, and vanished just as easily as he appeared. I had faith in Ink grabbing Mark and holding him, but I'd have to be the one to stop him. Permanently.

Thumbing open my spell book, I turned down an alley. Trying to read while running was stupid, to do it in the near dark while dyslexic seemed to be impossible. I clenched my thumb in my fist to try to beat down the nausea as I read through how to end a werewolf.

The entry began with a list. How to use a werewolf's tooth for a healing spell, a tuft of hair to curse a generation, a tail for...witch Botox essentially. My stomach churned at the cavalier sentences suggesting what a person's liver or spleen could do outside their body. It read like a macabre cookbook, the writer caring nothing at all that those nails they yanked off the paw belonged to a living being.

Ignore it. I had no intention to use any part of a werewolf for a spell. Ever. I just needed to stop one. There. A ward to...

A scream rattled from the very depths of the earth. It burst out of the ground in the form of red-hot steam erupting in jagged lines through the very cement. I tried to leap around the geyser, the shrieking whistle growing louder, when I spotted it. Ink hung suspended in the air, one leg striding in a full extend, the other curled up as if he'd been leaping. His face was contorted in a terrifying rictus and fire burned in his eye sockets.

What the...?

"You're not the only one who can use wards, witch," the voice threatened, bounding out of the alley. I stared at Ink, trapped in what looked like his own frozen hell. He couldn't even shift his pupils to focus on me, but I knew he was staring, directing me to remove whatever the werewolf had done to him.

I started to hunch over, to try to peel away the markings on the ground, when a laugh echoed from the fenced-in alley behind a vape and gun store. It shivered me to the core and I rose. No way was I letting him escape this time. No chance would I let Mark live.

A single bare bulb lit upon the man who'd pushed someone to their death without a second thought. He stood, not like a caged animal fearing the end, but with his weight off center and tugging on his coat to adjust it from the run. He looked like a professor waiting for the class to filter in.

"You killed them," I said, jabbing a finger at Mark.

He paused in dusting off his shirt to home those cursed eyes at me. "Witch, witch, come to hunt. Witch, witch, what a cunt." Mark leapt off his heels, his hand slashing wide.

Anger snarled through me, and I slammed my spell book forward, prepared to bash his wrists until they shattered. He got another step in, his toes cracking apart the cement as he jumped into the air.

Another body launched off the roof and smashed into Mark. "Don't you fucking touch her!" Calvin screamed. He tried to strike Mark, but they were too close. The pair rolled on the pavement, smearing themselves in muck and trying to trade blows.

It was Mark who slammed a foot out, stopping their punching tumble so he was on top. He folded his fists together and raised them above Cal's head. "Listen to me..." Mark said, when Cal slammed his palm into his brother's throat and hurled him off.

Shit. I started to run to Cal's side to help him up, when a growl burst from Mark. It ripped through his coughing fit, shaking away whatever minor damage

Cal had done. He glared at me, and dark shadows sprouted across his body.

"What did I tell you?!" Mark screamed. "Stay away from him!" His voice, warped by the shifting larynx of the half-man, half-wolf, rasped down my spine. I couldn't move as he loped onto all fours and sprinted for me. The teeth, fangs in a human mouth, opened to bite down on my leg.

"Argh!" Cal shouted. He leapt onto his brother, locking his arms around the wolf's chest. Fisting the back of Mark's dark brown hair, Cal slammed the jaw into the ground. "What the fuck are you doing?" he screamed, refusing to let go even as Mark tried to buck him off.

The longer they struggled, the more the wolf receded until Mark looked fully human and pinned below Cal. "Let me go. You don't understand!"

"What have you done, Mark? What?" Cal kept screeching in his brother's ear. Despite his best efforts, Mark couldn't get free. We had him. I took a step closer, the book opening as it sensed what I needed.

"Brother?" a voice rang out from the roofs.

It was only for a second that Cal and I turned in shock, but it was enough. Mark slammed an elbow into Cal's stomach and crawled free. I started to dash closer, prepared to attack Mark, but he scurried to his feet and flattened against the wall.

Cal turned on his ass and glared at his brother. Blood dripped from Mark's nose, which he let fall into his mouth as he screamed, "Get out of here, Claw! For fuck's sake, you have to leave!"

"Mark, what have you done?" Cal growled, the words shifting as he did. Even knowing what he was, it was a shock to watch gray and white hair erupt from his face and back. To see his ears climb up the side of his elongating skull. To tense at the claws and sinew of a predator rippling over the body.

In full werewolf form, Cal took to his four paws and stood directly in front of me. Most of his clothing was in tatters, shreds drifting on the wind, though the Bellpepper polo strained against his rearranged chest.

"I'm doing what has to be done," Mark shouted, pounding a fist to his sternum. "What we should have done years ago! I'm saving you and Eli from him."

Cal's growl rolled through me, his haunches tightening as he glared up at his brother. The werewolf couldn't speak, so I had to. "You're murdering people."

"Stay out of this, witch!" Mark shrieked.

"Brother?" a man called above our heads. We all strained up to find those same men who'd stalked us through the woods standing on the roof. "Is the deed done?" the first one asked, not caring about the wolf, witch and demon below. All his eyes were on Mark, who tried to pinch off the blood spurting from his nose.

Mark stared at us. "Yes."

"Then come, before the unbelievers arrive," the man said and bent to his knees to extend a hand. Cal growled and sprang forward, when a shot cracked through the alley. Concrete dust erupted from a bullet embedding between the divide of brothers. *Fuck.* I didn't even see the second man was armed.

We froze, trapped in the crosshairs of the rifle, while Mark turned to reach for the proffered hand. He quickly climbed up the wall, moving more like a cat than a canine. Just as Mark was about to leave into the welcoming arms of the cult, Cal jumped forward. He lashed his teeth onto Mark's shoe and tugged.

For a second, it looked like his brother would fall back to the cement. But Mark grabbed onto his new brother and tried to shake off the werewolf. Four hundred pounds of fang and muscle weren't easily dislodged.

Even with his teeth locked on, a growl reverberated from Cal. "Let go," Mark ordered. "Let g —"

A shot.

A whimper.

Blood.

Cal's teeth opened and he dropped to the ground. "No!" I screamed, forgetting the armed man, the murdering werewolf, the deadly cult. Running under them all, I threw myself to Cal's splayed body. Crimson stained his soft gray coat, dripping down his leg and onto the pavement.

"What the fuck!" Mark hollered and he slammed a fist into the gunman. "That's my brother!"

"We're your true brothers," the first man said. He cuffed Mark on the back of the neck, tugging him away while the rifle remained aimed at the both of us. "Besides, it's only a flesh wound. Should heal in a month or so. Nothing to worry about."

Mark glared at his keeper as if he intended to shred his neck in his teeth, but he remained human even while huffing. "Let that be a lesson to you, Claw. Stay out of this."

I needed to save him. To stop the bleeding. My pen. With my Sharpie in hand, I leaned over Cal's blood-soaked leg and was about to draw, when a voice said, "On second thought. I believe the Father would like to have this one returned to him."

"No." It didn't come from me but Mark. "He...he has no interest in this one. Leave him be."

"Is he not of the blood?"

"And you shot him. How do you think that will go for Lu…the Father?" Mark snarled, striding closer to the man struggling to stay balanced on the roof. What was he doing?

Think, Layla. You need a way out of this. A spell. Anything. Get rid of them. Save Cal. Heal him. Do it all fast, and without looking.

Laying my palm flat behind my back, I started to draw the only symbol I could think of. My thumb provided a steady tracer, but my arm wouldn't stop shaking as I watched Mark and the cultist argue over who would get Cal.

"Very well," the man sighed, sounding weary of the entire problem. "The wound should be enough of a warning. But if he interferes again…"

Cal tried to snarl, except it erupted from his lips into a whimper that stabbed into my heart. *Ignore him. Focus. There. The last line.* I swept the edge of my thumbnail over the middle of my palm and pressed inward.

"What are you doing?" the gunman shouted at me. A crack of thunder shattered above our heads, but all eyes were on me.

I dropped my marker to the ground and raised both my hands. The symbol vanished from my palm, revealing nothing. From the heavens, a single raindrop landed on my cheek. Then another. Cal cried out, his hot blood hissing from the cold storm picking up. I shifted to cover him, when the gunman demanded, "Don't move."

My heart pounded in my chest as freezing rain drenched my hair and dripped down my cheeks. Useless, I extended my hands up to the skies, while the three men shivered.

"I'm tired of this. Let's get out of here," the cultist said.

Mark took one last look at his brother bleeding out. "Agreed."

"Incidentally, do you care if we shoot the witch?"

He didn't even look at me. "No."

Fuck. I squeezed my eyes tight, the narrowing slit of my vision catching the barrel swinging to shoot me dead in the heart. My hands fell, and I dug them into Cal's wiry fur. The warmth wrapped up my arm, promising me a safety and peace I'd known for a brief second in his bed.

A gun shot splintered the rain-soaked air. I rocked back on my heels, waiting for the blood to drip, the pain to wrack my body, my shattered ribs to stab into my lungs. *Death.*

When I pulled in an obstinate breath free of all of that, I opened my eyes and was greeted by a demon's ass. Ink stood before me as a shield, his wings wide to cover all angles. "Try it again," he said, his chin crooked to the side.

"Forget it," the lead cultist ordered. He placed one hand to the gunman, lowering the weapon, and the pair turned to vanish over the horizon. I glared at Mark, who leaned off the edge and stared back.

I will find you.

I will kill you for this.

"Are you coming, brother?" was all it took for Mark to turn and run like the coward he was.

A single fat drop of rain splashed onto my nose and I collapsed to the ground. The rain I'd created kept picking up steam, even though I didn't need it to wash away the ward that'd trapped Ink. *Worry about shutting it off later. For now…*

"Should I go after them?" Ink asked. He spun to me, his hands holding mine and his body pumping warmth through me. The wings vanished in the cold air, but the fire in his eyes wouldn't douse.

"No," I said, shaking my head fast and trying to drop over Cal. "We have to save him first."

Ink tipped his head to me. Without any argument or insisting he didn't answer to my bidding, he scooped Cal's shivering body into his arms. "I will take him home," he said.

I brushed my fingers along Cal's head, my heart screaming that I might not see him again. The side of his tongue slipped from his limp snout and he tenderly licked my wrist. A laugh of pain burst from me, and with tears in my eyes, I nodded.

As Ink vanished with Calvin in his arms, I whispered to the wind, "Thank you."

Chapter Twenty-Three

A single clock hidden in the gothic manor of Cal's house ticked. Every second birthed and died a million fears. I folded my hands tighter together, staring at his chest. The stretched green polo would lift, hang upon the breath and fall. It sounded stupid, but I knew if I looked away, it wouldn't rise again.

"Why is this taking so long?" I glared at his leg, human and naked. The healing spell was nearly vanished, only a faint blue line blending in with his vibrant veins. It circled around the bullet wound, which frothed and churned from my magic, but wouldn't stitch up.

"What if I...?" I reached for the marker and Ink caught my hand.

"Your magic is strongest when siphoned through you. Parting into others requires time."

I stared through him, my eyes too exhausted to pull him into focus. Sighing, Ink lowered to his haunches and he cupped both my hands together. "The werewolf body is resilient," he said, taking my marker and placing it on the floor beside Calvin's bed. God, the sheets were still tangled from our gentle lovemaking earlier.

Ink had placed him there without pause. To my surprise, he hadn't made a single crass remark about the stains. When he said he was taking Calvin home I thought he'd meant our home. It left me in a panic, breaking the speed limit to get from my apartment to Cal's house. The only saving grace was the fact cops didn't want to be out in this shit weather catching speeders on Thanksgiving.

"You are weary and require sustenance," the demon declared.

"No. I should stay here. Keep watch." Shaking him off, I twisted back to gazing down at the pale man crumpled in pain. A voice in my head kept telling me to take him to the hospital. The myriad questions of how he was shot while half-naked didn't matter. Only his life did.

Warm fingertips grazed the side of my neck and rolled down to my shoulder. "There is chilled flesh of the turkey remaining. I shall gather some for you."

My stomach rumbled at the idea without my brain's input. Ink snickered as if that was all he needed, and turned to creak down the stairs. He didn't need to make a sound, but every time he walked across the bedroom, the floorboards reacted. Was he doing it for me?

"What Greed said," I began, causing him to freeze in the doorway. "You really are a demon."

"A sin born of mortal flesh," Ink responded, "which is close enough."

"So you don't...feel for people? Do you just see us all as meals? Food in plastic bins."

Ink's gaze darted down the dark hallway. "A true huntsman appreciates his prey. Finds joy in its life, protects its offspring for the next season, makes the end clean and precise. To treat them as only food is to be little more than a killer."

"What does that mean?"

Light passed over his face, casting a golden sheen everywhere it landed. "That you are more than food to me." With that, he slipped down the stairs to get me some.

None of that made any sense, but my mind was fogged from the endless buzzing rolling through it. That Ink was a demon, no matter how much I wanted to pretend otherwise, felt like a later problem. Right now, I had a dying werewolf. A werewolf who'd swept out of the sky to save me from his brother. Who my heart screamed in rage at for such a risk. Who'd shatter me if he died because of it.

Who would only be a friend as long as I kept a demon that could never love me.

What did I do to wind up with this much of a mess?

My hand did what it always did when I felt myself on the brink. It dug out my phone, scrolled through the mess of files and played one mp3 that existed only here. A woman's voice filled the room. There were no instruments, no backup choir, nothing but the shuffling of sheets from a child trying to pretend she was asleep while recording her mother's lullaby.

"Dion mo phaiste, bho olc nan rioghachdan. Ann an dorchadas, bi aotrom. Ann an tinneas a balm."

I had no idea what it meant, but I'd heard the words every night growing up until what was supposed to be the worst night of my life. Funny, I was so certain it couldn't be topped. Walking out of my bedroom to find

Aunt Didi talking to the cops. Knowing without anyone saying it that my mom was never coming home.

Tears swarmed my eyes like the emotional hornets they were. My knees gave out, about to jam my body onto the floor, but I was too exhausted to fight it. Giving in to the pain and anguish felt easier than pretending to be strong. I held my phone up, the song repeating, when a safe hand cupped to my back.

It didn't stop the fall, but lessened it. I scurried forward on my knees and caught Calvin's hand. A half-moon smile rose and he turned to shine his white-blue eyes on me.

"Thank fucking god," I shouted and pressed his knuckles to my salt-water-stained face. They rolled over the bags piling under my eyes, the puffy cheeks from all the tears I'd fought to hold in, my lips swollen from how hard I'd pressed to keep from sobbing. Every bump shook away a touch of the pain.

"I was afraid I'd wake to find a half-naked demon walking around," Calvin said. His voice sharpened at the end though his smile didn't dim.

Reaching for the glass of water that Ink had fetched and I'd never touched, I said, "The night's young."

A little laugh shot from him even as he took a long drink. While he drenched his larynx, I asked, "How are you feeling?"

"Like someone shot a bullet into my femur." Despite his proclamation, Cal started to sit up. I raced to try to push him down, but he barely even winced from the effort. "Though, I have to say it hurts a lot less than I'd have expected. Those cowboys are such babies."

I couldn't help myself and brushed my fingertips over the hair clinging to his forehead. It felt soft as down, and when I went back for another round, Cal looked up at me. What was I doing? "That's thanks to my healing spell. You should really avoid getting shot from now on."

"I'll take that under advisement, nurse," he said with a slow dip of his head.

Neither of us wanted to say what we had to. Just keep trading little quips back and forth until somehow the world fixed itself. That seemed far easier than the giant wall of truth bearing down upon us.

"I can't believe he did that." Cal was the first to crumble from the lumbering silence. I reached over to soothe his back, and froze. Was that a friend thing to do? *He got shot, stop making it weird.*

Rolling my palm over only the high part of his back and shoulders, I said, "I'm sorry."

"What do you have to be sorry about? I didn't listen to you. Again. And you were nearly... How did you not get...?" Cal tugged his lip into his mouth and bit down, as if he couldn't say that I'd almost been shot like him.

Clawed up one day, shot the next. Maybe cap the month off with some good old disemboweling.

The sarcasm stung in my throat and I stared at my fingers. They played with the edge of his sheet, winding it back and forth between them. The same one I'd held on to for dear life when he gently screwed me to nirvana.

"Ink," I said. The demon that'd come between us. "I managed to free him in time so he could shield me."

"Thank god for demons," Cal said. He swept his hand over mine, his fingers slotting perfectly between my knuckles.

"G-d has no part in such matters," Ink said, breezing into the room. He carried a full platter of food on one hand. "You should be thanking your repressive human fear of an innate biological function."

After dropping the tray filled with handfuls of cold turkey, a mountain of mashed potatoes, a pile of figs and a river of honey running through it all onto the bed, Ink turned to me. "Or so I've been led to believe. You are welcome for my intervention," he continued, entertaining Cal while I snatched up a pile of the turkey. "Though I will send you the laundress' bill for my trousers."

Tension rose, Cal staring at the scarlet stains baked into Ink's slacks. I pivoted to the demon and asked, "Could you give me a minute with Cal?"

"That's all he requires?" Ink responded, his face knotted in surprise. Cal glared at the bed, his nose pinched at the bridge. "Very well. But I had higher hopes for you," Ink said, pointing a finger at the werewolf while he slipped outside.

It was doubtful he went far. Or maybe he went home. I could never tell what Ink wanted or did when I wasn't directly involved.

The creak of the roof from the rampaging storm outside filled the bulging silence. I tested my fingers, darting them up and down as if I feared they could suddenly seize up and I wouldn't be able to cast spells. The movement drew Cal's gaze and I froze. After locking my fingers tight in my palm, I stared at anything else.

"You must be hungry," I said, leaning to pick up the whole platter.

A low growl I'd anticipated at Ink's appearance rumbled from Cal. I half expected to find the same gray fur stuck to my jeans sprouting from his naked skin, but he was fully human. Aside from the monstrous snarl, anyway. "I can't believe he'd… How can he do this?"

It was a plea he unleashed on me, a cry for me to make sense of why his brother betrayed him. All I could do was shrug. "I don't know."

"Mark was the strongest, the most pig-headed of all of us. If anyone would fall back into the embrace of the cult, I'd think it'd be…" Cal's cursing at himself faded. He sat up higher in the bed, a good sign as far as healing his leg. *Less so his psyche.* Bunching his fingers in his hair, he started to rock back and forth. "I should have stopped him. I shouldn't have let him leave dinner. No. I should have ordered him to this house."

"Cal." I reached over and cupped my hand to his arm. My palm bunched up the over-stretched sleeve of his shirt. "It's not your fault."

"Yes, it is. I am to watch them. They watch me. We…" Horror sliced through his anger, his lips falling slack and he stared in agony at me. He kept tabs on his brothers, and they in turn on him, just like the cult did. I could see the idea crawling over his face, almost making it to his mouth. But he shook his head and turned from me. "They're my brothers. My responsibility."

I wouldn't understand. He didn't say it, but it was true. The closest I'd come to siblings were the fellow foster kids I'd spent maybe a month or two with. We'd passed from one house to another, never stopping long enough to last a full semester.

A painful wheeze broke from Cal and I turned to him. Was his body having trouble healing? I could cast the spell again.

"Did you…did you watch me transform?"

I wasn't expecting that. Giving my head a half-shake, I said, "No. Not entirely. The alley was dark, and I was focused on other shit." He winced at the reminder of his brother the traitor. "And Ink brought you here. I had to drive myself to heal you. When I got in you were already back to…you."

It hadn't even crossed my mind to find Calvin in human form. I figured I'd be drawing all over his gray fur. Whatever caused him to shift back couldn't be a conscious action.

That also meant it was my incubus who'd carried Cal in a half-naked state in his arms. I gritted my teeth, fearing repercussions for that decision, but he smoothed a hand down his blanket. A soft ghost of a smile played with his lips. "Good," he said. "It's not exactly a pleasant experience and I don't want you to look at me and feel…put off."

"Cal," I said, reaching to hold his hand. He moved the same moment I did, our bodies sensing the dance before we even began it. I raised my chin, he turned his to the right. Heat swept over my lips, his breath almost caressing them. Cal began to pucker his mouth and lean to close that last millimeter.

"Can I come in yet?" Ink shouted. My eyes snapped open and I stared in shock at how fast I nearly fell back into the werewolf.

Friend. It was what he wanted. His choice. Mine… I had enough problems to deal with. What I wanted felt insignificant.

"Yes," I called to my demon and slumped back to the ground. Pain radiated up my knees. For the first time, my body felt the rigidity of the floor.

Ink blew in, all smiles and sunshine. If he sensed the two of us crackling with unresolved tension, he didn't say a word. Or he delighted in it. Demon and all.

"Well?" I prompted when Ink did nothing but stand at the front of the room and stare at us. "What did you want?"

"Nothing. It was boring in the hallway."

Oh my god. I groaned, tipping my head back.

Cal shuffled in his bed, sliding his feet out from under the covers. "I should get out of here. Find...I need to talk to Eli. How the hell do I tell him what Mark's done? No, waiting will only make it worst. Is he in the kitchen?"

He looked up at Ink first, who stared blankly in response. A chill crawled up Cal's arms, setting off his goosebumps, and he slowly swiveled to me.

"Eli's..." I couldn't take the acidic glare in Cal's eyes and focused on Ink instead. "We didn't see him."

"He is not here," Ink declared matter-of-factly.

"What?" Cal shrieked.

"We didn't think he was supposed to be—" I began.

A flurry of arms and legs interrupted me. Cal threw himself out of bed while he chattered fast to himself. "No. I told Eli to stay here. That his hotel room wasn't safe. He was supposed to be here. If he's not here, then..."

I tried to rise to my feet, but the blood drained from them and I almost toppled. Luckily, Ink snagged me from behind, his body propping me up. Cal locked his fingers to my shirt, not to tug me to him, but to hold himself.

"Layla, where's my younger brother? Eli couldn't... he can't stand up to Mark. Ever. If he's taken him back to the— I have to find him!" Cal shouted.

"I can help. Let me help you," I said, practically begging for the opportunity. I had no idea how, but there must be a spell to find a wayward werewolf. *Right?*

"Eli's…he's not like us. Any of us," Cal said, and he swept his eyes back to include Ink. "If I don't save him from whatever the fuck Mark is doing…" He pressed a palm into his eyes and stumbled back. As if my words had finally reached through the panic ringing in his brain, Cal said, "Thank you. Thank you. We have to save him. We have to…"

He paused and stared down his fully naked hips and legs. "I have to put pants on," Cal sputtered, his cheeks turning neon pink. Ducking, as if it was suddenly vital to try to cover his crotch, he slid to his closet.

Ink tossed a hand out. "You needn't bother on my account."

Was Mark so cruel he'd kidnap his gentle younger brother and force him back into the life of abuse and brainwashing? If it got him what he wanted, why would he even pause? My stomach churned, fear rising that the chances of this ending with a happily ever after felt as remote as Pluto. I had to do what I could, for Calvin's sake. And to show not all witches were evil.

* * * *

"Will this work?" Cal peered over my shoulder, staring at what to him looked like a blank page. I was glad he couldn't make out the intricate steps laid out before me. I'd only had a quick moment to read over the spell the book found for me before he dragged all of us into the basement.

He lit the last of a series of candles, and placed the small tea light on the ground. "There. That should work."

"You could have just turned the lights on," I said and pointed to a blank bulb above our heads.

Cal craned his head back and stared. "Don't you need to set the proper ambiance for the spell to work?"

"I mostly use sidewalk chalk and Sharpies. No amount of dragon's blood incense or burning candles made from the tallow of a hanged man will overcome bright pink finger smudges."

His lips pursed in what looked like an attempt at a smile, but it wouldn't go. He hadn't been able to do anything but bark quick sentences since getting dressed. I'd stood in his hallway trying to find the spell to track someone, while Cal drifted through his house hunting for the person that wasn't there. He did it twice, poking his head into every room and calling for his missing brother.

What if Eli's already dead?

That is not helping, brain.

Not as if Mark wasn't above a little murder to get what he wanted. *You know it, and he does too.*

I darted my eyes up to Cal, who stopped nervously slapping his hands together and dancing on his toes. "What…do you need anything else?"

Holding the book closer to my nose to try to hide my fatalistic expression, I read off, "'A piece of freshly tanned parchment.' I think a notebook sheet would work. 'A quill of finest feather taken from a goose during its molt.' Um…"

"Here," Ink announced, passing over a dark gray feather. I didn't even hear him leave. "Oh, wait," he said and extended his claw. With precision, he cut off the tip of the feather to make a sharp edge.

"Where did you get this?" I asked even while accepting the feather he turned into a quill.

The demon didn't laugh it off but sneered and rubbed over his fingers. Before he did, I noticed a red patch. "A very obstinate bird. Do not ask me to involve myself with geese or any other waterfowl again."

"Noted," I said. In our brief time together, I'd seen him fight off mutated tumors with tongues, werewolf claws and a bullet. But with all those, there'd never been such obvious revulsion as he held for a single goose.

"What else?" Cal prompted. He jabbed at the page without being able to read it, highlighting a drawing of the best way to drain a fairy of its blood.

Hopefully that wasn't relevant. Wrapping my hands tighter to the book, I drifted down the page and my stomach plummeted. "'A piece of your prey's life force.' Fuck." I almost slammed the book shut in anger, but Cal's finger remained in place, pinning it open.

"Life force? What does that...what?"

"That which gives you your existence," Ink said without explaining.

The confused werewolf turned to me and I sighed. "DNA, more or less."

"So, things like blood, or a tooth." Which we didn't have. "What about a hair?"

"Can't be one that fell out. Those are dead. It needs to have been ripped free, skin cells on it."

Cal's nervous pacing paused and he turned to me. "How do you know that?"

I shrugged. "Stands to reason. If it needs DNA, like all the other spells that require life force do, then the hair would have to have it. I watched a lot of police shows when I was a kid, okay." Not that they were serving me well now. *Very few had an episode on how to handle a werewolf cult that kidnapped your werewolf friend's brother.* Shame there was never a *CSI: Transylvania.*

"Damn it all. I don't have any of that. Eli's...Eli travels light. I could run the vacuum over his room, maybe find some wolf hair?"

The chances of it working felt slim. More likely it'd pick up Calvin's, and we didn't need any help finding him. No hair, no blood. Wait a second.

"That thing you said, about a tooth!" I dropped to my knees and dug into my purse. Tampons and pads scattered onto the floor as I delved into the second layer. Cal was in such a state he didn't even blink at the menstrual relics falling into his bachelor den.

"I don't have any of Eli's puppy teeth here. They'd all be planted back at the compound."

"Planted?" I swerved my head from my mad search to stare up at him.

Cal's nervous pacing held, his foot hovering over the ground. "You don't plant your teeth shed from childhood?"

"We, we put them under our pillow for the Tooth Fairy."

"Very unwise." Ink suddenly spoke up. He was tugging on the chain Cal would put around his neck, and about to lock his throat in himself. "One should never invite a fairy willingly into your house, unless you're tired of your bone marrow."

Okay, maybe that exsanguination drawing wasn't macabre dark magic after all. Shaking it away, I raised up the two pieces of scotch tape stuck together. Bound between them was what I needed.

"A fang?" Cal asked carefully.

"From the wolf that attacked me. I knocked it out when I shot lightning at him," I mumbled. Cal beamed at me, as if I should feel pride for barely offering up a fight and almost dying at a roller rink.

"But that's not Eli's."

"No, but if Mark took Eli, then he's most likely with…"

"Yes!" Cal shouted, before backing down fast. "Though the…father," he mumbled through a clenched jaw, "will most likely be at his compound now. That will not help us."

"Oh, but this is a special spell," I said, ripping the tape apart with my nails. The tooth tumbled into my palm and I closed my fist tight around it. After laying the notebook paper in the circle, I held the tip of the goose feather just above the pure white sheet. A wind twirled through the basement, catching upon the thin threads of the feather. It tried to dance out of my fingers, but I pinched them tighter and began to recite the incantation.

"Indita mihi locutus est dominus vitae huius."

The feather's tip stopped shivering. It locked onto the paper as if magnets held it in place. Slowly, I opened my fingers, but the feather remained upright. Holding my second fist above the quill, I clenched it tight, then opened. The tooth shattered into dust which sprinkled onto the paper in golden flakes.

When they touched the feather, it zipped off. A line blacker than any black ink scratched into the paper despite the blank quill not touching it. Cal peered closer to the feather drawing its way to the edge of the paper, then zipping back.

Like watching an old dot matrix printer, it took time. But Cal suddenly clenched to my shoulder and cried out, "That's the stream by the compound!" His wide eyes swung to me in joy and I realized I wasn't impressed by a magic quill drawing a map for us. What happened to me?

"It'll fill the page with an exact location of the tooth owner."

"But, like I said, he's…"

The paper shimmered and the trees the quill was turning into a forest shifted down the page. A new path emerged, drawing over and erasing what had been. "It's…it's self-updating."

"Yep," was all I could manage. Using his shoulder for leverage, I stumbled to my feet leaving Cal to watch in awe.

"This is amazing."

"When we're done, it's easy enough to stop. Just have to burn the page," I said, my feet drifting me away from the werewolf crouching on his haunches.

Ink unhooked the chains he'd had wrapped around his wrists and let them thunder to the floor. "My bond," he said, his tone pressing and serious. "I must speak with you."

Company had never stopped him before, from talking about anything. But I gave a quick glance to Cal, then jerked my head to the stairs. At the base, I said, "What is it?"

"Whatever may come of this fight in brother against brother, my only concern is you." It almost sounded sweet. Even knowing his reasons, I couldn't deny that it made me feel better to know someone would be watching my ass.

Ink leaned so close his mouth pressed to my ear. "I will not risk your safety for their lives. Any of them."

"The green-eyed monster finally rears its head in you?"

He scoffed and tossed his head. "I find your werewolf mate quite agreeable, truth be told."

That surprised me. Ink behaved as if he didn't like anyone, always giving snide remarks and quick glances. Or maybe that was how he treated people when he did like them? What the hell did he do to people he didn't care for?

"But if he decides that his brother's life is worth more than yours, we will have a very quick and bloody disagreement on that matter," Ink declared, his voice as set as the final seal locking away Armageddon. There was no breaking it without heavenly interference, and I didn't expect that tonight.

I watched Cal rise from the ground, the magical map flat in his hand. He kept darting his finger over the dancing quill, that half-moon smile rising to full. My lips twitched in response, when I felt the piercing eyes of a vengeful incubus.

"Okay. I get it. But...do you really fear being banished back to hell that much?"

It wasn't as if *he'd* die. I'd be the one to pay. Gone, no more. Did witches have an afterlife? I didn't see any mention of it in the book.

Ink snorted. "If you knew of what you speak, you wouldn't ask that question. But I am glad you see my perspective."

"What if I ordered you to save Eli or Cal?" I'd never tested the limits of this bond he kept talking about. I'd never had a reason.

But judging by the slow slide of his eyes from me to Calvin, I knew the answer. Ink would protect me, because all he cared about was saving himself.

Another cold wind rattled through me, and I wrapped my arms tight. Death was oiling up his dancing shoes and there was going to be one hell of a performance tonight.

"Here," Calvin said. He held the notebook paper out for us. The quill was trying to keep up, the image barebones as it kept drawing two hard lines and one dotted one up the middle. "I know where he's going. Where we can stop this, once and for all."

"Cal, are you…?" I wanted to warn him, tell him that I couldn't trust I'd be able to save him should the worst come to pass. But acid rose up my throat and I chickened out. "Are you ready?"

He threw his hand open, revealing claws straining from his fingers. "Let's save Eli."

Chapter Twenty-Four

Cal took the passenger seat, calling out directions while he kept one eye on the map re-drawing itself perched upon his lap. He wasn't the issue.

"Take a right," he said.

My blood hummed with energy, an internal clock ticking down to what I couldn't stay. But it caused me to go full *Fast and Furious* style down the soggy roads of the early morning. Cranking the wheel while barely pushing the brake, I knew my car could handle the momentum from the turn. Ink, however, could not.

His claws stabbed into my headrest and he struck the backseat door. I'd barely righted the vehicle when Calvin suddenly ordered a left. Wincing, I spun the steering wheel and waited for the twenty-seventh crash of the man in the back. He was bouncing around like a free-flying bowling ball.

"Will you sit down?" I shouted, glancing into the rearview mirror and catching the piercing red eyes of a demon. Ink raised his head, showing off his perfect smile.

The incubus shrugged. "No."

It'd be his funeral if anything could damage him. A little tick box formed on my mental to do list. *Figure out what harms demons.*

"There!"

The thought snapped away and I turned my car off the street onto a barely paved road. We passed between a pair of iron gates, the entrance side tugged open. At that point, the pavement vanished to gravel, my car's barely-there suspension threatening to leap to its doom from this mistreatment.

"Stop the car," Cal ordered.

I slammed both feet to the pedal, my heart flying into my ribcage as if I was about to plow into the man we were hunting for. All that kicked from the tires was a spray of muddy water, which splattered over an embankment wall. I started up it to a red brick building stretching beyond my sight. Two smokestacks rose from the factory building's innards. But only the half-moon passed between them.

No one was pulling a late-night shift.

The sound of the door opening drew me from the imposing building. With his nose in the map, Cal was already outside and about to move farther on. *Damn it.* I struggled to unbuckle my seatbelt, then remembered my car wasn't in park. Or shut off.

Fucking hell.

Both the men smoothly slipped to their feet and trailed off into the dead of the night while I had to remind myself of the steps necessary to park a goddamn car. "How do all of those destined-to-save-the-world girls make this look so easy?" I muttered to myself, opened the car door, stood and remembered I didn't win the fight with my seatbelt.

It snapped against my sternum, almost sending me flying back to my seat. But I managed to unhook it, grabbed my spell book and the purse crammed with anything I thought I'd need and finally got out. "That never would have happened to Buffy," I said to myself, shaking my head and hoofing it up the sodden hill.

Cal stood under a single flickering streetlight, his head craned back. "I know this place."

"Please don't tell me it's a meat packing plant."

He winced while turning to face me. "Close. They make dog food."

Well, I was never getting the stench of burnt chicken byproduct out of my clothing. Cal shuffled away, as if I intended to abandon him now because of a minor setback from him smelling like a Victorian meat pie maker's furnace. Reaching out, I caught his elbow. His hands were both wrapped up in the map, that trusty quill slowing in its drawing.

At my touch, he tried to smile. "The cult used this place," he said, directing us to start walking for a side door. His sight burned into the map, but he kept sweeping the edge up, as if he expected to find a man standing on the roof…or a monster.

"Do I want to know what for?" I tried to not shiver at the numerous possibilities. We reached the door which had a three-inch-wide deadbolt in place. "Ink, can you…?" I jerked my chin to the door handle, fairly certain the demon could yank it free.

"No need," Cal said. He pressed a code into the box on the side, and the lock released.

"How did you know that?"

"They always use one of three sequences, and never change them." As he pulled open the door, the stench of charred corn chips and chicken burnt to the bottom of the oven overwhelmed me. I swiped at my nose, prepared to cover it, when I paused. If it was bad for me, I couldn't imagine how hard Cal was fighting it.

Biting down the disgust, I slipped inside first. Ink took the door from me and waved Cal in next. "You'd think a secret cult of werewolves would know to use proper security procedures," I whispered. Low-level lights hummed from the rafters above our heads. Metal conveyor belts full of exposed wheels ran both beside us and on the second story. I peered through the darkness, spotting the rickety scaffolding circling all along this section.

"When you think you're the true god sent to cleanse the earth, you don't worry about someone stealing your passwords," Cal muttered beside me.

What a grim thought. And he'd grown up under that. Was probably taught to believe such a ludicrous lie about his...the man we were hunting. "Can you see where he's gone now?" I tried to whisper, but my voice caught on the cement walls and floors. It echoed through the building, striking my ears multiple times.

Cal's flat eyebrows furrowed and he stared harder at the map. The quill stopped its drawing and waited. "This way, near the back," he said and led us down a hallway cut off by chain-link fence ten feet high. I tried to stare out into what looked like the main floor, but red machinery blocked most of the view. A single bulb burned out there, brighter than the soft fluorescents barely casting more than a candle's glow from above.

"There is a matter that has me perturbed," Ink spoke up. He'd had his hand on my back to act as a guide while we slipped through the darkness. I didn't turn to look at him, our bodies crammed one by one through this small pass, but he kept going. "Does your would-be god often travel by foot?"

Cal scoffed. "He wouldn't dare let his five-hundred-dollar shoes touch mud."

"Then he must be capable of teleporting, because there were no vehicles but ours outside."

Wait. That's right. I locked on to Cal's arm to keep him close, then stopped to look at Ink. The demon's eyes glowed in the darkness, the orange radiating. "Does that mean...?" I started, when a barrel struck the ground.

"There!" Cal shouted. His arm wrenched from my touch and he took off. *Damn it!*

The last time I'd chased after someone, he got shot. I started to pick up speed, but ordered Ink, "Stay behind me and look out for demon traps."

"Already ahead of you, colloquially speaking."

Calvin pulled in the lead, unsurprising as I was trying to both look for wards and keep from accidentally impaling myself on any errant meathooks. I could only watch as his fading black jacket turned a corner. *Shit.* What if this was all a trap too?

The tipped-over barrel rolled in my way. I skirted to the side and dashed into an office. The killing floor gave way to cheap, unpadded carpeting. A desk and couch took up most of the space. I looked to the old computer monitor and a printer on the desk, when I caught movement.

Wrenching Calvin's shirt to get his attention, I pointed to the back of the desk. He nodded grimly and slunk forward. "You cannot—" he shouted, when a blond head popped up.

"Eli?" Cal gasped. He leapt for his brother, wrapped the blinking man in his arms and pinned him in a hug. "Holy shit, I thought…" He tugged Eli back to stare into his eyes. The same ice-blue stare blinked furiously from the glow of the emergency lights ringing the office. "What happened to you?"

"Mark—" Eli chirped, which was enough to cause Calvin to embrace his brother tighter.

"I know. I know what he's been doing. I'm sorry I didn't stop him. Catch him. This is all my fault."

My stomach churned at the well of emotions leaking from Calvin. He held his younger brother with such relief, but his words radiated the guilt and fear of his other brother. As if Cal had been certain when they found Eli, he wouldn't be in one piece.

"Well, this wrapped up rather neatly," Ink said, popping up beside me. "Shall we adjourn to—"

A loud, metallic bang shattered through the air. The sound of straining wheels followed and I realized someone was tugging open the main door. Hands grabbed me. I glanced at my left to see one belonged to Ink, and on the right was Cal. Together, they tugged me back behind the desk, just as the voices began.

"Prepare the site." Father Lucien. My blood ran cold at the words of the man who'd tried to murder me. An ache rose in my thigh, as if it suddenly ripped open just being near the asshole.

"Yes, Father." That was one of the men from earlier tonight. The one that had ordered me shot.

I rose on my haunches and tried to peer over the desk. All I could make out were the lights rising over the main floor of the factory. But I knew he was out there, in his same stupid robe with the silver runes on it. Probably glowing with glee while the people he'd brainwashed flocked to his every whim. My nails dug into the desk, clawing at the cheap plywood.

"We have much to celebrate," Father Lucien spoke. "Prepare the ring."

A low growl slipped from Cal. What if they heard it? I ran my fingers over the nape of his neck, trying to soothe him. The noise paused, but his sneer didn't drop.

"What does that mean?" I tried to mouth to him.

He risked only a quick glance of his narrowed eyes. "Mark," was all he had to say.

"Not to play the part of Legate, but have we not achieved what we set out to do?" Ink said.

"Mark is —" Cal began, when Ink interrupted him.

"A man who tried to kill Layla. This is hardly the place or opportunity to enact revenge."

"Ink," I tried to whisper a shout at him, "this is not your call."

"No," Cal said softly. "He's right. All that matters is getting Eli to…" He turned from me to his right. "Where is he?"

I tried to peer past him, expecting to find Eli's hunched-over form hiding in the shadows. But all I saw was a dusty cardboard box. "Eli?" Cal called, whipping his head around the empty office. When did he sneak out? How did he? "Damn it, he must have run at the sound of him."

Cal jumped to his feet, but I latched onto his hand before he could run straight into the death squad. "What are you doing?"

"I have to find Eli. That's all that matters. Find him, get him home. Layla, please. He's…I have to."

Shit. "Fine," I said, releasing him. "But let us—" Before I could even finish, Cal bolted. "Help," I whispered to myself. "Ink?"

"Oh, no. I am remaining by your side through every inch of this comestible dungeon."

Groaning, I rose to my feet. "I didn't expect anything less." I swore I spotted Calvin darting through the giant hoppers on the west end of the building. Which left me and Ink to try to wiggle through an array of extruders and the conveyor system.

"Eli." I tried to whisper loud enough that he could hear me while also quiet enough that the pack of evil werewolves wouldn't. Which meant I more or less mouthed it, so even Ink asked what I said.

This wasn't working.

Wiggling around the machines almost pressed to the wall, I spotted a potential answer. I locked around Ink's neck and pulled him until his ear fell against my lips. "What if we head up?" I said.

His incandescent eyes darted to the catwalk above and he nodded. I expected that to be the end of it, when he turned, wrapped his hands around my waist and kissed me hard. My mind jammed and my body melted in his savage grip. I opened my mouth, about to lick down the center of his tongue, when Ink pulled back.

Going from a 'fuck me' kiss to Ink calmly threading his hand onto the ladder in a second left me completely confused. "What...was that?"

"You're tense," Ink said, his body rising to the grating over my head. "I thought what better way to help alleviate that problem than—"

I wrung my palm over the cold steps and took one up. "With a kiss?"

"With a promise of what I intend to do to you once this is finished."

I oozed onto the catwalk, slithering on my belly and hooking my hands to the railing. It was a long way down, true, but my bigger concern were my shoes clanging above the murder-wolves' heads. Ink had no such qualms. He stood above me, his head cocked to the side as he stared down in bemusement.

"At that angle, this will take us all night. I imagine the Eli man will either be found by your wolf, the men there, or he will perish from arteriosclerosis."

My face puckered at Ink's annoying sarcasm being right. I planted a foot to the ground, froze at the whine from the fixtures and stared at the men down below. No one looked up, so I kept going. "How do you know about arteriosclerosis?" I asked once I got to my feet.

Ink chuckled and turned to take the lead. "You speak of it in your sleep."

"What?"

"I dare say, after the past week, I could pass your healers' examination."

I didn't talk in my sleep. And I didn't snore either. A part of me wanted to point that out to Ink. To tell him that he would hog the covers whenever he felt like lying beside me. To pretend that we weren't facing death just a few feet below.

My vantage point was almost directly over the gathering of wolves. Father Lucien, unable to hide his combover from me at this angle, stood on the highest step. He was flanked by the wolf that had ordered my death and a woman I didn't know. The man wore the same jeans and hoodie while she dressed like an escapee from a biblical play. A coarse linen sack stained the color of weak tea covered her, as if to hide away the shame of the female form.

They all stared at the cause of me locking my hands into fists. Mark waited almost on the edge of the light. His head hung low, like it had in the roller rink, but the Father beamed at him. Whatever Mark did, Lucien liked it. Which meant it couldn't be good.

"You know, it's weird," I began, needing to talk. Ink tipped his head without responding. Maybe he picked up on my desire to nervously chatter. "We followed the direct life force of the man's tooth. But he arrived after us. Instead, it led us directly to—"

"You cannot hide from me, little one," Lucien boomed.

Fuck. I crouched down, snaked my hands to my chest and tried to stop the creak of the catwalk with pure mental power. My mouth opened to call for Ink, but I wouldn't risk giving it any breath. He didn't shift from his peering stance in the shadows. So much for my theory that he could read minds.

"This is your destiny. This is why you were gifted breath. I know you struggle," Lucien kept on. He folded his hands into his robes' gigantic sleeves. "This society, this backward world of greed and hunger, is not meant for you."

What the shit is going on?

Pressing my face between the bars of the railing I stared just at the side of Mark. He turned his head and watched, when the sound of shoes dragging on cement squealed through the building. All the werewolves knotted their faces and reared back, but it didn't last long before…

No!

A body was tossed into the middle of the circle. Blood welled up in his white hair lit by the single bright bulb. I watched a line of scarlet drip until it stained the ground while he struggled on all fours.

Father Lucien jostled down his little dais. "Take heart, I do not blame you for your abandonment. It was not your choice to be so cruelly ripped from my side. To have your life's existence challenged, your reason for being stolen from you."

He stopped beside his victim, Lucien's robes soaking up the spilled blood, and he bent down. Hooking a finger under the man's chin, he raised a slashed face to the light.

"We welcome your return to the pack's loving embrace, Calvin."

Chapter Twenty-Five

Cal!

He spat at Lucien's feet, splattering his blood on the golden slippers. "I'm not here for you, or any of your 'pack,'" Calvin snarled and tried to rise. His body lurched to the side, but he slammed a fist to the ground to catch himself. Lucien didn't even flinch to try to help him. Only stood with his arms crossed watching the man, the son he'd had beaten, fight to get to his feet.

Cal rose to a teeter above the cult leader, his head even higher to direct his glare as he swayed. Fighting for dominance, Lucien stood on his tiptoes and he stared at Cal. "You always did fight the un-winnable battles. Second son, challenging the first for the rights of the pack." A horrifying smile graced Lucien's lips and he twisted around to beam it at Mark.

The traitorous asshole had enough sense to stare at his feet. But Mark being unable to lift his head didn't stop Cal from hocking another blood clot in his direction.

"Your strength has served you well in life," Lucien said, his hand reaching out to pat Cal's shoulder.

Without pause, Calvin threw it away. The two guards shifted closer, one about to grab his arm, when the cult father glared to keep him in place. Cal didn't care. "Shut up. Shut the fuck up. Stop fucking talking! You don't know a damn thing about me!"

"No?" Lucien snickered and shook his head, the mane of gray-white hair fanning out. I hissed from the memory of the white wolf nearly biting into my throat. Arms locked around me and I was about to slam my elbow back when I smelled brimstone. Ink. He had me.

But what about Cal?

Leaning to his second son, Lucien flicked a finger against Cal's forehead. A low growl rolled, but Cal kept from lashing out. He'd probably be beaten to a pulp if he moved. "Why did you return to your ancestral home? Why leave the relative banal safety of...New Mexico?"

Cal's body snapped rigid, his fingers knotting into a pose as if he planned to slash out Lucien's throat. The cult leader didn't react at all. He swept around the kill floor, his robes dragging in more of the blood. "You don't know why you toil in instinct, but I do. I know why you, your eldest brother, and even that worthless husk of a youngest are here."

The claws came out and punctured Cal's jacket. Lucien yanked him to his face, his eyes widening. In a voice that rattled the heavens, he said, "I made you. It doesn't matter how far you run, how delinquent you fall." For that he turned to Mark who was staring at the pair from below his lowered brow. "You can never escape me. I am your blood, and I command it."

Lucien yanked Calvin closer, the shorter man trying to overpower him. He didn't need to bother, the two guards on either side were enough. But I could practically feel Calvin winding up his muscles for an attack. His legs bunched in the thighs, his arms hardened at the biceps. When one hand locked onto Lucien's wrist, I knew what was coming.

And he didn't stand a chance of surviving.

"You command nothing!" A voice stronger than mountains ripped through the factory. Every head swiveled, trying to find the culprit. It didn't take long before a shock of white-blond hair marched into the light.

"Eli…?" Cal called to his brother. "Get out of here! Run!"

"The runt of the litter. You were such a disappointment," Lucien said, his lips tugged up in a snarl. But as Eli slammed his foot down, Lucien released Calvin and stepped back. "I knew you were weak of heart and mind, but to have you fall under the sway of Mr. White…"

"You killed her!" Eli roared, his hands locked into fists. He kept a slow, determined march to his father. "You strangled her, plunged your thumbs into her throat and buried her face in the bed!"

What the hell is he talking about?

Lucien knew. Whatever control he thought he'd had snapped. His entire face burned white and he whipped his head around to the gathering followers. "This coward killed two of our kind!" he shouted, jabbing a finger at Eli.

The quiet, gentle brother didn't stop. "They held my mother while you strangled her!" he screamed, his spittle striking Lucien's face.

"Those women were mothers themselves," Lucien said, turning the blame back on Eli. Reason, empathy, a dash of pathos seemed to be all that Lucien had left as his youngest son advanced on him.

Eli didn't even blink. "I don't fucking care," he said and leapt into the air. Lucien tried to backpedal, but he wasn't fast enough. Eli punctured his claws through the ermine fur, the holes giving him a strong enough grip that he raised his father off his feet. "I will kill you!" he screamed.

Three red dots swung onto the tuft of ice-blond hair. The lasers swept over Eli's forehead and one circled down his chest.

"Eli, stop," Cal said.

"He deserves to die. We all agreed!" Eli shouted back, unable to notice the guns trained on him.

I dropped to my ass, snatched onto Ink's shirt and pulled him too. "The snipers are up here," I tried to whisper at him.

"So?"

"So deal with them." Last thing we needed was gunfire.

Ink's haunted eyes darted to the darkness. No doubt he could see them all in predator-style infrared. "I can only take out one at a time," he said slowly.

I'd assumed as much.

He sighed and stared harder at me. "Which means when I attack one, that will leave two armed men who will fire wildly into the dark."

Fuck. I hadn't thought of that. "Can't you do it, you know, quietly?"

"Two hundred pounds of bone and liquid striking the ground is never silent."

Damn it. I tried to pierce through the gray shadows to find slightly darker ones hunkered in their sniper's nests. What could I do?

While I knocked into my brains, Father Lucien danced out of Eli's hold. Fury burned in the youngest's eyes, but he wasn't so far gone with rage to attack when it'd be half a second before a bullet pierced him. Aware of his literal captive audience, Lucien's smug levels hit critical.

He sighed patronizingly and raised his palm at Eli. Cal lurched forward even with the sniper dot swinging to him. But instead of a hard slap, Lucien calmly patted Eli's cheek. He tugged the frozen man closer and tried to whisper in his ear. Due to the acoustics of the place, every one of us heard him say, "I should have drowned you in the cradle."

A growl rolled from Eli's lips, fur white as a polar bear's erupting down his spine so it could stand straight up. But Lucien knew the threat was toothless, the man stepping back to his dais. "Luckily for our people, one of our forsaken has returned to find forgiveness."

"I did what you wanted," Mark huffed.

"Yes, your new brothers told me that you struck a blow against White's forces. We need not live in fear of him invading our territory any longer, now that the blood of purity has been restored."

That was the kind of shit a man covered in his own feces and licking knives said. But the werewolves hardened, the humans between them raising their heads. They all believed it. All but Eli and Cal. The latter kept tightening his fists and poor Eli, whatever had been guiding him seemed to have vanished. He stood helpless in the spotlight, trying to not stare at the traitor.

"Wonderful," Mark said, his voice rampant in sarcasm. That caused Lucien to swivel his head, and Mark bowed. He added quickly, "My Father. Have I not earned the right to return to the fold?"

Lucien's cruel lips ticked up, his false smile trying to paint over the sneer. "Not quite. Brother Mark, child of the prophet." Lucien didn't turn to Mark but the dark-haired woman standing to the left of the steps. "Before you can reclaim your place in this war, you must rid us of our weakness."

A knife appeared in Lucien's hand, one that glittered like a pool of mercury in the light. Was that silver? Pressing the knife into Mark's palm, Lucien said, "End the traitor who slaughtered us in the shadows." Grabbing Mark's shoulders, he spun the man to face Eli.

Fuck.

A spell. What do I have that could stop this? Freeze Mark in place? No, I'd have to draw a ward and they'd still shoot Eli. A sleep spell? What if it doesn't take at once? Wait. I got it.

Hunched over my book, I yanked out my pharmacology textbook and ripped out three pages. Furiously drawing, I tried to keep one eye on my work and the other on the man ordered to slaughter his brother.

Mark didn't take a step for Eli. He stood rooted on the spot, his fingers wringing over the white leather handle to the knife.

"Are you refusing?" Lucien prompted.

He didn't respond, but the words of his cult leader shook Mark awake. One step. Then another. *Write faster, Layla.*

"Don't do this!" Calvin screamed, his voice overrun with such agony, my eyes welled up. I couldn't look at him, I couldn't protect him. I had to finish this.

Mark snarled at Cal. "You don't understand. You shouldn't even be here."

"Silence your tongue," Lucien snapped, anger bubbling over his calm facade. "He is as welcome back into our arms as you. Once you finish the job."

One down. I yanked away the page about glaucoma drugs, now sporting a spell, and took to drawing the next. *Come on. Stall for time, Cal.*

"What the fuck is wrong with you? Mark. Look at me. Look at me, right now!" Cal shrieked at his brother. He tried to ram at Mark, but the guards locked onto his arms and pinned him. Still, he fought with all the fury he could even with his blood spreading on the floor.

For a beat, Mark's gaze drifted from roundabout the floor to his panicking brother. "How can you listen to him? How can you fall for his shit? You can't really believe that bull he'd spout about us being some kind of werewolf princes. He will kill us all."

"Claw..." Mark's voice dropped to the earth's core. Shadows darkened down his brow and he said, "Stay the fuck out of this." He swung from one brother to the next, his tone lightening. It sounded like he was about to recite a nursery rhyme as he said, "Eli?"

A soft whimper rose from Eli. I tossed the second paper at Ink and got to work on the last.

"What do I do with these?" my incubus asked.

"When I say so, you pop in and slap them to the back of every sniper."

267

"Layla, that is…"

I scribbled fast, my heart throbbing to finish and save them. "Trust me."

Mark's sickening sweet tone ordered, "Eli, look at me."

"No. No…"

"Come on, Eli. It's time," Mark said. He cupped a hand to Eli's shoulder, the other brandishing the knife drifting closer to his brother's ribs.

Fuck, get it close enough. Magic didn't need the drawing to be perfect.

"I don't, I want to…" Eli whispered.

"How long have I been there with you?" Mark prompted. "Look at me. You have to or…"

"But the asshole's already found us," Eli said softly, his eyes raising to stare directly into Mark's.

Mark brushed his fingers through his brother's hair. "I know. I know."

There! I threw the last of the drawings at Ink. He shuffled them into place and started to vanish.

"It's why…" Mark tugged Eli to him, the knife vanishing from view. No! "I'm going to end this," he whispered.

I waited for the gasp.

For the blood.

For Eli to tumble from his brother's arms.

But only silence rang through the factory. Every breath held, every tongue stilled. When Mark stepped back, the knife appeared without a single blood stain on it. He roughed the back of Eli's neck, pulling his brother close to say, "I'll protect you."

"No matter what," Eli repeated.

"What is this?" Lucien shouted, realizing one brother hadn't killed another.

Mark spun on a dime to face his father, the deadly silver blade raising to slash at anyone who dared to get close. "It's called a fucking double-cross. And you're going to pay for every second of hell you made our lives."

"You…you arrogant, brainless, waste of seed," Lucien roared.

"Shut the fuck up," Mark spat back, his knife leveled at the man he'd always intended to murder.

"Kill him, kill them all!" Lucien cried, the coward panicking at the possibility of facing real justice.

"Who turned out the lights?" a voice shouted from the catwalk. Another answered in kind further away, and the third tried to spin to take on a demon. His body tumbled over the railing and smacked into the cement, the force splitting open his belly and scattering his intestines.

Pandemonium erupted. Cal swung back with his claws trying to strike at his guards. One took it in the gut, but the other danced back and wound up to punch him. Mark tossed the knife in the air and caught it on the downward trajectory. In better stabbing position, he broke into a run at Lucien.

The father of this mess turned white as a sheet. He tried to leap back, stumbling on his robes. But there was nowhere to run from the man armed to slice him to ribbons. "I've waited twenty-seven years for this," Mark screamed.

Suddenly, the dark-haired woman flung herself in the way. Mark pivoted, half of his body struggling to follow with the rest. The knife remained in his grip, but it stuck between them. Reaching out, the woman wrapped her arms around Mark and clung to him.

"What are you doing? Let go of me! Mother!" Mark tried to kick her away—he even attempted smashing his head into her, but she took every attack with a dull thud.

A chuckle of pure malice rolled through Lucien. He once again had the upper hand. "You fool. You could have had an empire at your feet, but your inability to let petty grievances pass has doomed you and your brothers from ever reaching peace."

I had to get down there to help. Ink finished dispatching the gunmen my spell had temporarily blinded. I caught him staring from farther down the catwalk, his eyes warning me to stay put. But I leapt to my feet, only armed with my spell book and markers. Running hellbent for the ladder, I heard a low growl and the sound of fabric ripping to shreds.

A voice that'd shatter bones said, "You deserve death." Eli's body twisted onto all fours, thick fur that'd shake off a knife attack bursting over him. When the growl rolled off his tongue, my legs trembled. I'd found the white wolf that had attacked me, and it was going to kill his father.

Chapter Twenty-Six

The white wolf launched itself up, saliva dripping from his extended jaws. All the guards once worried about stopping Cal and Mark suddenly swiveled to try to impede the new threat. They threw themselves in front of their boss, who was trying to escape. Eli treated them like stepping stones.

His massive paws cracked into spines, legs and skulls until he stood upon the groaning men. Raising his head and whipping his tail caused the white fur to radiate under the light. Eli's entire body puffed up in his anger. He swung his eyes left and right, keeping Father Lucien forever in range. Mashing a paw into the back of one of the men until a crack rang out, Eli worked his wolf shoulders lower.

"Stop!" Lucien ordered.

The wolf trembled, his body frozen in place. I looked to Cal to find him doing the same. Only Mark kept moving, struggling against his mother. He tried to push her away without hurting her, which wasn't working.

"You are a disappointment, child," Lucien snarled. He folded his arms into his sleeves and stood taller. Or was he growing in height? "To your father, to your brothers and sisters." He glanced to the groaning men under Eli's weight. The wolf looked down once, and a whimper rolled free.

"Disappointments must be corrected," Lucien ordered. He reached for his belt, and the whimpering reverberated from all who saw. Even Mark cowered at the memory of what that belt had done. "Your mother would agree."

Eli's head snapped up, the lips curling back until both rows of sharp teeth glistened for Lucien's throat. I watched the father's eyes widen. His rote speech didn't work anymore.

"Wait, wait..." he shouted, stumbling away.

Bunching onto his back legs, Eli leapt into the air. His legs extended, claws ready to eviscerate Lucien's intestines. The teeth opened wide, Eli's tongue lashing faster than the whip Lucien threatened him with.

The mass of white fur eclipsed Lucien, almost blanketing him in a fluffy snow. I turned my head, my stomach already in knots at what was going to spill out.

A gunshot burst through the building. It rang off the metal, echoing in my ears like a siren screaming men to their deaths. I wrapped both hands over my head, and turned...

To watch Eli crash to the ground. Black coated his stark white fur, red bubbling from the hole in him.

"Eli!" Cal screamed. He madly kicked at anyone in his way and ran for the brother bleeding on the ground. "Eli, don't do this. Come on. Eli," he begged, rubbing his fingers through the coarse coat.

I leapt for the ladder, and opened my hands. The metal scorched my palms, but I had to get to the ground fast.

"We have to go home, Eli. Mom needs us," Cal pleaded. "Remember. We were gonna surprise her for Christmas. Brother. Please."

My feet struck the ground, jarring up my bones. But I didn't hesitate, turning while yanking out my Sharpie. I just had to get to Eli, to draw the ward, and he'd be fine.

Shoving past the bags of grains, I rolled over the last stack, and...arms wrapped around my midsection. "No!" I screamed, flailing my elbows back.

"I cannot allow this," Ink, that bastard, whispered in my ear.

"Let go of me!" I lashed out to fight him, but I couldn't move a muscle the tighter he squeezed. "I can save him. I can help!"

A cold voice twisted in my ear. "Look." Ink lifted my entire body off the ground to face first the guards rising to their feet without Eli to pin them. Then he twisted me to Lucien who still held a gun. "They will kill you."

Tears streamed down Cal's face. He kept absently brushing his palm over his dying brother's back and rocking in place. It made me fight harder and I shrieked, "I don't care!"

"I do."

"You're a coward," I sneered, digging my nails into his skin. They didn't even make a dent in the demon flesh, two bending back. "A chicken-shit coward."

"And you have no idea what lurks in hell."

Dipping, Cal placed his cheek to the wolf's barely rising chest. Blood coated his hand and leeched up his sleeve. But Cal didn't stop. He worked his other arm around until he held his brother. "You're not alone, Eli. I'm here. We're..." He glanced to Mark who'd fallen slack. He barely hung on to the knife and stared in shock at his dying brother.

"We're here with you," Cal said, rocking his brother. A painful whine and wheeze rattled from Eli even as he darted his tongue out to lick his brother's hand. The scene sliced me to pieces, but Cal didn't blink. Speaking through a rain of tears, he said, "I know it hurts. But it won't soon. Rest, okay. It'll be better in the morning."

Eli's tongue dropped. A single shudder rocked through the wolf's body, and it slackened in Cal's arms. He bent over with it, guiding his brother to rest in peace. "I'm sorry. I'm so sorry," Cal said in a gentle whisper to Eli. Every tongue held, every breath stopped, only the gut-wrenching cries and barely held-in sobs from Cal made any sound.

I slammed my elbow into Ink's gut, and his hands finally parted. I was about to run to Cal's side, but what could I do? What could any of us do now?

"A messy matter, I am afraid, but come, my sons. We must move past this entanglement your disobedience has caused."

"Disobedience?"

I expected that rage-snark to come from Mark. But he stood slack jawed, his face knotted in pain. Cal hunched his shoulder higher, and he said again, "Disobedience?" His head lifted, all the grief replaced with an inferno of hate. It crackled in the air, cindering to ash. Cal released one hand off Eli and slammed it to the ground.

Gray hair burst up it, his fingers folding in to make the paws. "You speak of disobedience as if you don't rape, murder, beat, starve and mutilate all of us!"

Lucien shifted like Cal struck him, his eyes opening wide. But he still brandished the nine mil at his second son. How much murder did that man have left in him?

"I am your leader, your alpha," Lucien said.

"You're a fucking coward. A sniveling, terrified narcissist who hides behind his goons and threatens women and children to feed his limp dick," Mark shouted.

That struck deep, Lucien swinging his arm and the gun at the new threat.

"You'd shoot me through my mother? Your supposed new favorite?"

"If you are a threat to the pack..."

"Fuck the pack," Mark said.

A howl burst through air, drawing all eyes to the gray wolf standing watch over Eli's body. Cal snarled at Lucien, who turned his gun on him. *No.* I wouldn't let him get shot too.

Dashing closer, I stretched out my fingers just as Cal started to move. I barely moved my lips to recite the spell, but the power surged through me. Lightning zapped into the air. But I forgot to ground myself and the blowback sent me spiraling. Electricity struck everywhere—the scaffolding above, over Mark's head, across Cal's back and into Lucien's hand.

It caused the gun to clatter to the ground, which was when Calvin smashed a paw to it. A great crunch revealed the smoking gun now in pieces. The scent of burnt fur swirled around Cal, who didn't stop walking closer. Lucien threw off his robes and leapt to the top of the stairs.

"If you think yourself worthy to take my place, then try, pup."

Cal tipped his head back and howled. Its power reverberated through the floor, echoing off the machinery until the sound blurred into a single word. "Kill," bounced off every surface and straight onto Lucien.

The leader's eyes opened wide even as he fell to his feet. White fur, much like Eli's, sprouted over his body. Cal stood watching, his jaws opening to finish this, when Mark ran forward.

Silver glinted off the light, the knife raised high to slice into Lucien's chest before he finished transforming. A paw bigger than a dinner plate raised into the air. It struck Mark's face, slicing through him and peeling back his skin. The knife tumbled to the ground and down between a grating. Mark slammed a hand to his wound to try to quench the bleeding, when Lucien raised his paw for another disfiguring attack.

Cal's jaws locked onto Lucien's foreleg. He shook his head, all but ripping the werewolf's leg out of its socket. Lucien howled in pain, and the mass of guards that'd stood watch suddenly jumped up. "Ink," I shouted.

"I will dispatch them," he said and leapt in front of the men. One man swung a punch that should have shattered ribs. Ink merely stared down at the fist almost inside of him, then shoved the man back.

I had to get to Cal. No, Mark. I had to… I turned to Eli left lying between the two raging fronts. I had to stop this. Clenching my fists, I slid across the ground and started drawing. Legs darted around me. A foot slammed onto my chalk, splintering it. But I picked up the pieces and kept going.

This better fucking work.

A snarl followed by a whimper burst from behind me, but I didn't turn around. Movement. A guard from the side caught me trying to hide under my incubus. He picked up speed, a knife in his hand. I swung the chalk around, finishing off the circle. A hand latched on to my ankle, the man pulling me. My body slid, but I slapped my hand to the ground.

Magic sheered through the air. It burst into golden sparkles which rained down on all the fighters. Hands dropped, weapons fell. One by one, every person collapsed to the ground dead asleep.

The crack of bone sent me spinning in place. Cal was hobbling, one foreleg dangling up in the air, as he gnashed his teeth toward Lucien. My spell didn't work on werewolves?

Lucien's wolf form was easily a foot taller and a hundred pounds heavier than Cal's. He didn't stand a chance. Even with blood dripping from Lucien's eye, the old wolf didn't pause.

You will die.

The words didn't slip from the snarling lips of Lucien, but I felt them bouncing in the air commanding and manipulating everyone he could reach.

Cal didn't answer, even if he could. He limped to the left, his body bowing in pain, and Lucien snapped his jaws. Cal bit back, his mouth open to get a lock. But the father with four good legs danced away.

Fight. As I taught you.

I had to do something. Lucien was boxing Cal in, his back scraping against the railing. All Lucien had to do was lunge and Cal was trapped. He struggled to protect himself, forced on the defensive for every attack from Lucien.

It doesn't matter. Lucien's acid words rattled in my brain. *I can still use Mark.*

Cal slammed his broken foot to the ground. His body crumpled, but he rolled with it. Lucien rose higher, trying to pin Cal further. On his back, Calvin pierced his teeth into Lucien's throat. The lead werewolf whimpered in shock, his body instantly falling limp while the tail tried to pathetically wag. To convince Calvin to let go.

Mark, with a hand still slapped to his mutilated face, shouted, "You don't have to…"

With a simple toss of his head, Cal ripped the larynx and trachea clean out of his father's neck. The second white wolf fell without anyone to shed a tear.

Chapter Twenty-Seven

"That tickles!" Mark tried to pull away from me, smudging my marker down his nose.

"Will you stop doing that." I scowled and locked my fingers tighter to his chin. The wolf tried to sneer, but I ignored him and focused on dragging the ink line across his cheek.

The second that Lucien…fell, his followers stumbled out like drunks at two a.m. None of them had the strength to fight. They just collected his body, even with the meat and stringy larynx dangling like party streamers, and trucked out.

"Do you have to draw all over my face?"

I ignored more of his bait, and finished the ward. Releasing him, I sat back watching ecstasy of relief crawl across his features. The skin was already knitting back over the open wounds, vanishing away the disfigurement his father would have left him with.

Plugging up my Sharpie, which was probably on its last leg, I said, "Look at that, a witch saved you from a life of wearing bags over your head."

The growl brought a macabre smile to my lips.

"If you'd like, I could put the scars back."

"No!" Mark shouted, dodging away from me. I knew how he was feeling, to go from facing months of healing to the problem being gone in an instant.

Why didn't I have any spells that would do that for the heart?

It was silent behind me, as it had been since the gray wolf had faded into a broken man on his knees. He sat beside Eli's body, gently brushing the fur of any snarls. None of us knew what to say to the man who'd killed his father and hadn't been able to save his brother.

I frowned at that and watched the demon wandering just outside the group. Ink kept a close eye on the parting cultists, making certain they all really did leave. I'd focused on tending to the silent Cal, then the whiny Mark. It kept me from having to think about what he did.

"Hey." Mark pushed past me to walk beside Cal. "Your witch is annoying as shit."

I should have re-slashed him. Shaking off any expectations that I'd be thanked, maybe even praised, accepted as a good and helpful witch, I left the two alone to mourn. My problem was stalking the shadows.

Ink drifted back and forth through the gaps in the machinery, never pausing. I folded my arms tight to my chest and waited. The heat of the moment. Anyone could panic. Even a demon. Surely by now he'd realized what happened and would own up to it.

"Well…" I said.

For the first time since he'd trapped me, Ink glanced my way. His mouth remained obstinately shut, so I said, "How about an 'I'm sorry.' Or an 'I can't believe I did that. I was wrong.'"

He snorted. "You expect me to apologize? I would grovel at your feet and beg forgiveness for the wind mussing your hair. Prostrate myself for flagellation because the rain wet your shoes. But I will never in all my days apologize for keeping you alive."

"He's dead," I said, then folded in on myself. Neither Cal nor Mark reacted, but I didn't want to risk them overhearing this.

"It was not I who brandished a firearm." The fucking demon fell back to his trusty nitpicking. He wasn't getting away with it this time.

"You let him die."

There was that goddamn snicker and toss of his hair. Somedays he reminded me more a spoiled brat than a sex monster. "Tell me this, oh mighty witch. What makes you believe your spell would have worked? It requires strength to heal. Stitch some skin, a few muscles, that's not much. Removing a lead shot out of a broken heart…that's another matter entirely."

I hadn't thought. No, no, he was wrong. "You didn't even let me try."

"And I never would have allowed you, even if your skills could revive an entire village on the brink of death. They would've slaughtered you in a second before your magic marker appeared."

"You know that. For sure?"

His eyes glowed with fire, the flames of hell. "Do not question the knowledge of a demon, mortal."

"I'm not a mortal."

"Then act like it."

Oooh! I wanted to punch him. *Fold my fist up and barrel it straight into his chest. Have him feel just an iota of the agony wracking Calvin. A pain he didn't need to know if the demon tied to me had trusted me.*

"You're freezing, Claw." Mark's voice inserted itself into our fight. I glanced over to watch the only brother with clothes on strip off his trademark leather coat and place it on Cal's shoulders. He barely shifted, extending his arms when asked only for them to fall back down. The pain must be squeezing him from the inside out.

Police talking to Aunt Didi. I'd spotted the sirens out in the alley and had to see what was going on. The living room was a better view. They didn't want me to hear. To stand in the doorway to Mom's room and listen to how she was mangled in a car crash. That the one who killed her drove away without even checking on the family he destroyed.

"When I was trapped in that cage of the wolf's making." Ink spoke, ripping me from the broken glass memory. I turned to find the demon with his head bent, his hands limp. "I feared what would happen if you went on without me. For an entire ten minutes, I couldn't reach you. Couldn't help you. But I could hear you, your heart beating in terror, your mind desiring only salvation. A salvation I was unable to provide."

He raised his head, his fire eyes burning through me. "I will never allow that fear to take hold again. Hate me to the end of days. I can work with that."

I scowled at his flippant response, but his smile fell.

"But I will not let you risk your life with such reckless abandon for another." Ink swept my hands up in his and I let him. The caress of his fingers over the back of mine sent shivers of assurance through me.

He'll always be there – because he fears hell. He'll save me – to save himself. He'll catch me – until he doesn't have to.

I knew it was stupid, but I wanted to believe there was more there than just a demon trying to save his skin. To think that something inside Ink wanted more than a witch to feed upon.

"What will it be? Hate? Banishment? The flagellation?"

"You..." I didn't know. He leaned in, as if he expected to steal a kiss. I slipped my hand over his mouth, leaving his lips to seal to my palm instead. "All I care about right now is healing a broken heart."

Ink shrugged. "I'm not much of an expert. Demons don't have hearts to break."

Even with him saying it, I clung to my silly belief that he was wrong. But Ink and his lack of a heart could wait. Mark managed to get Cal to his feet, both brothers gazing down at Eli. I kept expecting the quietest brother to shift back, to fade to human form as Cal did. But he seemed to be stuck in his wolf body even in death.

"We need to bury him," Cal said, the first words he'd spoken since the duel with his father. "I know a place. We used to...to run there, a top of the hill. We'd look out over the city and pretend we lived down there. All Eli wanted to try was ice cream."

"It didn't live up to the hype," Mark responded.

"I can't believe he...he was hunting the asshole. Killing the acolytes to get closer."

"Revenge." I inserted myself without thinking. Mark narrowed his eyes at me, but Cal gave a gentle shake of his head. I slipped closer and wrapped a hand around his back. He lay his cheek on my shoulder in exhaustion. "They murdered his mother. If I ever found the guy that killed mine I'd...I don't know if I could stop myself either."

"But it was years. Eli went to counseling. He got a good job."

"He buried it," Mark said. "Eli tried to forget it, and you tried to fight it."

Cal glared at his brother. "And what did you do, Mark?"

The dangerous brother, the threat that had turned out to be a sheep in wolf's clothing, sighed. "I followed Eli. He was going out of his mind with every full moon. Clawing up hotel rooms, screaming at the top of his lungs." Mark bit his lip and stared away. "I fixed his mess."

"What are you talking about?"

"The bodies. Eli wasn't trying to hide the crime. He wanted the bastard to come for him. He was...he was all wolf. Like everything that made him Eli was gone. Replaced with pure instinct and bloodlust. So I cleaned them up. Then I heard the call."

Cal gained enough strength to stand off me, but he kept a hand around my waist while focusing on his brother. "What call?"

"There you go fighting it again. I know you heard it. The chains? Yeah. It got to you too. The blood turning. We all boiled with one thought..."

"So help me god if you say it was to serve the alpha—"

"Ha," Mark snorted, "No, it was to kill him. I knew I had to get close, to finish him and his 'call' before we went out of our minds. But that asshole was always surrounded by guards. He was such a fucking coward." He finished by spitting a fat glob where

284

Lucien's blood stained the cement. "May he rot in the forest with maggots chewing on his eyeballs."

"Don't," Cal began.

"What about that Mr. White?" I said. "Was Eli... working for him?"

"The asshole was fucking crazy. Seeing things that weren't there. Thought the pack was going to be conquered by an invisible fairy living in his head. Eli never worked for anyone but the ghosts our bastard created."

The reminder of their brother caused Cal to grab his stomach and lurch forward. "This is such a mess," he muttered to himself, sinking lower. His gaze pinged between Eli's body and the bloody spot where his father died.

"I did it," Mark said, his head raising higher. We all stared at him but his resolve didn't waver. "I killed the asshole. I ripped out the throat of the alpha."

"Come on, Mar..." Cal said. "This is my burden."

"Are you out of your fucking mind? You have a home, a job, you're going to be a nurse and save lives! There's even a witch's shriveled pussy hanging around."

I growled at him, which made the dick smile a little brighter. Though, it wasn't at my expense, but from a pink rising on Cal's cheeks. The first sign he was coming out of his fog.

"Claw, I did it. I slaughtered Father. Do you hear me? If the pack want to hunt anyone for their moon-given vengeance, it'll be me."

"How will that work?" I said. "They were here, they watched what happened."

Cal gave me a pitying look, and Mark rolled his eyes. "You tell anyone a lie enough times and they'll believe it. People who've had their brains mashed to compliant goo for decades will nod their heads and agree with whatever they're told. I killed Father."

"Mark, you didn't…"

"Say it!" Mark ordered, and he shook Cal.

The younger brother didn't fight back, his body waving in Mark's grip. "You did it," he whispered. "You ripped out his throat. You drank his blood and spat it on the floor. It was you."

"Now, you believe it. None of this is on your soul, Claw. Eli, he…he had his demons to fight. And mine never stop. But you've got a future."

Cal winced, not believing for a second that his brother did the deed. But he wrapped his arms around Mark and the hard-edged tough guy hugged his brother back.

"You know what taking the blame means?" Cal asked.

"Don't worry. It ain't the first time I've been on the run. A couple of wolves don't scare me."

Despite Mark's cocksure attitude, I didn't believe him. He hunched tighter into his collar, already darting his wary eyes to the side, and it hadn't been an hour since the slaughter. "I should leave soon, but after we give Eli his rest."

Cal nodded slowly and he bent down. A grim knot wound up his features as he slipped his hands over his brother's cold, stiff body. I tried to turn away, but there was nowhere to go. Mark gripped the other side of Eli and together they raised him off the ground. Eli's silent head plummeted down, his purple tongue licking up the dried blood.

I scurried to try to pick it up, to help, when Cal brushed me aside. "Layla, this...this is something we have to do alone."

"Oh, okay." My vision shattered, cracks forming on the edges. I wound my hand up in the drawstring of the hoodie, wrapping it tighter and tighter until I couldn't feel anything.

Silently, the brothers carried the body past me and through the factory. To that hill Cal talked about, or maybe somewhere safer. I couldn't do anything but watch helplessly. "Cal..." I called once.

Please let me help you. Tell me you'll be here tomorrow. And the next day. I don't want to lose you.

My tongue fell silent. The only dirge to accompany the procession of the three brothers made two was the sound of grates rattling under their shoes.

Chapter Twenty-Eight

Rain splattered the gray-washed streets, no sun breaking through the dingy fog that had blanketed over our heads for nearly a week. I scrunched my back in, trying to keep out of the rush of drainage water pouring from the gutters. But I also didn't want to stand directly beside the door either.

If you stay out here any longer, you're going to freeze to death.

No one had seen Calvin in the past week. He hadn't been in class. He hadn't been at Grizzly's where this mess had begun. And he hadn't been at home. Not that it'd stopped me from walking past every day and knocking.

I had a warm meal and a hot incubus waiting for me at home, but I chose to stand in the freezing rain hoping for…I didn't even know. There were no *sale* signs on his browning lawn. No paper taped to the door declaring it abandoned. He had to be living somewhere.

"Are you home?" I shouted, my voice trampled by the splash of truck wheels finding all the puddles. "Cal, I...I want you to know that you don't have to do this alone. You've lost..." Practically his entire family. One brother dead, another on the run after taking the blame. The only unmourned one was his father, who deserved worse.

"Damn it," I muttered to myself, the resolve fading to nothing. What was I supposed to tell him? They didn't make "Sorry your brother was killed by your father" cards.

A cold drop slithered between my coat collar and neck. It caused me to jump back from his door, dooming myself to the chilled rains. I needed to get out of this. When...if Cal wanted to talk, he knew where to find me.

I tugged up my purple hood, trying to stuff my explosion of hair under the rain already drenching the thin fabric. Giving one last look to the house of the werewolf, its lights dampened, its curtains pulled, I slunk back. Past the overgrown shrubs, around a cement statue of an obelisk and under the trellis. Dead vines hung off the wire frame arcing over my head, but a single blue flower clung to life. Shaking off the urge to pluck it from its dying roots, I turned to march down the street.

"Layla?"

My feet moored to the ground from shock. I had to twist to glance over my shoulder. An umbrella black as the reaper's cloak shifted back to reveal the man underneath. In this gray, foggy world, Calvin's eyes blazed like two will-o'-the wisps.

"You've been following me," Cal said. I tried to curl deeper into my hood, wanting to hide from the man I sort-of stalked. But he strode closer, and extended his umbrella between the both of us.

"I was…" I risked looking up into his eyes. Red etched inside them, the way the pain clawed him apart. "I was worried about you."

His slack lips flushed into a smile. Not the half-moon one I'd give anything to see again. But he tried. "Worried I'd do something foolish enough you risked returning to the compound?"

How did he know that?

Cal snickered and tapped his nose. "This is better than any Facebook stalking, most of the time. I've smelled you…" He sighed and tipped his head. "Everywhere."

Was that good? Bad? Did he think I'd been trying to stalk him again?

His unreadable voice hardened. "Mark did what he promised. He's gone. The cult's in a frenzy with infighting to pick a new leader. When they finally do, they'll go after him."

"What do you…?" Rain struck through the heels of my socks. I stepped closer, and cupped one hand around the umbrella above Cal's. The heat of his body practically made the air sizzle. It beckoned me closer, but I resisted. "What are you going to do?"

"I thought about challenging them myself. Upending the entire thing. Putting an end to this reign of terror before it could infest another generation." Cal pushed back my hood, releasing my hair into the wild. "Go with Mark. Build our own pack to fight the cult when they come for us."

He brushed his palm to the apple of my cheek, his fingers trailing back around my ear and tickling my neck.

"That's a lot of options," I said, my heart cracking inside. He needed to leave, follow his brother, vanish into the werewolf underground. Abandon me.

Tipping his head at my stupid point, Cal swirled his thumb at the edge of my mouth. "Vengeance is…not a life. Even in the dark hours of the night, when I'd prowled the streets hoping for one of the cult's lieutenants to cross my path, I felt empty. The same way I did in the cult. And I never want to feel that again."

Clouds opened up beneath our umbrella, rain falling from Cal's eyes. "I want you, Layla. I want to fill with giddiness from making you laugh. To know safety whenever I wake with you curled in my arms. To cram my heart with so much that it can never empty."

The rain found my cheeks too, my eyes stinging even as I gazed up at Cal. He wanted me, to be with me, to let me help him. But… "I'm still with Ink. That hasn't changed," I said, my heart plummeting to the ground.

"I don't care," he declared, shocking me to the core. He wrapped me in a one-armed hug, pulling me closer to his chest. I placed my hand to his shirt, the flutter of his heartbeat pulsing over my fingers. "I've paced these streets up and down for days wondering, questioning myself and…I need you. If that means sharing you to keep you, then I don't care. I'll do whatever I must to have you."

"Cal!" I leapt up, kissing his lips with all the force left inside of me. His sweet words and tender mouth swept the heat of him through me. The wolf inside growled in need, Cal parting my lips with his tongue so he could swirl the taste of him inside me.

"Look at you," he whispered, grazing his mouth across my cheek as he traveled up to my ear. A series of pants overwhelmed me, causing me to moan in response. "You're soaked to the bone." Cal started brushing his fingers over the rain-soaked patches on my hoodie, but as he kept going lower, he started kneading and tugging to find my skin below.

"Do you know what you need?" he asked, dragging the tip of his nose up mine.

I stared into his eyes, watching the hunger prowl through them. "What?"

Cal locked a hand over mine, leaving me clutching the umbrella myself, and he started to run us for his home. "For me to draw you a hot bath, dip you into the steaming water and wash your delectable body."

"Only if you join me in the tub," I said, kissing him on the doorstep of his house. Cal shoved the door open without breaking from me. He threaded his hands through my hair, tugging on the roots and setting off a chain of explosions. The umbrella slipped from my fingers, landing outside and rolling in the wind.

Cal paused in tugging me up the stairs to his bathroom. Turning on a dime, he shoved my back against the wall and kissed me with the same ravenous need from our first kiss. But it wasn't going to be the last.

I bit my lip, holding in an unimaginable agony. Cal's ragged pants strained his chest under his shirt, my palm finding its way to caress down his pecs. I wanted him here. Or in the bath. Or that slow, gentle, all-afternoon sex in his bed. But another problem kept clanging through my brain. "There's a chance that Ink might...show up," I confessed, fear rampaging through me that he'd call off the whole thing.

That half-moon smile burst across his cheeks. "Well," Cal said. He lifted me up into his arms and turned for the stairs. "He'll just have to wait his turn."

Chapter Twenty-Nine

No jewels sat perched upon the top. The arms and legs were not coated in gold. There were no pelts of a white tiger or black-maned lion strung across the back. But make no mistake, it was a throne. And all who entered the office at the top of the glass building towering above all others knew it.

"Sir," a voice from the countless millions called to him.

He didn't rise from his executive suite leather swivel chair. He wouldn't have for anyone, unless it was the Man in Black. No, he only had to lift a finger for the underling to fall silent. A scrap of sugar tumbled from his meal, meager and unimportant to all but two ants that discovered it.

They squared off over the single grain, pinchers gnashing together until only one would win. It didn't take long for the stronger of the two to emerge, its teeth slicing through the other's midsection. Caring nothing for bifurcating its colony brethren, the ant scooped up its prize and toddled off.

He smiled and dropped another granule on his desk.

"We've received word that the leader of the Endless Moon cult is no longer with us."

The interruption was bothersome, but he smiled at the news. Abandoning the second round of ants fighting for dominance, he rose from his desk with a map of the ancient world inlaid upon it. "Excellent."

"There's already word of rebellion ripping through their ranks. It won't be long now until…"

He held up a hand, silencing the man telling him what he already knew. Of course there was rebellion. Get the prince to murder the king, wait for the rest of the pieces to come tumbling down. Hardly sporting, but *honor* was his louder brother's *raison d'être*.

The phone system buzzed, and his secretary spoke up. "Excuse me, Mr. White. A gentleman says he had an appointment with you, but I cannot find it on the calendar."

His smile rose, clipping up the sides of his face like a snake slithering around a bucket. "Thank you, Janet. Please send him through."

"Is it the lawyers? Because I swear, if I have to sit through one more 'this counts as a monopoly' meeting I will…"

He didn't need to say a word to tell his lieutenant to stop speaking. The man sensed the moment to stop. He had worked by his side for the longest of any of them — almost three years. Perhaps he was due a gift, a company car, a bag of jewels or a small village with a poisoned well.

The guest blew through the doors without a care for protocol. His lieutenant tried to stop the man, but it proved fruitless. It was why he was chosen out of the three.

But the man had enough sense to tip his head in deference to the king amongst them. "He's dead."

"Congratulations. You must be ecstatic."

The muscle snorted, his hair standing on end. "It didn't exactly go according to plan."

"That is not my concern. All that matters is the end result. The strongest ant comes out on top, and the rest are left to dry in the sun." Rising to his feet, he met the man and wrapped a tight, controlling arm around his shoulders. "This is a win for you. Something you've been attempting to achieve for years."

"Decades."

"Celebrate. Take the time to revel in your win," he said, guiding the man to the door. His constant secretary appeared, concern rising. "Janet? Would you be so kind as to round up the usual entertainment for my good friend Mark?"

Janet took the wolf in her weathered but talented hands. "I've got reservations for you and a lovely woman at T's steak house on fifth."

"That sounds…" His head spun back. "What about the cult?" This one had more sense than the others on White's payroll.

"Do not worry. We are moving on phase two, after your small vacation. Please. Time is not a concern. And do order the T-bone. It's particularly delicious," he said, slipping back into his spacious office.

The lieutenant stood beside one of a dozen computers, data and charts projecting onto the black screen behind his throne. "Mr. White, what exactly is phase two?"

He returned to his throne, folding his fingers together in thought. Light struck off a gold ring so weathered that only the hint of a galloping steed was visible. "Conquest."

**Want to see more from this author?
Here's a taster for you to enjoy!**

Some Like it Haunted: Ink
Ellen Mint

Excerpt

Ten minutes to midnight.
Ten minutes to Halloween.
Ten minutes to my birthday.

"Ah, shit!" I fumbled, my phone slipping to the unfinished staircase. Luckily it bounced, and the three zombie sours sloshing through my system didn't stop me from catching it.

"Careful, Layla!" my fellow nursing student Fariah called.

Dana stuck her head out of the back window and shouted for the entire block to hear, "Sorry your gift's late. But I swear, you'll *love it* when it arrives. Ten or twelve times a day until the batteries run dry."

I waved a hand at the girls, which was supposed to insist I didn't mind the lack of a gift, but that shot of whiskey rebounded and I slapped the mailboxes instead. "Sonnofa...!" The second curse of the night snapped to growling as I inspected the rising red welt thanks to my drunken buffoonery. Luckily, Fariah — our eternal DD — was already slipping off to shuttle the rest of the group home.

If they'd seen me, they'd have pulled out our anatomy books and come up with a dozen different treatments for 'drunk girl punches a wall'. Not that I was any better, my soggy brain wondering if I had a wrap back in the apartment while I stumbled up the stairs.

Slapping a wall, nearly breaking a phone and making a colossal fool of myself in front of the hot bartender would probably dim most people's birthdays. But honestly, compared to past ones, this year's was almost palatable. It helped that I'd stopped celebrating on the thirty-first when I was six. Last thing anyone wanted was to go to a kid's birthday party when they could be trick-or-treating.

As I rounded the stairs, checking twice that it was the right floor, I thought back to the bartender I hadn't been able to stop staring at. He'd had that whole 'I could model for a surf club' esthetic going on, complete with thick, medium-length dark hair and olive skin. But what'd had me drooling into my vampire bite were the tats. He'd known how to stylize his body, relying on black ink and the right amount of whorls and lines to draw the eye to all his best spots.

Shame that the rest had been covered by his shirt and the chance of me getting a peek had been negative billion. *Don't try to flirt when there's a pile of latex gloves in your pocket, is all I'm saying.* I can't even imagine the freaky shit he'd thought I was into.

"Seriously?"

Sitting before my door was a brown package, which was always supposed to be dropped off with the manager to cut down on theft. Not that it stopped him from refusing to keep said packages and just dump them off if we didn't collect within an hour. I checked the apartment number, thirteen, then the name on the box.

Layla Leeland. That was mine even if it was written in a super curly script my drunk ass had to turn around a few times to read. I'd bitch out the manager tomorrow... *No, that's Halloween. I'll bitch him out on November first.*

With that decided, I fumbled into my apartment. The door rattled open and smacked straight into the pile of laundry baskets I foraged from. Nursing school really took a bite out of everything in my life. Time, energy, the ability to connect with another human being.

I didn't even have a cake for my birthday. Most years I'd at least pick up a chocolate cupcake with orange frosting and cram a candle in it. But I couldn't bother this go around. Eh, what was twenty-five anyway but a reminder that a quarter of my life was over?

Dropping the box on my counter caused a trash bag to splatter to the floor. *I should really clean this place up. Put away my scrubs and dismantle bra hill. See if my vacuum even works anymore or if the spiders own it now.*

A yawn ripped from my throat, shattering any illusions I'd get my life in order. "I'll deal with it tomorrow," I declared to my apartment and the mystery box. It was probably more textbooks that cost the same as a new phone.

Shambling like a zombie on its last leg, I stumbled to my bedroom. Without bothering to shed my scrubs, or even wipe the makeup off, I fell face first onto my bed and embraced the ambivalence of sleep.

* * * *

What was that?

The sound of Jell-O shot out of a slingshot at speakers rocketed through my apartment. My heart jumped into my throat and my body tried to leap up. But I was still buzzing and had minimal control of my limbs. It was more of a graceful ooze to the floor.

In the process of righting my eyes, I caught a flash of light breaking from the living room. It kept strobing as if a lightning storm had crashed on my futon. If I wasn't partially hungover and drunk at the same time, I'd like to think I'd have done the smart thing. Called the cops, called the building manager, grabbed a weapon. Not walked out into the weird lights and sounds armed only with my exhausted hand on my hip.

As I stepped into the hallway, noting that my front door was still closed, a shadow crawled across the wall. It looked like a man rising to his feet when a pair of giant bird wings erupted from behind his back. They stretched wide, every shadowy feather straining as if this intruder were about to fly.

Did I turn around, grab my phone and wait for the police to sort this out?

Of course not. I ran straight into my living room and my jaw hit the floor.

It wasn't because a giant bird flew into my apartment and flapped about in pain. Or that one of my old angel costumes from a past Halloween had come to life and started dancing around. No, this was even weirder.

A gorgeous man with sun-kissed skin stood on my yoga mat. His hair was lush and reached his collarbones. His very exposed and cut collarbones. Which drew my eye lower down the rest of his body.

I could have offered to check him for moles for how naked he was. His chest glistened the only way hairless skin could, which he had puffed out to display his impressive pecs. A single line of dark hair revived itself under his labyrinth of abs. I tried to count them but lost track as I followed the treasure trail down to a pair of red satin briefs that barely covered his shame.

And it wasn't just because the fabric was tiny enough it revealed nearly his full bush to the world. No, whatever pipe he was swinging bulged so tight below his underwear it looked like it was vacuum packed for easy transport.

What if that wasn't the full show he had?

What the hell is wrong with me?

I lashed out with my hand and snatched up the first thing I could…which happened to be a pillar candle. Waving it about as if it were a club, I shouted, "Who the fuck are you?!"

The man laughed, his voice that deep 'roll through every nerve in my body' baritone. "Highly accurate," he said, raising and lowering his sharp eyebrows while a smile perched on his lips.

I shook the candle around, prepared to attack him if he didn't give me an answer. The stranger eyed it up, then said, "I am your incubus."

"What?"

"And I must say…" He placed a hand to his ab-alicious stomach and peered down. "I quite like your preferences. Ooh." His hand slipped under his red briefs and he started to jerk his hand along his full cock. Those dark eyes rolled back into his head and he shook his black hair while moaning.

I could nearly see the tip peeking above his underwear, his large hand yanking the waistband lower and lower. My toes raised my body up, trying to get me a better view, when I scowled. "Stop that!" I shouted as much at him as my own train-wreck libido.

The man pulled his hand away instantly then extended both out as if I had him at my mercy. *Ha. Sure.*

"Let's start again. Who are you?"

His infectious smile wavered, drawing my attention to how hawk-like his features were without the raised cheeks of a grin. I clenched my toes, afraid of what his anger would bring, but any ire snapped away in an instant. "I am yours, Layla. What more need be said?"

"Mine? How the shit are you mine? I've never seen you before in my life!" I shouted again, still brandishing the candle. To my surprise, he kept acting like it was a real threat to him.

His eyes stayed steady on the sweet pea pillar while he spoke. "I am here to answer your every desire."

My desire? Who the shit breaks in and... *No.*

Ah fuck, no. Dana and the rest did not chip in to get me a...an incubus, as he called himself. Did that mean a male prostitute?

She said my gift would arrive later, and I did give her a key to my apartment in case of emergencies. Did sneaking a male whore inside count as an emergency? I whipped back to my front door, noting the locks in place.

"Look, this is all very..." *Humiliating that my friends know I can't get a date to save my life.* "Flattering, but I don't—"

The stranger stepped closer, and my senses flooded with him. His heat burst across my skin like a warm bath. His scent, rugged as an alpine mountain, tingled down my spine and lit a fire inside me. And his look...*fuck me,* but he was even hotter out of the shadows.

Those eyes that'd been dark as night were in actuality an otherworldly amber. His sharp nose and harsh cheekbones combined with the full bottom lip made the word *pretty* almost perch on my tongue. But then I glanced down his body, the muscles taut and proud, his gait strident, those full-to-bursting briefs, and he was nothing but fire.

"I am yours to command, to will, to dance to your every desire, my lady," he announced, his head bowing low. My fingers ached to rummage through the thick hair before me, to tug on the roots and crush him to my lips.

His head popped up and a smirk greeted me. Shit, did he read the stupid horny thought on my face?

I stared at the candle. He didn't seem to be a threat, and if Dana booked him…?

I mean, it's never nice to return a gift unused, right? It seemed very impolite.

He rolled his hand around the candle, plucking it from me before I could even put it down. "I don't believe this is necessary, unless you were hoping to set the mood?" After placing the pillar on the coffee table, he turned and smiled. "Or intended to pour hot wax on my body."

"What…?" Fucking hell, what did she get me? Okay, the hottest incubus at the dude ranch. But, still—

"You seem…" he whispered while rolling his hands through my hair. It'd been a matted mess from a long day of school and drinking, but under his fingers the curls felt smoother and sleeker. Hot breath curled against my neck, causing me to shiver down to my toes. "…as if you require some relaxation."

Strong fingers dug into my shoulders, kneading away the stress. A moan slipped from my lips, this stranger making fast work of unraveling the tension I'd carried since I was nine.

"Now that is music for the ages," he said behind me. His hands released from my shoulders and flat palms caressed my weary ribcage before rounding right at the side of my breasts. Dressed in little more than an old bra and scrubs, I could nearly feel his skin on mine. It sent my heart racing.

"What's your name?" I spat out, clinging to the idea that if I knew who he was, then it couldn't be so pathetic. All the while, my body begged for him to touch more of me.

"Do we need names?" he asked and that pouty bottom lip caressed the shell of my ear. He didn't bite down, didn't lick, just placed it there telling me he could do anything at a moment's notice.

I spun in his hands, which settled right on my hips. The fingers kept tugging on the waistband of my scrubs, this incubus slapping the elastic back and forth. "What if I need to call you? Give you directions?"

His eyes blazed as the amber shifted to fire. "That should not be a concern. But if you are wondering what to shout to the rooftops while I devour you…?"

Fuck, how did he know that?

"I believe Ink will suffice."

"Ink?" I repeated, while staring the man up and down. "And…what are you going to do to me?"

Swooping his fingers under my shirt, he dug into the small of my back. I flew forward, his lips a breath from mine as he said, "Whatever you desire."

Home of Erotic Romance

Sign up for our newsletter and find out about all our romance book releases, eBook sales and promotions, sneak peeks and FREE romance books!

About the Author

Ellen Mint adores the adorkable heroes who charm with their shy smiles and heroines that pack a punch. She recently won the Top Ten Handmaid's Challenge on Wattpad where hers was chosen by Margaret Atwood. Her books, Undercover Siren and Fever are available at Amazon as well as a short story in the Lucky Between The Sheets anthology. Married, she lives in Nebraska with her dog named after Granny Weatherwax. Her hobbies include gaming, painting, and halloween prop making. The basement is full of skeletons because they ran out of room in the closets.

Ellen loves to hear from readers. You can find her contact information, website details and author profile page at https://www.totallybound.com